FAMILY AFFAIR

Elle M Thomas

Family Affair

Family Affair Copyright ©2021 by the author writing as Elle M Thomas

The moral rights of the author have been asserted.

All rights reserved. No part of this publication may be reproduced, distributed or transmitted in any form or by any means, including photocopying, recording or other electronic or mechanical methods without the prior permission of the author, except for brief quotations embodied in critical reviews.

This is a work of fiction. Names, events, incidents, places, businesses and characters are of the author's imagination or used in a fictitious manner. Any resemblance to actual persons, living or dead, or actual events is purely coincidental.

Cover design and editing by Bookfully Yours

Formatting by Lia V Dias

This is an Elle M Thomas mature, contemporary romance. Anyone who has read my work before will know what that means, but if you're new to me then let me explain.
This book includes adult situations including, but not limited to adult characters that swear, a lot. A leading man who talks dirty, really, really dirty. Sex, lots and lots of hot, steamy, sheet gripping and toe-curling sex. Due to the dark and explicit nature of this book, it is recommended for mature audiences only.
If this is not what you want to read about then this might not be the book for you, but if it is then sit back, buckle up and enjoy the ride.

Other titles by Elle M Thomas:

Disaster-in-Waiting
Revealing His Prize

Carrington Siblings Series (should be read in order)
One Night Or Forever (Mason and Olivia)
Family Affair (Declan and Anita)

Love in Vegas Series (to be read in order)
Lucky Seven (Book 1)
Pushing His Luck (Book 2)
Lucking Out (Book 3)

Love in Vegas Novellas (to be read in timeline order)
Winters Wishes (takes place during Lucking Out)
Valentine's Vows (takes place around three years after Lucking Out)

Falling Series (to be read in order)
New Beginnings (Book 1)
Still Falling (Book 2)

New Beginnings/Falling Series Novellas (to be read in timeline order)
Old Endings (prequel to New Beginnings – Eve's Story)

The Nanny Chronicles (to be read in order)
Single Dad (Gabe and Carrie)
Pinky Promise (Seb and Bea)

For Holly, the best friend a girl could ask for, in good times and bad.
Thank you for just being you, Hol x

Prologue

Declan

Pacing the corridors of my club, Dazzler, I can't disguise my nervousness that everything needs to go off without a hitch tonight. My brother, Mason, is coming over. Not that he knows it yet, and his girlfriend, Olivia, is going to propose.

Mase has no clue what Liv has planned for him, but he will accept her proposal. He is totally smitten, a much happier person now, fulfilled. I don't go in for one true love and all that shit, but if I did, I'd say that's what they have. He has been married before, to Arianna, but honestly, it was never like it is with Liv. Mase has had countless girlfriends but from the second he set eyes on Olivia, he changed. His sole purpose in life appeared to be capturing the very beautiful brunette, but if I am honest, I have no clue who caught who really.

There will be a full-on party here tonight and we'll have the run of the place as I don't open the club on Tuesdays. An adolescent titter escapes me as I recall almost catching Mase and Liv mid shag on a previous Tuesday when they had used it for some *private dancing*. Yeah, that is what my brother assured me they were doing. Although, having seen Olivia dance I can vouch for the fact that it's akin to shagging to music.

Olivia has had a shit life all in all. Her parents split up when her and her brother were kids, the father disappeared and then the mother moved into some religious commune where the head of the 'church' systematically abused, beat, and raped Olivia, amongst others. When his crimes began to catch up, he,

Raymond Daniels, went on the run, but only as far as Olivia who he beat and assaulted. She lost the baby none of us knew she was expecting that night. Yes, they definitely deserve to be happy. And Raymond? He is being sentenced today for his crimes and that is where Mase and Olivia are now, along with her long-lost brother and father and his new family. I suppose some good has come from it, although I know Mase still has reservations about the brother and the father, but Liv wants to be one big happy family so he will play ball unless they cross him.

With a frown, I wonder how a parent does that to their kid; abuses, facilitates the abuse, or simply moves on to build a new life without their child. Mase and I have had four stepdads and numerous stepsiblings over the years, but not once have we felt anything other than loved and safe. As if by maternal magic, my phone rings and it's my mother.

"Hi Mum, are you okay?"

"Yes, darling, fine. Have you heard from Mase?"

I can tell from her voice that she has or has at least heard something about him.

"I haven't," I confirm.

"Your dad called. That awful man has been sentenced to more than eighty years."

"Wow…how's Liv, and Mase?" I ask, unsure what else to say.

"Your dad said Olivia is remarkably holding things together, Mase not so much so…he's quiet and brooding," my mother reveals and is clearly concerned.

"Mum, he'll be fine. We'll all keep an eye on him and after tonight he will have everything he wants," I say in an attempt to settle her nerves and worries.

"He won't have the baby Olivia lost, neither of them will," she whispers, sadly.

"No, but they will have other babies and I think that will be sooner rather than later."

"Of course. Are you okay, Declan?" she asks, and I smile at how fortunate we are to have her as our mother. She is unconditionally loving, has always put her children's needs first and there is no element of doubt in my mind that she would move heaven and earth to ensure our happiness and safety. Who could ask for more in a parent?

"I am great, Mum." It's not a lie. I am happy. I have my business and an endless supply of pretty girls, speaking of which a very hot little brunette has just entered the building. "Mum, I have to go, but I will see you later. Don't worry about Mase, he's got Liv, so he'll be fine."

I immediately go in search of the pretty dark-haired girl dressed in shorts and a very tight vest. I find her in my kitchen, with her back to me, chatting to Kelly who usually works behind the bar but is helping me out with decorations today. I stand in the doorway and take in the scene before me. Clearly the girl I saw is from the catering company which is owned by Olivia's father who is at court with her. I have no idea what Kelly is talking about with the other woman as my brain refuses to think, see or hear anything that isn't her sexy as fuck arse that is hanging out of her tiny shorts. This woman is a serious contradiction with her dark hair and fair skin, her short height and fuller, voluptuous curves that seem to be screaming to be touched and caressed.

The noise of her laughter startles me, mainly because the sound that resonates from her is the most divine thing I have ever heard. I cough in some kind of shocked and nervous reaction, alerting them both to my presence.

"Hi, Dec. This is Anita, she's the caterer." Kelly reveals the beautiful lady's identity.

She has the darkest brown eyes I have ever seen and a face that could and probably does stop traffic. I lower my glance to her chest which is tightly ensconced in a vest that only emphasises her boobs. They really are magnificent and equally as curvaceous and inviting as her behind, both of which are in total contrast to her tiny waist and frame. She is like an adult doll maker's blueprint for immoral thoughts and as I prepare to delve into immoral and quite possibly depraved thoughts, she, Anita, smiles a sweet and seriously hot smile that has me hard in an instant.

"Kelly, could you go and collect the balloons and tea lights?"

She grins, confirming she knows exactly why I want the place to myself. More importantly, why I want Anita to myself.

I am a man whore and have no issue with that. I like sex, a lot; hot, frequent, all variations on sex, but most of all I am looking for uncomplicated sex. The idea of sex with one person for the rest of my life brings me out in a cold sweat. The monotonous, formulated sexual encounters that so many couples are grateful for is not my thing at all. I want excitement, unpredictability, and no emotions.

Kelly leaves us alone and then I speak to Anita, a simple introduction. "Dec," I say with an outstretched hand, and only then do I notice that she is in no position to accept it.

With her hands full of a piping bag, I see her grin. Then with a glimmer in her eye she licks her lips until they are glistening with her own saliva, and it takes all my powers of restraint not to go and add my own. This woman is a strange one with her innocent expression and knowing eyes. She's teasing me.

"Like she said, Anita." She proceeds to pipe what looks like lemon butter icing onto a huge tray of cupcakes.

I am rooted to the spot watching her navigate the piping bag, the off-white creamy mixture oozing from the nozzle under her control. God, I need to stop watching porn I decide as I consider my narration of what she is doing. With the last cupcake completed and another tray being started, she stops to point the bag at me and allows a little icing to dribble from the end. Yes, I really need to reduce my porn viewing.

She fixes me with a gaze and quickly lowers it, as if somehow shy or scared by the sexual tension that's crackling between us.

We remain silent, her focusing on the cupcakes and me focusing solely on her. She is beautiful, stunning, she really is. Her shoulders suddenly stiffen as if she has become aware of my gaze on her, even with her back to me.

It is taking every ounce of my self-restraint not to pounce on her, ripping her clothes off to devour her, but I fight those basic urges. It's not that I don't think she senses this sizzle between us, she most definitely does, and yet, she seems wary of it. So, for now, I will be a gentleman—not an actual gentleman because I don't think that is in my repertoire. Instead, I will rein in my primal urges and stop staring at her quite so much.

Moving from the door, I head for the fridge where I grab for a bottle of water. Holding it aloft in her direction, I gesture to it?

"Drink?"

"Yes, thanks," she replies and continues to wield the icing bag on goodness knows what tray number of cakes she's on.

Placing the bottle on the countertop near to where she works it dawns on me that her hands are kind of full.

"Would you like me to open it for you?" I point to the water.

"Please."

Without giving it another thought, I twist the lid off and put the bottle to her mouth, tipping it up and allowing her to sip the liquid from it. She drinks some down, her neck moving in the most delightful way as she swallows it down and in that second my mind is back in the gutter, conjuring images of this woman on her knees, still swallowing, but certainly not water.

I could swear she knows what I'm thinking as the blush creeps up her face, then she pulls back, ending her drinking but not before a small drop of water escapes her lips, dribbling down her chin.

Fuck me! This woman has done the simple thing of having a drink of water and has me rock fucking solid.

So much for ridding myself of pornographic images! If I don't put some distance between us, we are going to end up naked, and yet, I can't bring myself to leave. What the fuck is that all about?

"Would you like a taste?"

I must look like a rabbit caught in headlights as I absorb her words and allow them to register in my mind. I am sure she must mean the icing but one look at her glittering dark eyes and the way her tits are almost heaving out of the confines of her vest disputes that.

"The icing?" I ask, thinking that this girl is a stranger and potentially she could just be teasing me, and the last thing I need is a slap or for Olivia's dad to tell Mase that I have been sexually harassing his staff.

"If you like." She grins and I am reassured that I am not going to get slapped but I might just get lucky.

"Why not?" I close the distance.

Slowly and deliberately, she squirts a small blob from the bag onto her finger to offer it to me. I immediately accept the sweet and sticky substance, sucking and lapping her finger in the most sexually explicit way I know, which considering the depths of my deprivation is pretty disgusting. The sound of her moans echo around us in the otherwise silent kitchen, spurring me on and she actually groans when I nip her fingertip confirming that we are both imagining that it is not her finger in my mouth. I pull her digit free and reach for the piping bag. With none of the finesse she showed when she wielded it, I am streaking the sticky sweet concoction on the skin between her breasts. She shudders and whilst it might be down to the temperature of the icing, I suspect it's more to do with sexual arousal and expectation. I quickly lean forward and then with a single, deft upwards stroke of my tongue I consume the icing, which is, as I suspected, lemon.

"Mmm," I rumble against her skin causing her chest to rise and fall which satisfies me hugely.

I am like a starving man here, in need of sustenance and she is the only meal that will satisfy my appetite. With her low, gravelly whimper, I am almost crippled. I don't need any further encouragement it seems as I lunge forward and cover her lips with mine whilst lifting her, my hands full of her fleshy behind that I am using to hoist her up onto the counter where we begin to devour each other.

We are like animals on heat. Within seconds we are shedding clothes, briefly breaking our lip-to-lip contact in order to facilitate the removal of barriers. I am losing it here I realise when I end up fumbling like a fourteen-year-old boy, unable to find the clasp on her bra when she pushes me off.

"Front fastener, Stud," she announces as she pushes her breasts towards me, the fastening now obvious.

I frown at my failure to figure her bra but then grin at her calling me Stud, which is ridiculous, but I don't care and choose to reciprocate with nicknames. "Very nice, Cupcake," I tell her as in one deft movement the clip is undone, the lace fabric gaping, allowing her glorious tits to come into view. "Fuck!"

The sight of the perfectly full globes of her breasts, complete with tightly pulled, erect nipples that are as hard as bullets is truly glorious.

"Foreplay first." She grins. "Foreplay, an orgasm and then the fuck," she tells me before grabbing my head and pulling me back in to kiss her again.

I know that Kelly will give us enough time, but I don't want to risk her, or anyone else busting us and I love a woman who knows what she wants so I need to get a move on with foreplay and an orgasm before we consider the fucking. Quickly, I relieve her of her sexy little shorts and even smaller pair of pants and am taken aback again to find her completely bare. Not that I haven't known a bare woman before, but this woman is all contradictions with her big innocent eyes and naked pussy.

Slowly, deliberately she spreads her legs for me, and I am stunned to see her glistening pussy opening before my eyes. Yeah, she is a total paradox of a woman, but I find it hot. I reconsider my porn viewing and think I might just need to watch more, with this woman maybe. I lean in and kiss her again, but this time I worship her breasts at the same time, cupping, stroking and then squeezing the heavy, full globes before closing in on her tautly pulled nipples that have her crying out when I eventually reach them. I am deliberating feasting on them when she pulls one of my hands from her breast and places it between her splayed thighs.

"Dec, she whines. "Make me come before anyone else arrives."

I am reminded by her words that we are at serious risk of being discovered and the last thing either of us wants is to be rumbled in such an obviously compromising position.

Clearly, I pause a little too long before replying because I feel her tense before she breaks our kiss and in a low whisper says, "Sorry, I don't know why I've done this."

She sounds on the verge of tears and her glistening eyes seem to confirm this, but there's more, she looks embarrassed, ashamed and that is what bothers me most because we have done nothing wrong.

"Hey, ssh," I say to reassure her. "If you don't want this then you say and we'll forget it," I add, really hoping she finds her earlier bravado because apart from the feeling that this might be the best thing either of us could do, I am more concerned that my balls will drop off if I don't get off soon. I really am harder than I can recall being before and all rational thought, not that I am prone to that, well it disappears at the second my dick gets hard. "Do you want me, Cupcake?" I ask with my best endearing smile and she nods. Thank fuck.

I recall that she wanted foreplay, orgasm and then fucking so drop to kneel between her still spread thighs and pull her arse to the edge of the stainless-steel counter she is still on so that I can feast on her to tick off foreplay and orgasm for her, after all we don't have time on our side.

Anita

Today started off as being totally shit, well, today was just the icing on the cake after several shit weeks but it's kind of picking up now with this handsome barman wedged between my thighs. He is clearly aware of the lack of time we have judging by how quickly he gets to work. Glancing down I smile at the top of his head that's covered in thick, dark brown hair that I am tempted to tug on as his tongue sweeps the full length of me.

With the whole of my sensitive and intimate flesh coming to life as his tongue dips into my core I feel my legs trembling and hear a whimper escape from my mouth. My handsome friend appreciates my enthusiasm, and his approving glance up confirms that. I feel suddenly self-conscious to be under his scrutiny, although he has now averted his eyes from mine.

Closing my eyes, I wonder what the hell has got into me. I stifle a very juvenile giggle and response when I feel a finger slide inside me. But this is not me, I don't do anything wild, unpredictable, or reckless, not anymore. I used to but then fate or karma decided to kick me in the arse and my behaviour caught up with me and changed me forever.

"Oh God!" I cry as my thoughts of the past are broken by the burn in my pelvis radiating up and out until I can feel that I am about to combust in sweet ecstasy. *Stud*, as I named him is sliding another digit inside me as his tongue begins to lap against me. My nub of pleasure is swelling. I can feel it along with the soft tissue around it. "Yes, yes," I chant as his tongue forms loops and laps around my clit, driving me crazy with desire as every touch drives me closer to release. "Don't stop," I plead, and he doesn't disappoint me, in fact his efforts are increased in speed and quantity until I am literally riding his face I realise with shame and horror but am helpless to do anything but continue, pulling his face further into me whilst grinding into his bloody genius tongue, fingers and face.

I can barely think, see, hear or talk now as the whole of my body convulses and twitches, inside and out. It is like someone has plugged me into the mains. Electricity surges through me until I am a mass of sensation, burning, aching, and stinging that courses through my core and everywhere beyond until I am limp and spent.

Deep, warm eyes are on me again, the handsome barman stands before me, between my still splayed thighs. I wonder if I have had some kind of seizure because I have lost minutes. Precisely the minutes between him giving me the best orgasm of my life and right now. Him standing here, smiling, clearly appreciating the view I am affording him, not that I understand why because he is gorgeous enough that he could have any woman he wants. Before I go down the well-trodden road of self-deprecation, he laces his fingers through my hair to pull me closer and closer until I can feel his breath on my face, and honestly, I can smell my own juices.

"Cupcake, you are seriously compromising my schedule for the day," he tells me with a slightly lopsided smile that makes him even more attractive. "Are you sure you want to do this?" he asks, shocking me because he doesn't seem the sort to question doing this. He is confident enough that I don't doubt he does this regularly and his skills would support my idea that he has had lots of practice.

I nod. I am sure. This might be the one thing I have been sure of for years.

"Yes," I confirm, and he is sheathing himself with a condom, easily sliding into me, inching into me slowly, but never once taking his eyes off mine.

"You feel so good, Cupcake," he tells me, and I smile, a full-on toothy smile that confirms I love him calling me Cupcake, regardless of how pathetic it might be.

"Hmmm, you're not so bad yourself, Stud."

He grins his reciprocal appreciation of my use of Stud again, then he begins to move in earnest.

From the first stroke I am gasping and moaning. My hands are reaching for him and with them on his shoulders I am pulling him closer until there is nothing between us and my legs are winding around him tightly, drawing him closer and closer until there is almost nothing to separate us.

"Jeez," he hisses through gritted teeth as my short nails dig in more firmly as I feel the fluttering low in my belly beginning to gather pace. "Come on," he whispers against my neck where his mouth is nestled tightly.

His thrusts are quickening, becoming slightly less controlled telling me that he is almost there, but I need a little more so slip a hand between us to find my drenched sex. With two fingers moistened with my own juices I am circling my clit. He is pulling back slightly, to watch my fingers between us. Quickly he adjusts our position so that he is pushing my thighs wider, opening me up, giving himself a ringside seat to me arousing myself while he fucks me with increasingly faster thrusts.

"You're so fucking beautiful," he tells me and that is the thing that makes me blush...I am okay, average in terms of attractiveness but I don't believe I am classically beautiful, I know I'm not. "Shit! I'm going to come," he warns, advises and threatens at the same time.

The sensation of the tissue around and beneath my clit swelling gives me the final push and while he is hissing and shouting indecipherable sounds I am screaming and crying in blasphemous and quite foul terms about just how good I feel.

It's probably only a matter of a minute that we remain joined in our strange little huddle until his phone rings, breaking the moment. He ignores the insistent ringing but passes me my clothes and then we both redress in silence.

He keeps looking at me, as if he wants to say something and

just as he begins with a simple, "Shall we grab a drink?" Kelly calls through to him.

"Dec, balloons and tea lights are here."

She appears in the kitchen and looking between us, smiles a knowing smile but before she can say anything his phone rings again and this time, he reaches into his pocket for it and answers. "Hey, bro," he says with an easy grin before mouthing a *see you later* to me, but I have no clue if that is simply his version of goodbye.

Chapter One

Declan

I am struggling to eat breakfast, much to the amusement of my brother who has already cleared his plate, him, and our father who I am sharing a table with.

"Is this because you need to make a speech?" my dad asks but before I have the chance to reply, my brother chips in.

"Dec, you do know I'm the one who is supposed to get pre-wedding jitters, not you, don't you?"

Him and my dad laugh again as I try to think of a plausible explanation for my inability to eat which is being caused by the dread in the pit of my stomach at being reunited with Anita.

"I'm going for a walk!" I growl and am already leaping up and turning to storm off but have no clue where I'm going.

I am barely out of the hotel restaurant when I feel Mase on my heels.

"What the fuck is the matter with you?" he snaps as he reaches my side and tugs me back to look at him. "Is it the speech? Because if it is, don't make one. In fact, don't do anything you don't want to. I am getting married today and so long as Olivia ends the day as my wife, I don't give a shit about anything."

I immediately feel guilty that I am stressing him out with my wobble rather than reassuring him through his own, not that he has any.

"Sorry," is all I manage to mumble as my brother leads me towards a quiet corner table in the hotel foyer and I try to think of something else to say, an explanation to offer. "I'll be fine." I want to kick myself for being what I perceive as deceitful and a bit of a dick.

"Dec, I mean it. If you don't want to speak or do anything that is fine by me. Just stand next to me at the top of the aisle. I'll even look after the rings if that's an issue." He smiles and adds, "Even if you lose the rings, I am still marrying my girl so there's nothing you can do to cock it up."

I admire his determination to marry Olivia. That is his only intention, and he won't let anything stand in his way. I am also slightly jealous of his obvious happiness and contentment, but who wouldn't be envious of the huge smile on my brother's face, especially when you consider the reason for it comes in the beautiful, sexy, funny and talented form of the brunette he met at my club.

"It's the bridesmaid," I blurt out and Mase simply laughs.

"I know there's a certain tradition, little brother, but not only would Sarah kick your arse if you tried it on, her husband is considerably bigger than you and he is possessive of his pregnant wife so I really wouldn't recommend it." He laughs, clearly confused by who I mean.

Mase and I are close, and we don't really keep secrets. We can and do talk about anything, but this, well, I have chosen to keep it to myself since it happened on the night of his engagement because I have no clue how he is going to react to it, especially if Olivia finds out and takes exception to it.

"Not that bridesmaid," I confess in a hushed voice that I only know is loud enough for Mase to hear when I see his startled expression.

"Assuming you don't mean our niece, I would say if you like Anita there's no reason for you not to act on it, you're both single…" He trails off and I assume my face has given away the fact that I have just made my previous move quite clear.

"What?" Mase asks, his tone is growing agitated, confirming that I might have already outed myself.

"We might have already hooked up. I didn't know who she was, and it was an accident," I stammer as I see his expression darken.

"What?" he asks again but his voice is raised, drawing attention to us, but not as much attention as his next question. "An accident? You accidently fucked my wife-to-be's sister? How does that work exactly? Did you trip and accidently slip your dick inside her?"

I see the security man, concierge, whatever he is, approaching us and both Mase and I hold up a hand to assure him that this isn't getting out of hand. That it is no more than raised voices.

"Come on."

I dutifully follow him outdoors onto the terrace and once we have sat down together, he turns to face me. That look alone tells me all I need to know. It's time to spill my guts.

"It was the day of your engagement party. Before the party. She arrived at the club, the caterer, and I had no clue who she was. I knew Olivia had stepsiblings, kind of, you mentioned them, but I had no idea who they were or what they were called. We were alone and ended up getting together, she was frosting the cupcakes," I say, and immediately regret it.

"The cupcakes for my engagement party? You shagged her while she was icing them? I hope to fuck you didn't contaminate them, Dec. I ate them, Olivia ate them!" He grimaces and I can't help but smile.

"That butter cream shit was seriously tasty." I smirk and I'm relieved to join in with my brother's laughter.

"You are disgusting, you man whore!" he accuses, but I simply shrug.

"Guilty as charged and you weren't always so conservative," I tell him as I recall my brother's like of pretty girls in the past, pre-Liv, although she is his ultimate pretty girl.

"Declan, do not mistake monogamy for conservative," he replies with a grin of Cheshire cat proportions that tells me that my brother is in no way deprived or missing out between the sheets, but that's not for me. I still don't get the attraction of one woman forever, not anymore. "So, you and Anita, do you plan on pursuing it? I have no objections if you do, and I can see the attraction. But for fuck's sake do not mess her around because if you do that will piss Olivia off and that would mean your actual fucking would end up fucking with my life."

"I'm almost tempted to do it if only to piss you off," I taunt but immediately back track. "Afterwards I missed her leaving, but intended to find her on the night, if she was working and if not, I figured I could find her via Liv or her dad. I really liked her, fancied her, had enjoyed what we'd shared. However, she rocked up for the party as a guest and was introduced as Liv's sister, which threw me, both of us, really, and we avoided each other mainly."

"Mainly?" Mase asks.

"Hmmm, yeah. I spoke to her, apologised for what had happened, explained that I had no clue who she was and assured her that I would never have touched her had I known." Hearing my own words along with my brother's expression I can see for the first time that Anita might have been offended, which would explain why she simply shook her head, gave me a death inducing look and walked away from me.

"Bet that made her feel special." Mase frowns. "If she shares this with Olivia you are fucked and I would guess that I am too and not in a good way, so I am telling you now not to make this worse, not today. I am getting married to a woman who deserves to be happy, the same woman I have been kept from for the last seventy-two hours meaning if you piss her off and I don't get laid tonight, I will kill you!"

I laugh at his almost pained expression at the thought of not getting his special time with Liv tonight, but he is deadly serious making me laugh louder and harder until I consider how amazing that one time with Anita was and how my words might have made her feel. I vow to myself that I will speak to her, make amends because there is no way anything I say could make things worse, is there?

Anita

I have been cooped up in this hotel for the last two or is it three days and I am beginning to go stir crazy. My dad is driving me mad because he is flapping and is now rechecking everything that has already been checked. I understand his need for perfection for Olivia, but honestly, Mase is paying serious cash for that to be achieved and Liv herself has double checked everything.

A small smile curves my lips when I see Olivia give our dad a rather harsh sideways glance when he asks if the caterers have come with references and then goes on to suggest that we could have self-catered. I refer to him as our dad because he is Olivia's natural father and my stepdad. Olivia lost touch with him when she was about ten and her mother and stepfather threatened him with claims of abuse to keep him away. He became my dad shortly afterwards. Olivia finally loses the battle of biting her tongue and snaps at Dad.

"Dad!" she growls. "The catering is fine. The company is one Mase has used countless times. The menu is set, everybody knows what they are doing and if they don't, we're fucked because I am getting married in two hours."

I watch my mum shoot my dad a warning glare as he prepares to reply and possibly tell Liv off for swearing.

"Nigel, I think Liv and Anita might need to start getting ready," my mum suggests even though we all know it's simply a ploy to put some space between them.

Fortunately, he doesn't argue but simply follows my mum out and leaves us alone. Liv let's out a huge sigh that makes me laugh, laughter she joins in with.

"I don't actually know why we needed to take up residency here for so long before the wedding, but I swear, had I had to stay any longer I might have said some really bad things to Dad and run away back to Mase," she confesses.

I know how much she and Mase love each other, and I know that our dad has been driving her crazy since we arrived here, but my face must betray something else, maybe the fact that her need to be with Mase might be viewed as a little pathetic. Although the truth is that I am a little jealous of what they have. In addition to that, I can't get over the fact that I shagged her husband-to-be's brother on a stainless-steel kitchen countertop without knowing who he was, and it was fucking fabulous. The downside is that he was a complete and utter tool afterwards, not immediately afterwards but when he found out who I was, who my sister was.

"Are you okay?" Liv asks with a concerned frown in my direction.

"Yes, fine," I reply with a forced smile. "Sorry, just nerves, I think. I hope I don't let you down."

I feel slightly guilty as Liv moves to sit next to me on the bed where she wraps an arm around me. I am worried I will let her down, but I mean letting her down by behaving in such a way that will show the world that I have shagged her brother-in-law.

"You'll be fabulous," she reassures me. "You look bloody marvellous in your dress and if you get nervous you will have Sarah to lean on, but if you really don't want to be a bridesmaid I understand. I know I'm not really anything to you," she says genuinely with no intention to sway me or gain sympathy or pity.

"No, no. Of course, I do," I say in a rather high-pitched voice. I quickly change the subject to something that will refocus her, Mase. "Can I ask you how you knew Mase was the one?"

Olivia's face breaks into the biggest of smiles at the mere mention of her fiancé's name. "We had a connection from the second we met," she begins and then laughs. "He was my first one-night stand, only one-night stand, then I went to work, and he was there. It really was a done deal from that point on, although we did have a few false starts."

"Really? A one-night stand?" I ask a little disbelievingly at that nugget of information because ever since I have known them, she and Mase have very much been a proper couple and she doesn't seem the type, to trust so easily and with good cause.

"Clearly, this is not common knowledge, and I don't think Dad needs to know but we didn't even trade names," she says with a gasp and a giggle that suggests she still can't believe it. "We met at Dazzler, so I figure Dec knows, plus he and Mase are close. That better not feature in his wedding speech, either of their speeches."

"Bloody hell!" I reply wondering if there is something about those Harding boys because when I met Dec that day in the kitchen at the club, I was powerless to resist or maybe it's the club rather than the Harding boys themselves. "No, Dad would have a heart attack or something if he was faced with that information." We both laugh until Liv turns conversation to me.

"Are you okay, really?" she begins and then expands, "you seem sad, distant...if ever you want to talk. I know I am smugly in love and for that reason alone I want everyone to be as happy as me, but I really do want you to be happy."

"I'm fine," I protest dishonestly and sensing more probing from Liv, I divert attention back to her and her favourite topic of conversation, Mase. "So, are you saying you knew you'd marry him before you even knew his name?"

"God no! I never wanted to get married!" she shrieks. "Like I say there was something; a connection, a pull, but it was after that night. He took care of me, made me feel safe. What I felt with and for Mase was like nothing I had ever known. I have dated before, been kissed before, but when Mase kisses me it's like I am being kissed by a man for the very first time every time."

I smile at her words and sentiment because apart from anything she deserves to be happy more than anyone else in the world after what she's put up with. Her next words have me roaring with laughter that she joins in with, but her glittering eyes and dazzling smile suggest she means every word.

"And the sex is abso-fucking-lutely out of this world, mind blowing, shoulder clawing, I think I might actually fucking die phenomenal."

"I met someone," I clumsily blurt out and immediately Liv's eyes fix me to the spot, demanding I expand. "Your engagement..."

Before more words leave my mouth, the door flies open to reveal a very amused and flushed looking Sarah.

"You alright?" Liv asks her pregnant best friend.

"Yeah, but your husband-to-be is a pain in the arse. I had to feign illness to get ahead of him to stop him coming up here... he's missed you." She grins and in response both Liv and I do too. "He has given his dad and Dec the slip and was at a loose end so thought he'd come and say hi."

"I don't mind," Liv says with a very salacious expression.

"No!" Sarah screeches. "No way! As your chief bridesmaid I cannot have you walking down the aisle like you've just been fucked in a cupboard, like you did at my wedding."

"We fucked in a cupboard after your wedding, as well you know," Liv corrects but still has a huge smile plastered across her face.

My eyes are out on stalks as I imagine Liv and Mase huddled in a cupboard on the day I first met her, but all too soon, I actually wonder if there is any way I can get myself some cupboard action.

Chapter Two

Declan

After my heart to heart with Mase we regroup with our dad who seems to be the calmest man in the world. We are basically killing time until we need to get changed and make our way down to the orangery where Mase and Olivia's wedding will take place. A waiter is just placing a tray of tea and coffee before us when I see Liv and Anita's dad approaching us and his pissed off look immediately causes me to panic because the last thing I need now is for him to put me on my arse for shagging his daughter.

"Bloody women," he states as he takes a seat opposite me. "You're the only sane one amongst us," he tells me and explains. "Being single. And you," he says addressing Mase. "Bloody good luck because that girl of mine has a temper and a mouth on her."

I watch Mase bristle at Nigel's reference to Liv as *his girl* because as far as Mase is concerned she is only his. My dad and I both know this and exchange a small smile.

"There is nothing you can tell me about Olivia that will make me think I need any more good luck. I lucked out when I met her," Mase replies and grimaces at the saccharine sweet words and sentiment he has just shared. He quickly pulls his phone out and looks down at the screen before getting to his feet. "There might be a few less for the reception," he informs us. "Christian," he explains and walks away.

I know that Christian only made it onto the wedding guest list because he is married to our stepsister, Imelda, and Olivia was keen to put their associated past of him as her arsehole boss behind them in favour of family harmony. Although Olivia doesn't know that Mase has bought Christian's share in the interior design company she used to work for as a receptionist and now he owns a large controlling interest that is his wedding present to Liv.

Watching my brother walk away as my dad and Liv's dad launch into the wrongs and rights of the female half of the human race, I realise that Mase has ditched me. He is nowhere to be seen and that can mean only one thing…he's gone to find Olivia. I excuse myself and leave the two older men to set the world to rights as I hunt down my brother.

The sight that greets me as I turn the corner before Olivia's current room is of Mase sitting on the floor with the hotel room door barely open. I smile as I hear him talking to Liv.

"I just needed to see you baby, I missed you," he tells her as I hear female voices, Sarah mainly telling him he can't come in.

Olivia's voice is the one I hear next as I notice her hand creeping through the narrow opening of the door right into his. "I missed you, too. Let's not do this again, the three nights apart," she says, and I see Mase smile, it says he is in total agreement with her.

Sarah sounds more insistent now in her calls for Mase to go and then says something about him having to wait until after the wedding to shag Liv in a cupboard which is what makes me laugh, loud enough that Mase turns to face me.

"Come on, big brother," I call as I approach him.

He lands a single gentle kiss to his fiancée's hand and then gets to his feet.

"One hour Livy, don't be late," he tells her and then we leave, him with a contented grin on his face and me with an amused and slightly judgemental smirk on mine.

I love my brother and I really am thrilled that he has found happiness, but I can't deny that I am worried by his level of dependency and devotion where Liv is concerned. What will he do if things go wrong, if she stops loving him, betrays and leaves him? I know what will happen, it will hurt him, break, and damage him and he will never be the same again. He will never recover, that's what happens when you pin all your hopes and dreams on another person. They betray you one way or another and that is why I have truly embraced my man whore status. I will not be that man, the heartbroken shadow of his former self. I am and I will remain this man, the one who doesn't complicate sex with feelings, not again, once bitten...

****

"I knew Liv was different the second Mase met her...he became completely and utterly impossible to be around. He had dreadful mood swings, an uneven temperament and absolutely no interest in the opposite sex," I say, and I'm relieved when the owners of the dozens of sets of eyes on me laugh. "After a couple of false starts including Olivia almost breaking her hand when she punched him and then Mase drugging her, they realised they were meant to be together."

Some of the eyes are staring at me in disbelief, possibly unsure if I am joking or not. I'm not.

"If there was any doubt in my mind that my brother had met the girl of his dreams, a visit to his newly redesigned office convinced me that nobody would ever get him like she does. So, ladies and gentlemen, raise your glasses of overpriced champagne before my brother breaks with tradition to make his speech after the best man in order to have the last word. I give you the bride and groom."

Once I retake my seat I relax until I look across the top table and find Anita's eyes on me. God, she is fucking gorgeous, her big brown eyes are lowering now, avoiding mine. I really need to speak to her, to clear the air, but not now because Mase is in full flow telling everyone how fantastic Liv is and how she has changed his life. Try as I might, I can't take my eyes off Anita in her beautiful dove grey, full length bridesmaid dress that has a one shoulder waterfall detail that leaves one side of her neck and shoulder bare, daring me to kiss the expanse of skin. Thoughts of Anita's skin and my lips makes my trousers tighten and realisation that I know the detail on the shoulder is called a waterfall makes me frown just as she braves a glance up in my direction. We really need to talk, although I have no clue what I intend to say but I really need to say something to remove the tension between us and ensure that future family functions don't become an issue for anyone involved.

Anita

The sound of the DJ's voice announces the arrival of the bride and groom to the dancefloor. My parents are on the opposite side of the room, and I allow myself a smile as Dad takes Mum's hand to give it a gentle, loving, and reminiscent squeeze. They watch on, as we all do, forming a human wall around the dancefloor that Mase and Olivia are slap bang in the middle of.

Somehow, I have managed to avoid Dec since my sister became his sister-in-law, not that he seemed too keen to chat, not with me anyway. He looks horrified every time his frowning glance lands on me. When we walked back up the aisle, with my arm stiffly linked through his because Jed who was acting as an usher ditched me in favour of escorting his wife, Sarah from the service there was still no conversation, although I did think a couple of times that he was poised to speak. He didn't.

I chasten myself for allowing Dec into my thoughts again because not only does he cause ridiculous chemical reactions in my body, but he also pisses me off, makes me pissed off with me and him. Him because he was a complete dick to me after that day we shagged in the kitchen at the club. Or at least the night when we discovered who the other was, and he has made no attempt to make contact since and me because I shagged him in the first place. I think the thought and memory of that is embarrassing more than anything. Embarrassment and shame wash over me.

I refocus my attention on Mase and Olivia who are slowly moving together across the floor. Liv looks happy, happier than anyone I have ever seen. She's beaming with love as she gazes up at her husband who looks like he has just won the lottery, which he might have done.

The look of reverence and total adoration that is bestowed upon Olivia by Mase takes my breath away. I have never seen such sincerity in a single look. He looks at her as if she is not only the only woman in the room, but as if she is the only person that exists in his world. I have no doubt that I will never ever find someone who'll look at me that way because what they have is a one in a million kind of happening but it's so much more than that. I know I won't find what they have because people like me, people who do things like I have done don't deserve what they have.

The tears I can feel building inside disappear immediately when a hand settles on my hip and warm breath dances across my ear and neck before words follow.

"We need to talk," he says and although I already knew who was standing behind me, the voice confirms it.

"I have nothing to say. Not to you," I reply curtly, even if my hitched breathing and quickening heart rate contradict my displeasure.

"Then maybe you could listen," he says in response and his words are like a red rag to a bull causing me to spin to face him.

"Listen! Fucking listen? Maybe I could, *would* have listened had you deemed me worthy of your words when you realised the girl you'd fucked on your kitchen counter was your brother's soon to be sister-in-law!"

"You're mad," he says, overstating the bloody obvious.

"Mad?" I ask, amazed by his stupidity and timing.

No further words leave my mouth. I have no clue what to say or do to make him go away or at least erase the memory of him, of how he made me feel. My body is traitorous in its response to my memory of his touch, his lips, his hands, his dick.

My breathing and heart rate are erratic as they pick up and my body is heating from the inside out, from my face that I know is flushing down to my chest where my breasts feel heavy and achy, especially my nipples that are beading and pulling into tight points. My stomach is doing somersaults that make me nauseous and then flipping until I feel giddy with expectation. The familiar fluttering in my lower half is coiling and spiralling lower and lower until it settles between my clenching thighs. My sex is swelling and pulsating in anticipation, although it is going to be disappointed and unfulfilled. A sudden awareness of my own slick arousal escaping my body causes a low, gravelly moan to leave my mouth. In the blink of an eye, I almost miss Dec grabbing my arm to lead me away from the dancefloor towards a door.

Silently we ascend the stairs far too quickly for me in heels. That much is clear when I almost fall up the stairs behind Dec. Still, neither of us speak, even when Dec turns and picks me up, throwing me over his shoulder and then his pace quickens further, almost running down a corridor before he stops just long enough to open the door in front of him. Once the door closes, he places me back on my feet so that we stand, barely inches apart. Him staring down and me gazing up, and still no words are spoken.

I am unsure if he is angry, horny, or simply confused because his eyes suggest all three and then with a single step forward his lips cover mine and I know I am lost, done for, and hopefully screwed.

The sensation of Dec's tongue stroking my own causes me to reach up to pull his head even closer, preventing him from gaining anything resembling sense and order to his mind that might make him stop what he's doing. He pulls back but my grip only tightens further until I realise that he is attempting to shed some clothes when his jacket hits the floor. I lower my hands to undo the buttons on his waistcoat and then push it off his shoulders until it joins the jacket on the floor. Next is his tie and then his shirt that is still gaping open when my hands begin to trace the muscles beneath it.

His lips are now tracing a path along my jaw to my ear where he begins to speak as his shirt hits the deck. "Oh, Cupcake, I have dreamt of this moment."

His cool breath and his words have me gasping while my belly and sex are clenching.

"We do need to talk." I know he is right, but I don't need to talk at this moment in time, not unless that talk consists of moaning, gasping, and calling to deities. "But later, after."

I grin. I may not be in a cupboard, but I am getting some action and we are going to talk, assuming he doesn't do a U-turn once he's got his release.

With his lips tracing their way down my neck and shoulder I feel Dec's arms wrap around me as far as the zip of my dress and with one easy movement it is falling to the ground in a pool around my feet revealing my near nakedness bar my pants and shoes.

"Fuck me!" Dec says appreciatively when he takes in my appearance.

My grin only broadens with his words and hungry gaze. Taking his words literally I respond. "You seem to have forgotten the order of things, foreplay, orgasm, then fucking," I say, repeating my words from that day in the kitchen.

With a bravery I may not feel, I step out of my dress and manage to switch our positions so that Dec is leaning against the wall and I am standing before him, briefly. Quickly, I lower myself to my knees, leaving my face at the same level as his groin and then reaching forward I tackle his waistband with ease. Pulling his trousers and boxers down together I reveal his straining erection that is already glossy with his leaking pre-cum. Gently, I reach for it, taking him in the palm of my hand that I close around it. I slowly pump it before using my thumb to sweep his arousal around the tip of his dick. He hisses loudly, somehow encouraging me to shuffle closer where I replace my sweeping thumb with my lapping tongue.

Chapter Three

Declan

It really had been my intention to talk, to have a simple conversation where I explained that I had no clue who she was when we first met, but to apologise for the way I handled things once I knew exactly who she was. I need her to know that what we shared that day was not a mistake. She was not a mistake. Moreover, the only mistake was to suggest any of it had been. I don't regret that day and I don't want her to. Regret is a useless emotion; one I don't do as it only ever gets turned in on the person feeling it and ends up fucking them over more than the thing they regretted in the first place.

Looking down I still can't quite believe that my attempt to talk has got us here. Her on her knees palming my erection whilst sweeping her thumb around the crown of my still swelling dick. I hear the hiss that leaves my lips at her touch but am ill prepared for her next move, which is to move closer, one knee before the other and then her soft, wet, pink tongue leaves her mouth, and she replicates the sweep of her thumb with her tongue.

"Oh fuck, Cupcake," I say, but am already running my fingers through her hair, preparing to pull her closer.

Her response is to cover the very tip of me with her mouth and then she gently sucks. I am totally mesmerised by the image of her on her knees, naked but for her tiny pants and shoes, my dick slowly disappearing into her mouth that is slowly drawing me in, her cheeks hollowing as she begins to suck me whilst never taking her big, brown eyes off my face that I know is contorting in pleasure.

She seems to like the power she has over me at this moment in time because I am sure I see the ghost of a smile in her eyes if not on her mouth which is otherwise occupied. My grip on her head and hair tightens significantly when her hand reaches up to cup and stroke my balls while her mouth begins to slide up and down my length which I swear is still expanding in earnest. Her other hand is gripping the base of my erection and is sliding in perfect synchronicity with her mouth. I am embarrassed to admit that if she continues, I am going to come soon and as much as I like the idea of coming in her mouth, I'd rather fuck her and pleasure her before I find my own release.

It's only another couple of minutes before I am almost done for. My balls are beginning to tighten as I twitch in preparation for release and she knows it, the triumphant glint in her eyes says as much, as do her fingers that are starting to creep from my balls to my perineum which might just be my undoing if she continues to massage me there. Although her mouth bouncing up and down on my dick whilst her other hand is literally milking me are serious contributing factors to me being ready to explode. Then at the exact second her tongue stiffens on the up stroke, she sweeps her tongue around the head paying extra attention to my frenulum and she winks, an actual wink. Oh yes, she knows exactly what she's doing to me.

"Oh no, Cupcake," I tell her as I try to hold her head firmly enough that she can't continue with her movements.

She releases me with a loud and what I suspect is a deliberate *pop*.

Still on her knees with a small smile as her hands settle on my hips, she says, "I thought you knew it was foreplay, orgasm and then fuck."

"I do and so far, you haven't had foreplay or an orgasm," I reply.

"I think I was as big a part of the foreplay as you were," she says, licking her lips salaciously. "And orgasm wasn't that far away." She grins.

I have no idea how everything happens so quickly but before

either of us can say another word I have taken her hands in mine and pulled her to her feet. She stares at me like I am a mad man, and I am. She is driving me absolutely fucking crazy. I quickly spin her around so that she is facing the wall then bend down to slide her pants down her hips and legs before helping her to step out of them.

"Keep your shoes on." We might need some help with the height difference.

I reach for my trousers to find a condom and by the time I'm standing I have already torn the foil wrapper open so that when the time comes, I am ready to sheath myself.

"Put your hands flat on the wall and spread your legs, Cupcake."

She complies without hesitation which pleases me immensely. I can't quite believe the image of her waiting expectantly. Her bare sex mine for the taking and I fully intend to do precisely that.

"Lower your hands," I demand and in doing so her behind comes away from the wall as she ends up in a bent position that reveals her glistening pink entrance.

With a step forward she's close enough to touch. What I go with is to run my hand along her spread cheeks and moistening centre. My middle finger slips into her with ease, and I gasp almost as loudly as she does when her body clenches around my digit.

"Foreplay," I say as I begin to pump my finger in and out before adding a second.

"Yes, shit!" she cries as my pace quickens and I find her G-spot. "Fuck, please," she pleads.

"Orgasm before fuck!" I correct her with false sternness in my tone.

She lets out a little whimper that turns into a near growl when my thumb skims up to find her clit.

"Oh yes, please," she implores but her begging is unnecessary because I have no intention of stopping until she is coming apart and then I am going to fuck her.

With my free hand I reach around her body and find a large pendulous breast hanging beneath her and cup it gently at first and then more firmly as I hone in on her nipple that is stiff and beading. As I pinch and torment it, I feel her edging closer to release with her insides pulsing more tightly and her breathing becoming louder and ragged.

"Hard, pinch me harder," she whines.

I am only too happy to oblige because she is beyond sexy when she is horny, desperate, and about to come. My face is beaming at her words, her demand, but then I wonder just how she'll take to my sexually arrogant and bossy persona.

"Ask me nicely, Cupcake," I insist and am startled by her response.

"Please pinch me, hard," she gasps. "I'll do anything, I promise."

There is no way I can deny her now. Immediately I slip a third finger inside her whilst continuing to manipulate her clit, but now I am pressing more firmly into the soft fleshy tissue and then, finally I pinch her nipple hard enough that I half expect her to cry out in pain. She doesn't. Her cries are of simple, unadulterated pleasure as she is rocked sideways by her orgasm. Her pussy is squeezing me so tight I think she may cut off my circulation.

Once I have eased her down, I reposition her slightly and once fully covered with the condom I slide into her. My hands find her hips that I grip tightly enough that she might just have bruises tomorrow.

"Stroke your pussy, come with me," I tell her as I pick up pace.

One hand immediately leaves the wall and heads south and we are surrounded by the sound of flesh slapping against flesh and our laboured breathing. I won't last much longer at the relentless pace I have set but I am powerless to slow down as I chase my release.

"Come on, babe," I implore and as if on cue Anita is coming.

Her screams and cries as her body quivers and quakes can probably be heard beyond the confines of the room but right now, I couldn't care less because I am coming, longer and harder than I can ever remember and I have a really, really good memory.

Once we are a little calmer, I help Anita to move back into a more upright position. I am still inside her and can feel myself stiffening for round two, but I know we should probably talk first, establish some boundaries. Maybe I could invite her out on a date kind of thing before returning to the reception. My body is still blanketing hers and I am pretty sure she can feel my new erection forming inside her.

"Bloody hell, Stud really is an appropriate name for you, isn't it?"

We both laugh until the sound of the room door opening startles us both. Our heads snap in unison to see my brother coming into view and whilst we are shocked by his sudden appearance, he is absolutely fucking stunned by ours.

"Mase," we hear Liv say in a very sultry tone as he comes to a dead standstill.

My instinct is to cover Anita's mouth to stop her speaking and outing us. Mase's is to give me a death-defying stare followed by a shake of his head at what we've done, maybe where we are and that leaves me in no doubt that I am in the shit. If Liv makes it into this room and sees us, I have no doubt that he will kill me, especially if she revokes the consummation of their marriage tonight.

"Baby," Mase says whilst still staring at me and Anita who is crimson and trying to hide her shame covered face from view.

This situation is far from ideal but there really is nothing for her to be ashamed of.

"Why don't we keep up our own wedding tradition until later," Mase is now saying and although I can hear hesitation from Liv he continues. "There was an unlocked linen cupboard back there."

"I am a very happily married woman." She giggles.

"Yeah, well, you be sure to remember that Mrs Harding," he replies and with a final muttered *take me to the linen cupboard* from Liv the door closes, but not before Mase mouths to me, *we need to talk* which ironically is what my original reason for being here was, to talk.

Anita

I really wish a hole would open up and swallow me. My face is crimson with embarrassment having been discovered by Mase, but fortunately not Liv. I need to get dressed and out of here, quickly, but Dec is still pressed against me, holding me firm against the wall. God, he is still inside me! I really need to stop doing this with him.

"Dec," I begin but he is already lifting his weight from me, removing himself from me, allowing me to move.

He passes me my pants which proves to be a little awkward. As much as I would like to use the bathroom, I want to get out more than anything else. Dec helps me to step into my dress. While I slip my arms into it, Dec discards the condom and begins to redress. Once he has his trousers and shirt back on, he reaches for me to fasten my dress, then I turn to face him and can see he looks as awkward as I feel about Mase bursting in.

"Sorry," he says. "About Mase, I should have thought to lock the door," he adds as he picks his cravat and waistcoat up.

I nod as I watch him finish redressing and only then do I take in this room. It's beautiful, much nicer than the room I have, not that my room isn't lovely, but this one is something else. The bed is huge, a very grand four poster, but modern at the same time with dark wood and sparkling white linen with a pattern to the middle and towels folded into hearts. Beyond the bed there is a small balcony that looks out onto the lawns to the rear of the hotel. There is a lovely lounge area with a chaise and a couple of chairs in front of a fireplace and a bath. I have to do a double take at the bath in the main room and wonder if it is prone to flooding. My thinking is seriously skewed. The bath has a curtain thing that seems to partially separate it from the rest of the room and the bath itself is huge. Stretching for a better view I decide it might even be a whirlpool or spa bath, whatever they're called, but whatever it's called it blows bubbles. Looking back at the bed I realise that the linen is totally white and the pattern I thought it had earlier is actually confetti, rose petals in the shape of a bright red heart and then the penny drops.

Angrily, I reach for the door, opening it just enough to see the plaque adorning it and then slam it shut again, turning to face Dec to unleash my fury on him.

"You are fucking unbelievable! We shouldn't have been in here at all never mind locked the door. Why do you even have a key to the honeymoon suite?"

He looks guilty, maybe not at being caught by Mase, although he looked absolutely seething when he found us in here, but Dec's guilt seems to be in relation to where we are.

"I wanted to talk," he says defensively, which only serves to irritate me further.

"What? And fucking me just kind of happened?" I add a heavy shake of my head.

"It's you, I lose my mind when I'm around you and do these things," he explains and although my heart skips a beat at those words, at the sentiment I believe he is trying to convey, I am still mad at him so refuse to acknowledge it, for now.

"So, it's my fault that you brought me to the honeymoon suite to talk and your brother, the groom, who has married my sister caught us naked against a wall?"

"That's not what I meant, and you know it," he counters. "I had a key because I had planned to leave a few surprises in here for them, later, but I needed you alone. To talk. That really was my original intention, but once we were alone…"

He looks sad and confused now and I can relate to that. I am still pissed off about Mase finding us and am sure he will give Dec a hard enough time without me adding to it so decide to cut him some slack, a little.

"I know," I say, acknowledging that by the time we got to this room, and he looked at me there was nothing I could have done to prevent us kissing and once our lips touched, I was blinded to everything else. "It explains why this room is so bloody gorgeous," I add and offer him a small smile.

"Mase is going to fucking kill me," he replies with no hint of humour or jest.

I'm clearly not ready to let him off the hook completely. "Yeah. He looked really mad, and you do deserve it."

He looks stunned at my words and then he laughs. "Your support is duly noted, although if Liv finds out that you got lucky in the honeymoon suite before her, she may not be thrilled," he says and suddenly I am panicking that Mase might tell her. "Especially as her first sex as a married woman was in a linen cupboard instead of that luxurious looking bed, or the bath…"

"Shit! Do you think he'll tell her?" I wonder if Liv will tell my mum and dad too, which would be beyond awkward.

Dec is grinning at my discomfort now and just watches me cringing for a few seconds before putting me out of my misery. "Cupcake, it will be fine, don't worry. I'll take full responsibility because it was my fault really."

He is in front of me, and I am pressed against the wall again, his weight holding me firmly in place. If I don't put some distance between us soon, I am going to end up naked and shagging in the honeymoon suite again and this time I know exactly where we are.

"Dec," I whisper but am already reaching up to cup his face. "We really need to go."

He flashes me the cheekiest of grins but fortunately nods before kissing my cheek. "We do need to talk though."

"Not here."

He nods again before leading me from the room.

"Let me take you to dinner, whenever you're free…" he suggests as we make our way down the corridor towards the stairs.

He drops my hand from his so he can bend to refasten his shoelace that he has almost tripped over and then a nearby door comes flying open to reveal a very hot and bothered looking Liv and Mase. Clearly, he wasn't joking about the linen cupboard. Liv looks stunned to find us there, or maybe it's the fact that we're together but more than anything she looks uncomfortable as she figures we know why they were in a cupboard. Mase leans in to kiss her and I think whispers something that makes her blush and giggle before he turns to Dec.

"You and I need to discuss something before I go away," Mase says. "Baby, this will only take a moment, why don't you take Anita back to the reception."

Liv doesn't bat an eyelid as she kisses her husband and then links her arm through mine to lead me away but not before calling to Mase, "Don't be long or I'll have to dance alone."

Chapter Four

Declan

Mase is calling after Olivia, warning her about dancing alone but she completely ignores him which makes me laugh. He is seriously whipped. As his head snaps in my direction, I regret my laughter that has drawn his attention towards me.

"Mase," I begin, preparing to apologise, but he interrupts.

"Do not tell me it was another accident because the tiny grip I have on my sanity will slip completely if you do," he says with an anxious disposition I have rarely seen in my brother.

"Okay. It wasn't an accident, but it wasn't planned. I needed to talk to her, to explain that I didn't mean to make her feel shitty after last time."

My brother is staring at me expressionless, and the truth is that I have no idea if he is going to punch me or laugh. He does neither. With his fingers pushing through his hair, he shakes his head.

"I assume she bought whatever you said judging by how naked you both were when I came in?"

I feel guilty again as I realise that I didn't even achieve my objective when I sullied my brother's honeymoon suite. Not that I think anything Anita and I did would or could be classed as tarnished in anyway, but I can see that Mase might disagree. If he does, I hope he won't be too disparaging about Anita because she doesn't deserve his judgement or disdain and if he does, I will defend her.

"We didn't get around to talking," I admit warily and attempt to soften that particular blow. "We're going out to dinner though, you know, like a date."

I sound ridiculous to myself so am in no doubt that Mase will reach that conclusion too. He sighs with another shake of his head and leads me to the top of the stairs where he sits down and gestures for me to do the same.

"Dec," he begins as I sit beside him. "What are you doing? She's my wife's sister. You can't fuck her and then drop her like you normally do. This really is a case of crapping on your own doorstep, or at least mine."

"I know," I admit. "Did you tell Liv? Anita was worried about her finding out."

Mase stares at me once more. "If you continue to fuck her sister, she will find out and if you mess Anita around and hurt her, my girl is going to be pissed and if she finds out that you both enjoyed our honeymoon suite before we did, she is unlikely to be impressed. The fact that you are still standing suggests I haven't told her though."

"Thanks." I'm grateful that he hasn't told Liv about Anita.

"What do you plan on doing, Dec?"

It is a simple and fantastic question, and I wish I had an answer for him. I don't. Not a clear or concrete one anyway.

"I like her, but I like a lot of girls," I admit, knowing this is nothing newsworthy to either of us. I am, after all, a man whore. "That time in the club was amazing and today I wanted to talk but once we were alone…shit, the sex was inevitable and it was fucking superb, better than the first time which I didn't think was possible."

My face is a grimace, frown and scowl that amuses my brother judging by his grin.

"You're disappointed it was good?"

"Gutted." I attempt to explain myself. "I wanted it to be no better than good so that I could put it behind me. Since that day in the kitchen, every time I've had sex has been mediocre because it wasn't like it was with her. Today was the best…how the fuck am I going to go back to meaningless sex if my own hand whilst thinking about Anita is better than actual sex with any other person who isn't her?"

Mase is agog at my words. I'm pretty stunned myself because those words were not what I was planning to say and yet I said them anyway. My brother's laughter breaks my silent misery, but I fail to find anything amusing and my sullen expression confirms it. The same expression that seems to increase Mase's amusement.

"What?" I cry, irritated by his continuing laughter and my own words and thoughts.

I do not do this. I am not looking for permanence and I know that Anita is not a fuck buddy kind of girl, so what the hell am I doing? I am taking her on a date, and I called it that even though I don't really date either. I do nights out but usually with the forgone conclusion that the night out will be hot and satisfying but ultimately meaningless long term.

"You, little brother, are seriously fucked!" he states with more laughter.

Picking up on his inference, my irritation rises further, and my response confirms my mood. "Yeah, I was seriously fucked in the honeymoon suite before you were. In fact, I am two for two over you for shagging a Carrington girl first at your engagement and now your wedding."

All laughter stops and cold fury settles across Mase's face, clouding his eyes.

"Declan," he warns, my full name testament to that. "I am going to make allowances for the fact that you have been knocked on your arse by Anita. However, if you ever refer to the shagging of my wife like she's one of your usual slappers or make my fucking of her into a *who can piss the highest* contest I will put you on your actual arse, understand?"

I can see he's seething and regret my words. I regretted them as soon as they were out. "Sorry." I apologise guiltily. "What do I do?" I am desperate for a solution to my turmoil and confusion.

"Go to dinner if that's what you've agreed. No more sex until you've talked and if you can't agree on what you want, need, cut her loose."

"And if I don't want to cut her loose?"

"Then we're back to you being fucked like I was from the

second I set eyes on Livy."

"Shit," I hiss as I realise the enormity of things because I was there when Mase met Olivia, but me and Anita, it can't be the same, can it?

"Hey, there's my boys," our dad calls as he ascends the stairs. "Your mum was looking for you," he tells me. Turning to Mase he grins. "And your wife is setting the dancefloor alight."

"What did I tell her?" Mase asks as he leaps to his feet.

"Clearly you took too long." I laugh, reminding him of Olivia's words.

"Don't look so amused little brother…you've got all of this to come," he says but is already descending the stairs two at a time followed by me and my dad who has just slapped my back for no reason I can think of.

Maybe I should cancel dinner. This is a really bad idea. I am not Mase, and I do not want or need what he has, not now, not ever…not anymore, and Anita needs to accept that.

Anita

Liv leads me into the reception and immediately grabs us a couple of glasses of champagne before directing me to sit at a small table in the corner. She watches me closely, too closely meaning I am in no way surprised when she launches into a discussion on how I came to be upstairs with Dec.

"So, Dec?" she asks and like that I am busted.

My mouth curls into a huge smile, but I am already flushing and then taking on a very guilty expression, I can feel it so I know she can see it. I nod but say nothing. I have no clue what to say. What is there to say and what is she expecting? I am clueless as to what Mase may or may not have told her meaning I am at a serious disadvantage in knowing exactly what her *so, Dec,* question means. It could just be that she is curious to know why we were upstairs together, or it could be that she'd like to know why I thought getting shagged against the wall of the honeymoon suite she will be sharing with her new husband was ever an option.

My mind drifts back to our earlier, interrupted conversation in

Family Affair

the hotel room when I was talking about when she first met Mase, specifically the part where she said she expected that Dec knew about her and Mase which now makes me wonder if Mase knows about me and Dec. There's no doubt that he was surprised to find us shagging in his room, but with hindsight he didn't seem too startled to see me and Dec together meaning his brother knows that wasn't our first time, but just what does my sister know?

"Anita, I feel a bit uncomfortable asking this," she says nervously and my heart sinks as I imagine where this conversation is going. "Upstairs, you and Dec?" I can see an awkward flush creeping up her cheeks meaning she doesn't want to ask me, but she continues. "The honeymoon suite, you and Dec..."

I am crapping myself now because if she suspects what we've done and I confirm it she could go off on one, rightfully so, but I do not need my recent shag, as amazing as it was to be outed in this very full room.

"I can explain," I begin, but Liv is already picking up her earlier conversation.

"I can take a joke, so can Mase. We laugh, a lot, but if you've done something to our room, something bad it might not go down too well. Today has been perfect so far and I want it to continue that way. Mase needs it to be perfect, for me he thinks, but he needs perfection more than me. After everything with Raymond, losing the baby and the court case, Mase needs today to be the first day of forever for us both and our future babies," she explains with a grin and I realise that she thinks Dec and I were unscrewing the legs on their bed or filling it with condoms, or whatever else people do to newlyweds and the relief I first felt at her misunderstanding is replaced with guilt as I replay her words.

"Are you pregnant?" I ask her with a grin for hers and Mase's future babies and a suspicious glance in the direction of her untouched champagne flute.

Liv shakes her head. "Not that I'm aware of, although I haven't had a period for five weeks." She grins. "I might have packed a pregnancy test for our honeymoon though."

"Wow, that's great." I mean it. It would be great if she was pregnant, great for Mase and her and they'll be great parents whenever their time comes. I then think of our dad and just how thrilled he'll be to be a grandad. My smile disappears at that moment as a cocktail of emotions flood my brain.

Olivia is already turning the conversation back to Dec and doesn't seem to notice anything untoward in my mood or expression.

"I think Dec likes you, the way he looks at you…" and then the penny drops for her. "Oh my God, you and Dec, bloody hell. He was the one, wasn't he? At our engagement party?" She doesn't wait for an answer. Her mind is already putting the pieces together with a gasp. "Upstairs, you and Dec…Anita, please be careful," she pleads with a concerned frown. "Dec is a man whore. I love him, and he and Mase are close, but that's what Mase calls him, a man whore, which is fine…"

Oh shit, she is doing the rambling thing our dad does and I need her to stop before I end up confessing all my sins and hidden skeletons come falling out of every closet I've hidden them in.

"Liv, I know. I know what Dec is, but it's fine. We're going out to dinner, soon, to talk. We both know that it's complicated because of our families being linked and neither of us planned what happened and we weren't expecting what happened to happen, either time," I say, hoping I am explaining myself clearly, but with thoughts of the twice Dec and I have had sex I can't keep the grin off my face.

"Bloody hell!" Liv mutters and then laughs. "You've got that face…I had that face from the first time I shagged Mase. If he is anything like his brother, you won't ever be able to move on. Nobody will ever come close," she tells me with an arched eyebrow that is also questioning me further.

"It's like nothing I have ever known," I finally admit with the biggest of grins that my sister reciprocates and then we both laugh again.

"You are screwed," Liv finally says and then we laugh again, both of us knowing that I've already been screwed, twice, by Dec. "Just be careful," she tells me and whilst I want to wave away her warnings, I can't because I share them.

Dec could be the biggest mistake of my life and the fact that we're linked through my sister's marriage to his brother it will be further complicated for everyone if we make the wrong choices, and I am done with wrong choices.

A dance track suddenly sounds around us and in the blink of an eye Liv is up on her feet and dragging me off to the dancefloor where she manages to dance and move in a very seductive way, even in her wedding dress. She is attracting lots of attention as she moves to the music and at one point even Jimmy, Mase and Dec's dad joins her. He dances for a few seconds before whispering something to her and then with a kiss to her cheek he leaves to return a few minutes later with Dec, both of whom are behind Mase. He is heading straight for his wife who I remember was told not to dance alone but once he reaches her, he simply pulls her to him, takes her in his arms and dances with her.

I smile at the picture of them in love until I look beyond them and find Dec. His eyes, dark, intense, conflicted, and fixed firmly on me.

Chapter Five

Declan

I am trying to get away from Christian who has popped in. Although, I know, we both know that's crap because he never pops anywhere. He is my stepsister's husband and was Liv's boss, but was a total knob to her, always had been. However, once she and Mase got together he became worse until my sister-in-law resigned.

"I've gone solo," he says as he follows me through the club I am checking on before I go out for the evening.

"I'd heard," I reply without explaining that I know Mase bought his shares in the interior design company he once co-owned with my former stepfather and Christian's father-in-law, Nathan, and together with my brother's own shares he is gifting them to Olivia making her the majority shareholder.

"Hmm," Christian says and then begins to look around speculatively. "Have you thought of an update, a revamp for your interior?"

Suddenly the reason for him popping in is clear. He is touting for business.

"Not really," I reply shortly and hope he will take the hint and sod off.

"I could put some ideas together," he offers. "And a quote," he adds, presumably not wanting me to misunderstand his offer as anything other than a business deal.

"Christian," I say, checking the time that suggests I am now running late. "I really need to go. I have plans, but in terms of a design job, I'm not really thinking about it right now, but if I was, I would be inclined to go to Liv first."

He looks genuinely shocked that she would be my first port of call, but she would as she is seriously talented and to the best of my knowledge Christian hasn't designed for several years. I am thankful that Mase is nowhere within earshot when he continues to run his mouth.

"Why? Because she has managed to fuck her way into your brother's bed? That he has set her up in my business because she knows her way around the male anatomy? She was my fucking receptionist and don't think Mase was the first man she tried to use to advance her career," he accuses, and I am tempted to hit him myself.

Mase wouldn't hesitate and Christian deserves to be punched for his whole attitude towards Liv, but right now I have the other Carrington sister on my mind.

"Christian, don't be such a dick. If, when I decide to go for a design job, I will go to Liv first, but for no reason other than the fact that I like her work and she understands the name, brand, and ideas I want to use here. You really do need to stop this hating on Liv shit though because if you don't you are going to burn a lot of bridges and if Mase hears you talk about her that way he will fucking flip and he may not hold any interest in your business anymore, but you know he could make your life very difficult," I warn him. "And you are putting your wife and kids in the middle of this."

"Women like her..." is as far as he gets when I interrupt him.

"For fuck's sake, Christian! Women like her! She is Mase's wife. She should have been and will be in the future the mother to his children. You are barely related, buddy, so if I was you, I would shut the fuck up and back off."

He winces at my comments but recovers quickly enough that he turns back to his near obsession with hating Liv. "Was our absence noted at the wedding? I did call Mase, it was last minute though," he sneers.

"Oh right, yeah, you didn't make it, did you?" I say as if I had only just realised. "Christian, I really have to go, but think about what I've said if only for Imelda and the kids."

I am already leaving the club and Christian follows me out onto the street, but I now feel agitated and antsy after defending my brother's wife. This is why relationships are not worth it, they need commitment to love, support and defend, which is fine except the way I do things I can still support and defend, with sex rather than love but the expectation for it isn't there. Hopefully, Anita and I can get on the same page because right now she might be the only thing that can restore my equilibrium.

****

Anita and I exchanged numbers the morning after the wedding. I was a little disappointed that she wouldn't come back to my room with me, but then I can see why that would have been a bad idea with her room being next to her parents and mine being next to Sara and Jed's. Mase's words about no more sex until deciding what I was going to do as far as Anita was concerned also rang in my ears and I know he was right. With hindsight it was probably for the best because it was hard enough to get through breakfast with Anita opposite me without her having shared my bed, plus Liv also warned me off. After she and Mase had finished their shagging to music routine or dancing as they call it, she essentially told me that her sister deserved far better than a man whore to mess her around so to think very carefully about my next move. She had then kissed me rather than punched me, so I think she approves if I don't fuck it up.

I sigh loudly as I consider my own thoughts about not fucking up because that would suggest I want more than the usual fuck buddy I go for, but what does Anita want? I suppose I will find out soon enough I realise as I pull up outside the restaurant where we have agreed to meet.

I enter the restaurant and nervously adjust the tie I'm wearing which is something of a novelty. I don't really do shirts and ties unless I must and tonight, I think I do. I want to do it right. For everything to be right for Anita who has just arrived herself. I can feel her presence before I turn and find her looking perfect in a royal blue off the shoulder lace dress. I am staring at her, powerless to speak as I fully take her in; the hollowed-out effect that leaves her neck, collar bone and shoulders all on show. I am on my second or third rake of her body and allow a small smile to curl my lips at her sexy little legs that are bare from the mid-thigh down and her sexy little feet that are strapped into sparkly blue, heeled sandals. My eyes roam back up over her full hips, nipped in waist and lace covered chest that is heaving in what I think are nervous and anticipatory breaths. Even her arms are sexy, encased in yet more lace. Fuck she is gorgeous and standing there with her hair curled and cascading loosely down her back while she casually licks her pouting glossed lips all I can think about is fucking her and making her scream my name or calling me stud. She really is the image of redemption and sin rolled up in one perfectly beautiful package.

Anita smiles and then laughs with a flush to her cheeks as she speaks, and I realise that the maître d' has appeared and probably already spoken to me.

"We have a table booked," she explains and with me *back in the room* I take over.

"Yes, a reservation, Harding, Declan Harding." I am praying to everything I hold dear that they haven't lost my reservation.

The maître d' smiles, a little too much in Anita's direction and as I consider setting him straight, he is leading us to our table which is situated towards the back of the restaurant where we sit opposite each other. I feel my own tension and can see her anxiety in her breathing and nervous nibbling of her lip. I am reminded of her having done that when she attempted to control the excitement and sound of her release when we had sex, both times. With the combination of how fucking hot she looks and my own thoughts of her lip biting I am stiffening in my pants and really need to get my mind out of *her pants,* or we are going to end up shagging again with no chance of conversation. I think she senses my thoughts and concerns because she turns conversation to safe, non-sexual conversation, Mase and Liv.

"Dad said Liv and Mase had arrived safely."

"Yeah, he sent that message to our mum," I confirm, knowing full well that Mase refused to allow Liv to take her phone with her on honeymoon, but he did take one for emergencies that he had no intention of turning on once they arrived safely on the very small, secluded and exclusive little island he has taken his wife to.

"I have no clue where they've gone," Anita says, and I nod.

"Nobody does, not really, except our dad. Mase wanted them off the radar unless there was an emergency."

Again, she nods, and a strand of her hair falls across her face. She pushes it back slowly and I am back in that place where all I can think of is her and me naked and sweaty. The waiter appears as if on cue to get us out of each other and back on conversation. He leaves us with menus and that passes some time allowing me to calm down a little.

This is one of the reasons I prefer meaningless sexual relationships, because of the pretence a real girlfriend requires. When you both know and agree that sex is what you want and need it's easy, no strings fun. You shag, you shag some more, maybe even share the odd meal or night out but you both still know that the real point is the end of the night, the sex and afterwards whoever isn't home gets up and leaves. Easy, or it would be if Anita wasn't my brother's sister-in-law. That is the only reason I am thinking I might need to offer her more, isn't it?

Anita

We are sitting and staring at each other and have been for a while. We've eaten in relative silence and it's not a comfortable silence we've shared. I am desperately trying to think of something to say to break the heavy, awkward atmosphere between us. Unfortunately, I watch Dec for a few seconds longer and it's enough time for us to lock eyes and the atmosphere between us charges in an instant, meaning I need to speak, to say something before I end up sprawled across the table with no thought for our fellow diners.

"How's work, the club?" That is what I come up with as a safe topic of conversation.

His eyes darken and then he responds. "Good, work, the club, although the kitchen holds extra special memories that make it distracting to be in there," he replies and we're back there again. "Sorry," he says in response to the long sigh I release.

"No, don't be. We have a serious elephant in the room, Dec, so maybe we should address it," I say in one huge breath, knowing that if I don't get the words out, I am going to chicken out and still end up sprawled across the table.

"What do you want? From me?" he asks me with a huge sigh of his own as he rubs a finger across the bridge of his nose. Unfortunately, he doesn't give me a chance to speak, he simply continues himself. "I am not Mase. I am not looking for a happy ever after and kids and stuff. I like fun and uncomplicated."

"I see," I reply, unsure what to say because I don't really think that I am in a position to want the things he claims not to. He doesn't want them, and I don't deserve them.

"Look, Anita, I like you, I think that's pretty clear to us both and I would like nothing more than for us to leave here together, but I don't want to mislead you on who and what I am."

"Man whore," I say with a small grin tugging the corners of my mouth.

"Is that courtesy of your sister?" he asks with a small grin of his own but makes no attempt to deny it which is disappointing and reassuring at the same time.

The waiter returns to clear our plates and we both decline dessert, eager to be left alone once more to resume the conversation we'd been avoiding up until a few minutes ago.

"We could go and discuss this more, decide what the hell we want to do," Dec suggests, and I nod, not that I know what I want or what I will accept in terms of a way forward from this awkwardness interspersed with hot sex. "Where do you live?" he asks and I realise he means going somewhere private, secluded. Somewhere with a bed, although we've never had a bed before, so anywhere with kitchen counters or walls is a high-risk location.

"At home, with my parents," I admit and feel a little embarrassed that at almost twenty-four I still occupy a single bed in my parent's box room. "But maybe somewhere private isn't a good idea."

"Maybe not. So, what do you want Anita, from me, us?" he asks again, without any invitation to move on now.

"Not a clue, but I like you."

"I like you, too." His grin broadens. "Come on." He's already reaching for my hand as he stands. Clearly, we're moving on.

He throws down some cash onto the table and then we are on our way out, me trailing behind, smiling appreciatively at the sight of his glorious behind that is encased in quite tightly fitting suit trousers. My eyes lift to see the rippling muscles of his back showing through his white shirt.

"Dec, your jacket," I say with a giggle as he spins round and dashes back to retrieve it from the back of his chair.

"See, you are sending me crazy," he tells me as he returns, throwing his suit jacket back on before grabbing my hand again. "We can go back to mine," he says once we exit onto the street. "I assume your parents wouldn't thank me for coming into their home, defiling their daughter only to leave under the cover of night."

I laugh and shake my head as I imagine my dad's face at the reality of me having sex.

"I'll take that as a no." He grins leading me to his car that is parked nearby. "Are we doing this?" He pushes me back against his car, his body holding me firmly in place as his lips graze mine making me needy and desperate for more.

"I'm still not sure what we're doing," I reply, because I have no idea what we're embarking on or what I am agreeing to.

"This, us," he says with a small frown as he gazes down at me, his fingers lifting my chin so I am gazing up into his eyes. "I think we both know it's confusing and may go horribly wrong, but I can't get you out of my head, Cupcake."

My smile is beaming at his use of Cupcake, and he smiles back in response to my reaction to it.

"So, we'll keep it low key, casual."

I nod at his low key but am unsure what he considers to be casual.

"Play it by ear."

Again, I nod, but manage to interject something. "And talk, can we talk about things as we go?"

"Of course," he agrees. "Did you drive?" he asks looking around.

"Yeah, I'm on the car park around the corner."

"I'll drive you round to get it," he tells me more than offers.

"Or I could leave it. It's a secure place. I can collect it in the morning."

Dec looks confused and is frowning that confusion before he asks, "But how will you get home? It's likely to be the early hours when you need to leave and taxi—"

"What the fuck?" I screech, startling a rather loved up looking couple who are passing by. "You expect me to come back with you, shag you and then leave, in the middle of the night?"

He looks startled by my outburst or at least the meaning behind my words.

"Is this your idea of us? Low key and casual means a fuck buddy?" I ask, slightly stunned.

"I thought this is what we agreed," he says and honestly, I want to punch him for thinking that is what we've agreed to. What I've agreed to. "Although I wouldn't have said fuck buddy."

The guilty expression on Dec's face would disagree that he wouldn't have called us fuck buddies. I do not want to be a notch on his bedpost, on anyone's bedpost. I have misjudged men in the past and made mistakes, of colossal proportions but no more. No matter how good a shag he might be because experience has taught me that I only get hurt in those situations, hurt, and left to deal with the fallout.

"I did think we might be exclusive though, unless you'd rather not and then I would just request the courtesy of you telling me and vigilance with protection."

I am agog at his arrogance, stupidity, call it what you will. I have essentially just protested at being sent home in the early hours as a fuck buddy and he is still discussing details, specifically the details of being free to shag other people but without the inconvenience of picking up an STD.

"Un-fucking-believable! You fuck who you want, Dec, I don't care. No matter how good sex with you is, as amazing as it makes me feel, nobody has ever made me feel quite as cheap and worthless as you and I have known worthlessness and cheap, so no, no us, no deal. Goodbye," and then I slap his face, hard.

Determined not to cry until I get to the privacy of my car. I knew that I would break once I reached the security of my single bed in my parent's box room.

Chapter Six

Declan

The sound of banging is beginning to infiltrate my current state that is somewhere between drunk and hungover, awake and asleep. I think it must be the gremlins in my head stirring but as hungover and awake begin to win the battle, I realise it's the door.

"Shit," I mutter, realising that I am still in the club, having got drunk and fallen asleep here the night before. "Fuck!" I curse as I get to my feet and find both Lindy and Laura nearby, passed out and naked.

The banging continues and the thudding of my brain rattling against my skull is getting worse. I throw on last night's jeans and plod, barefoot to the door. Opening it I wince at the daylight hitting me.

"What the fuck?" I'm stunned to find him here. He's supposed to be on honeymoon, isn't he? "What the fuck are you doing here?" I ask as he pushes past me and is heading towards the bar where I left Lindy and Laura lying naked.

"Fucking hell!" he bellows.

Yes, he's found the girls and has woken them up judging by the series of sleepy, *Morning Mases* I hear. He spins so quickly that I almost collide with him and his angry face.

"Declan," he snaps, and I am unsure if he is pissed with me or the fact that he has just seen my sister fuck buddies naked.

"Girls," I say, already passing them their clothes and a twenty-pound note. "Go and get some breakfast yeah, and I'll see you both later for work."

They are good girls and don't pout or make a fuss, they simply begin to dress and take the cash for food. With one each side of me they kiss my cheeks with a *bye* for me and my brother who is following me upstairs to my office where I will find pain relief.

I am scrambling through the drawers of my desk, hoping I can find some headache tablets when Mase speaks, having remained surprisingly silent since we ascended the stairs.

"What are you doing?"

I take him literally, maybe deliberately misunderstanding him. "Looking for headache tablets," I reply as I find them. "Ta-da," I cry and immediately regret my own raised voice that won't be singing again anytime soon. I grab two bottles of water and offer one to Mase.

"I mean this, the mess of you and the girls?"

His serious frown makes him look like our dad and I laugh for no reason beyond the fact that my brother is truly whipped by Liv and marriage. My brain vibrating against my skull suggests laughter was also a mistake.

"Mase, just because your days of three ways are behind you, don't condemn us all to the same mind-numbing monogamous fate. Anyway, why aren't you on your honeymoon?" I hope I haven't missed something bad happening as I have been on a real bender, night after night since I royally fucked up my handling of Anita. It's for the best I tell myself for what feels like the millionth time since that night outside the restaurant.

"Grow up!" he snaps, and I assume that is in response to my monogamous comment. "My honeymoon ended yesterday and this morning my wife got a call from her father…"

"Shit, I didn't do anything, Mase," I plead, hoping he'll believe me. What the fuck is the matter with Anita and her father that she must make a big deal out of her hurt feelings and why would her father decide he needed to tell Liv about it all? Presumably she has then shared with Mase and here he is. "We went for dinner, and it was as awkward as fuck. I thought about what you said about being honest regarding what I wanted and could offer, and I was. I thought we were on the same page and then when I suggested she needed to bring her car to mine so she could go home afterwards, she went mental and slapped me. I haven't seen or spoke to her since."

Mase sits on the sofa, staring at me. He might be mildly amused judging by his face, or it could be wind or just his smug in love face.

"Well fucking say something," I demand and then hold my head as my raised voice echoes around me again.

"My wife received a call from her father who explained that he has a business issue...his kitchen at the catering company is knackered and his domestic kitchen isn't suitable," Mase explains and although I understand the words I am only concerned about Anita.

"What happened to the kitchen?" I hope to convey false nonchalance.

"Gas explosion," he replies flatly but I am beside myself now.

"When? How? Is she okay? Not Liv, Anita, is she okay? Was she there?"

Mase shakes his head. "She should have slapped you harder or taken a leaf out of her sister's book and punched you." He grins, clearly thinking of the time Liv punched him. "She's fine, they're all fine. It happened at night."

"So, what has the kitchen got to do with me?" Once I hear my own question, I know exactly how it involves me. "No, Mase, fuck, no!"

"You have the facilities. You're the only one I know who does and I said I would ask you."

"Ask? Is that what you're doing?" I feel certain he is telling me he's already agreed to it.

"It is. If you say no, I'll go back and tell them no. It makes no difference to me beyond the fact that Olivia will feel better knowing it's sorted, and I need her to be relaxed, but if I need to, I'll hire them somewhere until their premises are back in action."

"But then she'll know. Anita. She'll know I said no."

"And that matters, why? You fucked it up with her, cut her loose or at least let her cut herself loose. You've moved on or at least reverted to type. Does it matter what Anita thinks or knows?"

His question is reasonable. It shouldn't matter, but it does, and my smug and conceited brother knows that.

"Fucking fine, let them use my kitchen, but don't blame me if I end up fucking her again," I snap to a grinning Mase who is shaking his head at me.

"Good luck with Nigel around." He laughs, but then more seriously says, "Dec, don't mess her around. If you have licked your rejected wounds and want to try and make amends fine, but do not fuck her about, she doesn't deserve it. Plus, I have left Olivia with Anita so I am sure next time it will be a punch, not a slap. Oh, and as I say, I need my wife to remain relaxed."

"Why? Why does Liv need to be relaxed…oh, wow, should I be congratulating you, big brother?"

"Yes, you fucking should!" my brother replies with a smile of immense proportions, and I am pleased that he is so genuinely happy, pleased and a little bit jealous, the latter being something I reject quickly.

Anita

My legs feel as though they belong to someone else, but unfortunately my banging head is all my own. The walk of shame is never easy but is compounded when the final destination is your family home where your parents are and most likely, your brothers too.

Since that night with Dec, I have tried to spend as much time out of the house as possible. I had a couple of days where I stayed in, ate chocolate and cried, but then I picked myself up and brushed myself down and hit the town. I met a guy on the first night out and we've been seeing each other most nights since, work permitting. He's nice, kind of. His name is Jack, and he has just split up from the mother to his two kids so is looking for nothing beyond some fun, which is fine. I am happy with that. I briefly consider that Dec was offering me the same, but the difference is that Jack didn't plan on turfing me out onto the street once he was done. No, he lets me stay all night and even makes me coffee before I return home in last night's dress which is what I am doing now.

"Oh bollocks!" I cry as my heel gets stuck in one of the gaps in the paving. I pull my foot free and yank the thing out with my hand, completing the journey up the path wearing just one shoe and hobbling as though I have one leg longer than the other.

It looks like everyone might be home, my parents and certainly my oldest brother and stepbrother, Scott. All the cars on the drive and the road confirm that, but I figure none of them should be judging me and if they are, tough, because there is far more about me that they don't know that they certainly should and would judge me for if they were to discover, which they won't. Nobody will, not ever.

I'm unsure if I can sneak in at eleven in the morning, but to be honest, after the last couple of weeks my appearance in last night's make-up and clothes is unlikely to shock them. My parents are concerned, they have voiced them, several times a day. My brother, Aaron, who is just a year younger seems to be slightly disappointed, but he is with the same girl he was at fifteen, so I suppose I seem to be a bit of a slapper in his eyes. Joel is almost four years younger than me and seems amused, but I suppose at twenty and cute he's no stranger to the walk of shame. He, however, is discreet and always comes home to his own bed before daylight. I have no clue how Scott feels, he's a bit of a closed book and doesn't really express much in the way of opinions, although I imagine that in the religious cult place he and Liv were brought up, opinions were rarely encouraged.

Falling through the front door, I consider going straight up to bed but the sound of laughter filtering through the house draws me in as far as the lounge where I see Liv looking tanned, relaxed and happy.

She sees me straight away and is up on her feet and heading towards me where she pulls me in for huge hug that is accompanied by a whisper of, "Sorry if Mase busted you."

I have no clue what she's talking about but allow her to lead me to the sofa where she pulls me down next to her. Quickly, my younger brothers disperse leaving Mum frowning her concern at me again. Scott still says nothing but is chatting to Liv about some jobs he's applied for. My dad is glaring at me. Clearly, he is pissed off about my night out and I can see he is dying to say something but doesn't, for now.

I sit and listen to the chatter around me for another ten minutes or so and after failing to stifle my final yawn, I attempt to excuse myself which is when my dad decides to chime in.

"Maybe if you came home at night you wouldn't need to slope off back to bed," he snaps, and everyone suddenly looks awkward.

"Dad, I'm not sloping anywhere. I am going to take a shower and redress and then I will be ready to do that cake for Saturday." I'm lying. The only plan I had was to go to bed, but I do need to bake that bloody cake for the wedding we're catering on Saturday.

"How long, Anita? How long are we supposed to simply sit back and watch you do whatever it is you're doing with God knows who?"

I can see Mum literally stepping in. "Nigel," she warns. "This isn't the time—" she begins but he cuts her off.

"No, Carol! Enough is enough and it probably isn't the time, but this is unacceptable."

Scott looks beyond uncomfortable and is disappearing into the back garden, Liv looks like she might cry while Dad looks beyond angry, angrier than I have ever seen him. The words *you're not my dad* are swimming around my head, but I stop myself, just.

He continues goading me to say things that can't be taken back, not that he knows he's doing that.

"Why can't you be more like Livy? You don't see her behaving like this. She's found someone she loves; someone she has married."

The temptation is to point out that his precious Livy picked Mase up as a one-night stand and shagged him without even knowing his name, but I don't. Although I think Liv knows how close I am to the edge.

"Dad," she says, and he turns to face her. "Anita is a grown woman. You need to let her make her own decisions."

"Do I indeed?"

She is clearly shocked by his firm, terse tone and I am kind of hoping Mase will walk in to hear him speak to her that way, but then I remind myself that his current tone, although aimed at Liv is definitely down to me.

"Well, maybe everyone needs to remember that while you live under our roof, we have expectations."

I don't need to say anything because Liv does now and she stops our dad dead, so much so that I end up feeling sorry for him and guilty that my actions have caused this.

"Yeah, well I don't live under your roof. Haven't done for a very long time so your expectations don't impact on me, but whether you like it or not, she, Anita, is not a child and if you continue to treat her as one, she won't be living under your roof either." She then turns her attention to me. "You really do need to go and have a shower and maybe think about what he said."

I nod and am happy to leave the room, offering a single and heartfelt, "Sorry," to my parents.

The sound of Liv walking behind me up the stairs is a shock, as are her words to me. "I would like to know just what the fuck is going on with you!"

Liv follows me to my room, sits on the bed and waits for me while I have a shower and because I am not overly confident of my own body I quickly redress in the bathroom before returning to her.

"So?" No more words are required.

I tell her about my dinner date with Dec and how it all went tits up and she looks genuinely surprised.

"Wow." She exhales slowly. "I would have punched him," she tells me sounding slightly disappointed that I only slapped him. "He is a man whore but that's a bit shitty. He'll fuck you in his bed but doesn't want you to sleep in it." She is shaking her head when she suddenly seizes upon my night out. "Hang on, if you weren't with Dec, which is what I meant about Mase busting you…shit, I'll come back to Mase. Who were you with if not Dec?"

I explain about Jack, and she looks sceptical, but why wouldn't she be if I am.

"I am in no position to judge," she concedes. "I knew Mase intimately and he'd told me he didn't date girls who shag him on the first night before I knew his name. Oh, and thanks for not outing that to Dad. It must have been tempting. Although from that to this, happily married and preg— shit, I am supposed to be keeping this to myself until I've seen a doctor, but you're my sister, so it doesn't count." She grins and then physically beams as she says the word in full, "I am pregnant."

We hug and I mutter a variety of congratulations before Liv moves back to her earlier reference to Mase.

"Mase has gone to see Dec. Dad said it's been a struggle with the gas explosion at the kitchen so we thought you might be able to make use of Dec's kitchen, especially in the day. Sorry, I didn't know…"

"Shit. Let's hope he says no." I pout but then there is a knock on the door and when I open it Mase is standing there.

"Have you told her?" he asks with a nod of his head in my direction. "Dec says yes."

"Great," I cry, hoping I will be lucky enough to avoid Dec and if not, to at least remain dressed in his company.

Chapter Seven

Declan

I last a total of forty-eight hours avoiding Anita in my club. I finally give in to curiosity and enter the kitchen where she is laughing with another girl who works with her. When she looks at the doorway I occupy, the glorious sound of her laughter stops dead and that slays me. The knowledge that just the sight of me renders her unhappy and incapable of amusement cuts me deep. I have no clue if the other woman knows who or what I am. What I was to Anita, but she certainly knows there's something. Her speedy exit with just a couple of muttered apologies confirms that. We remain, looking at each other, maybe deciding what to say or do.

"They look good," I say pointing towards some kind of canapes I have no interest in whatsoever.

"What do you want?" she asks, her directness shocking me, but it's more than that, she's cold, detached almost.

Her attitude, whilst understandable on a personal level is pissing me off because the truth is that I am helping her out. Well, her father's company at least. I ignore my own acknowledgement that I agreed to help partly for Mase and Olivia but mainly to be able to do this, to see her and find out if my regular three ways with Lindy and Laura and countless other nameless encounters are really helping me to get past how it felt with Anita. They're not. Just the sight of her with her hair pulled up in a ponytail and dressed in baggy jeans and a plain blue t-shirt has got my dick hard and my heart hammering out of my chest which is pissing me off even more than her arsy attitude.

"Look, darling," I snap, already hating myself for where I am going to take this conversation. "I am already doing you the favour by allowing you to knock up your mediocre prawn vol-au-vents, so just remember your place."

If looks could kill I would currently be a rotting corpse because her look is murderous with a heavy dose of contempt thrown in for good measure.

Her reply is flat, short and to the point. "You made my place perfectly clear, Declan. On a countertop, against a wall, but never asleep in your bed."

She looks hurt and ashamed now which makes me sad and humbled. I need to make this right somehow even if all previous attempts to make things right backfired and seemed to only have the opposite effect.

"Anita," I say, having trampled down the Cupcake I wanted to bestow upon her.

She looks at me thoughtfully and I think possibly optimistically as she speaks, "Dec, just fuck off!"

My brain is still debating whether to laugh or cry at her words as her phone rings. She smiles down at the screen before answering it.

"Hey, babe. I thought you'd still be in bed after last night," she says with a sexy as fuck giggle, but the meaning of her words cut me deep, too deep.

She's moved on, like you have, I tell myself but dismiss that thought and do as she asked and fuck off, seething as I go, my mood darkening with every step that takes me further away from her.

Anita

I watch Dec walk away and feel a bitch at the hurt and anger filling his eyes, but then he started it with his *remember your place*. Arrogant prick!

The voice at the other end of the phone is calling to me and I can't believe I did that.

"Sorry," I begin. "Are you okay?"

"Yes, although that's what I called to ask you. To see how things were going at home and with Dec, but—" Liv's voice trails off and I assume she has figured just how things are going with Dec with the way I answered the phone to her.

"Home is better. We've agreed that my walks of shame need to be no later than daybreak. Either that or I need to take a change of clothes."

Liv laughs, loudly, slightly disbelievingly I think which is confirmed by her words. "I bet that wasn't awkward at all. And Dec?"

"It was great until he appeared and opened his mouth." I think that sums it up.

"I see, and Jack?"

"It's fun, Liv. Easy, but no more."

"Okay." I can hear the cogs turning in her mind.

"Olivia." I'm attempting to warn her off.

"I still think you and Dec could have something."

"No," I say firmly because as much as I want to be with someone who makes me feel like Dec does, it just ends up a bigger mess each time we try.

I laugh when I hear Mase's voice echoing my own, "No!" He does follow his up with more words though. "Baby, please, just mind your own business," he says, and I laugh again, louder.

"I can't," Liv protests. "She's my sister."

The genuine affection and concern she carries in her voice makes me smile at the love and warmth she extends to me.

"Yes, and Dec is my brother so back the fuck off and leave them to it."

"Alright," she says, seemingly compliant but I'm not convinced. "Hang on, Anita, this fucking coffee machine is conspiring against me again. Meet me for lunch one day. I'm back to work tomorrow but as Mase has made me the boss I can do any time so just let me know when you can do."

With our goodbyes exchanged and me giggling at Liv's constant battle with Mase's coffee machine, I turn my attention back to the potato cakes with smoked salmon and cream cheese canapes for tonight's function.

****

The next couple of hours fly by and by the time my dad arrives to collect the food I have almost forgotten about my earlier encounter with Dec. Not forgotten as such, but it's not as fresh in my mind as it was, except I might have just refreshed it. I help to load the van and as my dad heads off to the function room I run back into the club for my bag. Once I have it, I head out to find Dec in the bar with a member of staff. A very buxom blonde member of staff who appears to have his tongue in her mouth.

The horror I feel etched on my face is compounded further when another woman who looks like the first one appears behind them and seems to be nuzzling Dec's ear. I cough, genuinely shocked by just how big a man whore he is. They all turn to look at me but only Dec looks embarrassed to find me bearing witness to their exchange or whatever the hell it is they're sharing. Not that I am in a position to judge because I wouldn't expect to be judged by Dec for Jack.

A small laugh escapes my lips, not because I find this scene funny, but I now realise just how out of my depth I was and always would have been with Dec. I have been stung before by a man with no scruples or moral code. Never again.

"Cupca…Anita," he corrects himself and suddenly I only feel sad that I am no longer Cupcake. "I thought you'd gone."

"I am, right now. And Dec, me nor my canapes are mediocre, but this," I say bitchily with a sneer and a dismissive wave of my finger between the two women who are simply standing there wide-eyed, but seemingly unbothered by me or my presence. I'm unsure if they have even got my inference about them but don't wait to find out. I simply walk to my car and text Jack because the sooner I flush Declan Harding from my system the better.

Chapter Eight

Declan

"Oh God, yes, like that," I hiss as I feel my balls tightening and the warm wetness of a mouth sliding up and down my length.

I glance down at the brunette on her knees before me and curse myself for looking. Now I have seen her I am going to struggle to pretend that she's someone else, Anita. I can't even remember her name as I slide my hands through her hair, pulling her down onto me more firmly. I am so close to coming and she seems to sense it too. Her mumbling around my dick gives me a sadistic thrill.

A slap to my leg encourages me to loosen my hold enough for her to rest back on her heels.

"My jaw hurts," she whines. "Fuck me instead," she pleads, but I have no intention of fucking her pussy.

"Darling, suck me," I reply, just needing to come. "Blow me and then I'll make you come." The way she came earlier suggests the dangling carrot of another orgasm should be enough for her to finish me off.

She grins up at me and goes back to the task in hand, well mouth, and with my eyes firmly shut I push thoughts of what a bastard I am out of my mind and conjure images of my Cupcake when she was on her knees in that hotel room and that is the final bittersweet touch I need to get me there. I come hard, but there's almost an emptiness about it. That only increases when I watch her swallow my seed, almost resenting her for doing that.

She smiles and I know she's waiting for me to make her come and I will but before either of us make a move, the office door flies open, and Liv is standing there.

"What the fuck?" she asks, already covering her face but her fingers are splayed allowing her to see everything.

I am helping the woman on her knees to her feet and encouraging her to leave which she does reluctantly whilst I adjust my clothing.

"You might want to consider knocking," I tell Liv who is bright red.

"You might want to lock the door," she replies, making me laugh, especially when I remember Mase coming through another unlocked door into the honeymoon suite where he found me and Anita.

I close the distance and attempt to hug her, but she backs away from my touch and kiss.

"What?" I ask at her objectionable expression at the prospect of a kiss.

"I have no clue where those lips have been," she tells me, deadly serious. "Oh, and maybe wash your hands." She recoils making me laugh loudly, but I'm already heading to the small bathroom in my office where I wash my hands.

"So, how are you and my niece or nephew?" I return for a gentle kiss to her cheek and a pat of her belly.

"We're fine." She actually glows. "Did Mase tell you it's a secret?"

"Yeah, so my lips are sealed."

"It's just you, Sara and Anita that know," she explains with her expression clouding over, but she recovers quickly. "So, I was wondering if you're free to come out next week, Tuesday. We could check out that new club?"

"Are you allowed out to dance?" I know that Mase is beyond protective and jealous where Liv's concerned but a pregnant Liv is going to send him into protection overdrive.

"You leave Mase to me," she says with a suggestive wink that makes me laugh but also makes me envious of my brother's together life compared to my own chaotic one that I was more than happy with until a few short weeks ago.

"What the hell, yes. But if Mase kicks off it's on you."

She seems totally unbothered at the prospect of having to deal with an angry, overprotective husband and I envy that she has no doubts in her mind that she won't fuck up her dealings with Mase, moreover that she won't just make things worse, unlike me with Anita and suddenly my suspicions rise.

"Liv, you're not matchmaking, are you? With Anita?" I remember the time Sara did that exact same think to Liv.

"Dec, I love you, but really? After my sister found you with your temptress twins and what I've seen today, why would I fix her up with you?"

I can't really disagree with her observations as she leans in and kisses my cheek before excusing herself.

"I've got to go. I'm due to meet Mase for lunch and if I don't get there first he'll become suspicious and realise I've been using public transport," she says with mock horror and an aghast expression mimicking Mase's total opposition to Liv being unattended on public transport.

Anita

Somehow, I have avoided being alone with Dec since that day with him and the two blondes. I hate to admit, even to myself that seeing him hurts me. The knowledge that what we shared really meant so little to him, unlike me. Although I am still seeing Jack it is very much on the way out for us both, no more than a bit of fun really. The sex is okay, however, it's nothing compared to Dec, but then Jack is a nice enough guy, friendly and honest. I dismiss my own conscience when it points out that Dec is also a nice guy, friendly and honest. So why did I accept a casual fling with Jack but not Dec?

It is fortunate that before I can answer that question Olivia enters the restaurant looking happy, aglow, and stunning, as usual. The heads turning as she passes other diners confirms that.

"Sorry if I'm late," she gasps as I stand to greet her.

My dismissive wave of a hand suggests her time keeping is not an issue. Liv virtually growls at her phone ringing as she pulls it from her bag.

"Hi, babe," she says and smiles despite her furrowed brow for Mase. "No, I haven't. In fact, I'm about to have lunch with Anita. No, the same place where I met you the other day."

She is silent as presumably Mase speaks. The waitress appears to take our drinks order. I go with a fruit juice concoction dressed up as a cocktail and with two fingers held up Liv opts for one too. I love how much Mase loves my sister, but I think he would drive me crackers with his possessive traits, not that I imagine ever finding anyone who'd care enough about me to want to possess me.

"Mase, I have been in the office until ten minutes ago so no trains, tubes, buses or anything else. Right, I am going now... then don't make me hang up on you. Okay, yes, I love you too, bye."

I watch her as she drops into the seat opposite me, and she looks tired suddenly.

"Problems?" I really hope there are none because if Liv and Mase can't make things work then nobody can.

"Mase is panicking," she begins and sadly smiles again. "He is scared for me and the baby. After I lost the last one and his guilt that he didn't prevent it..."

Her voice trails off and her eyes glaze with tears for her lost baby.

"The other day I met him for lunch and before I did that I went out on the train." She grins knowing there is nothing wrong in that. "He doesn't like me using public transport after I told him about the time I was dry humped by a fellow commuter."

I stare at her recount and can only imagine Mase's reaction to it.

"Don't be surprised if he rocks up here at some point," she jokes, I think. "So, now he keeps checking up on me. Jimmy had trackers put on me once before," she says flatly. "I am sure Mase is seriously considering doing it again."

She laughs, as do I but sense her seriousness. Mase and Dec's dad, Jimmy, is a lovely man, but there's something about him that scares the living crap out of me and the fact that he could rather than would put trackers on my sister only confirms that my fear is well placed and totally warranted.

"Anyway, enough about my beautifully crazy husband and double O Jimmy. Tell me about you and your love life."

I am still talking by the time we've finished lunch. She now knows that I don't see a future with Jack, nor Dec, not really because he clearly sees no future with any one person anytime soon and that is my ultimate goal, no matter how unlikely. She doesn't attempt to dispute this. I also tell her about my disastrous fling at uni, just that there was one and that I loved him, thought he loved me, no more than that. She empathises but doesn't push for more.

We come full circle when she asks, "So, Dec?"

I sigh and cup my head in my hands because I want Dec. Like I have never wanted anyone else before. "He makes me feel things nobody else has, before or since."

She nods like she really understands.

"But I don't want to simply be another notch. I don't need to be his sun rising and setting and everything in between but I need not to be no more than a notch…even if I go home before breakfast, I need to at least be the only one who is sent home by him."

I had no idea all those words and thoughts were inside me, nor the tears that are running down my face. Liv is crying too as she rounds the table to hug me hard, a little too hard.

"You," she says on another squeeze. "You deserve to be somebody's everything and more and if Dec can't see that then he's a bloody fool and whilst he's a dick, he is nobody's fool."

Returning to her seat she fixes me with a stare. "Next Tuesday, come out with me and Mase. There's a new club. Come to ours for dinner first and maybe we'll find you your Mr Right."

My initial reaction is to say no but her face does this thing where it crumples when she's sad, like Dad so what I actually say is, "Okay."

I think she might have just manipulated me because her crumply face disappears in the blink of an eye and her regular face is reinstated leaving her looking smug, but then I realise

Mase has just walked through the door so it might just be her smugly in love face.

Chapter Nine

Declan

Mase walks into the pub, and I see him a split second before he spots me. He is alone, making me worry that something is wrong with Liv. The smile he greets me with suggests that he is happy, meaning Liv is fine, if absent. He sits next to me at the bar and immediately orders us both a drink and grabs the bar food menu.

"Olivia will meet us there. She worked late." He frowns.

"You're not enjoying having your wife as the boss of her own company?" I laugh making my brother's frown deepen.

"I didn't fucking think it through, did I? She is happy though and it was only because there's been a problem of some sort. Nathan seems happy with Olivia at the helm."

I nod thinking that our former stepfather, Christian's father-in-law. and now the junior partner in Liv's company, Nathan, will be more than happy to let my sister-in-law run things while he plays golf. I wonder if I should tell Mase about Christian's visit and the frown potentially causing permanent creasing to my brow alerts him to my confusion.

"What? You're surprised he's happy with my wife's work?"

I laugh at his bristling mood at the idea that I might have been in anyway criticising Liv.

"No. I was thinking about Christian. He came to see me, while you were on honeymoon."

My brother looks less than impressed but not entirely surprised.

"He suggested a little reworking at the club."

"I hope you told him to fuck off!" my brother snaps.

"Not quite, but I did say I'd probably go to Liv first. How is it going to work with him and Liv?" I ask because no matter what else Christian is, he's family, kind of, but he is involved and woven into the fabric of our immediate family.

"I anticipate it being awkward for a while, but ultimately she's my priority so if he chooses to make it too awkward, he will have made his own choice I suppose. Can we talk about something else because I still don't get his open hostility and total opposition to my wife and thinking about it pisses me off?"

"Okay," I agree and address the niggle in the back of my mind about the evening that lies ahead. "Mase, tonight, please tell me Liv isn't going to try and fix me up?"

With a shake of his head and the running of a hand through his hair he shrugs. "I'd like to say no. I have told her to mind her own business and she felt bad for Anita when she found you with Lindy and Laura," he says with an arched brow.

"I felt shit about that. I thought she'd already left. I wouldn't have done that to her, although she's seeing someone else anyway." I sigh thinking that the churning in my guts feels a lot like pain when I think of Anita with someone else.

"Yeah, but I think it was casual," he says, revealing that it is over by speaking about it in the past tense. "Nigel was pissed off about it, but she's a grown woman at the end of the day. Let's eat and then if you want to dissect you and Anita again, we can, but whether Liv tries fixing you up or not, you need not to make my sister-in-law feel any shitter than you already have."

He's right. I know he is and yet I can't guarantee that I won't say or do something in the future that makes her feel bad. I don't do it on purpose, it just happens. Like I told Anita, I'm not like Mase. I don't want or need to make this perfect family he has his heart set on and always did have. We are the product of a broken home, well maybe not quite, but divorced parents. Our mum married four more times and our stepfathers were okay, and we always maintained a relationship with our own dad but this whole need to be with one person and for it to be enough is not my thing.

Mase married his first wife even when he realised he shouldn't. They should have remained business only. He insists that when he met Liv it was a lightbulb moment, a second of complete clarity and he is happy, sickeningly so, but I don't believe that everyone has that one person and at what point is that soulmate simply a case of settling. He calls me cynical, and I am, but maybe that's not why I see things the way I do. Could it be that Mase and I are two different sides of the same coin? Whereas he wanted to prove our parents, their divorce and statistics for kids of divorce wrong, I am happy to accept that all relationships are flawed and that I will never, ever settle for one person to make me complete, no matter how good the sex might be and the best sex I have ever had was with Anita. I can't even describe what it is or how it makes me feel. I just know that when I kiss her, touch her, fuck her, everything makes sense. When I watch her climbing higher and higher until there is only one way for her to go and that is into a spiral of pleasure and arousal, she brings me to my knees. Knowing that I have done that to her. The feeling of being inside her will remain with me for the rest of my life. The perfection of how she holds me; soft and warm, tight, and yet gentle. She really is a conundrum.

"Come on, what do you fancy?" Mase asks, breaking my thoughts and all I can think of is her, Anita. She is very much what I fancy. I then see the menu in my brother's hand and realise he means food.

Anita

Olivia is in the kitchen, finding us something to eat. Some kind of pasta is how she describes it and then explains that Mona, hers and Mase's housekeeper, cleaner woman has left it for us. She looks nervous, on edge and I have no clue why, although I have wondered if she and Mase have had a disagreement since he is meeting us at the club and not having dinner with us.

Conversation is unusually sparse over dinner and it's not until we are in the bedroom getting changed that the usual topic of my love life is broached, by me this time.

"I properly ended things with Jack. No more going back," I seem to announce.

Liv seems quite shocked by that information. Her wild swing to face me and gaping mouth suggests shock. I don't wait for her to question me; I continue to explain.

"Mum and Dad were pleased when I told them. Jack was nice, but he is just out of a long-term relationship, and he wants fun. I want fun, but if I am going for fun, I want it to be toe curling fun."

"Like Dec?" Liv asks optimistically making me shake my head.

"Nah, I mean Dec can give me the toe-curling fun for sure, but I don't want to go from that high to the low of feeling like a whore and knowing he won't see me as anything more than a quick shag puts me off, plus I can't, *won't* share him with the blondes."

"Hmmm," Liv replies, thinking for several long seconds. "Maybe you should tell him that. That you want fun, but exclusive fun, if that's what you're really saying."

"I have no clue what I'm saying because I am a rubbish judge of character," I admit and can feel tears pricking my eyes as I drop onto the huge bed that my sister and her husband share. "My lover at uni, he was married, and I was in what I thought was a monogamous, loving relationship only to discover that for him I was no more than fun."

"Shit!" Liv sighs as she sits down next to me. "I am so sorry that you ended up in that position. Did he go back to his wife?" she asks and although it is a simple question, I am incapable of replying so allow my tears to silently roll down my cheeks and nod. She pulls me in for a hug as she asks, "You loved him?"

"I thought I did, yes. I did, but I can see now that it was infatuation. A naïve misinterpretation of love and he couldn't go back, he never left her."

Liv nods. "I went out with Sara's brother, Ridley and we were both young and immature. After Ridley I met Brad and we were together for a couple of years on and off, but they were nothing compared to Mase. He is like my first grown-up relationship so maybe your boyfriend, the married one was like

Family Affair

that, young and innocent."

Her expression is one of understanding and compassion, but she is totally wrong where my married man and I are concerned. She clearly thinks he was young and married and I need to set her straight.

"No." I shake my head. "He was older."

"Oh, he wasn't a student?" she asks and then aghast continues. "Anita, he wasn't a tutor, was he?"

I laugh. In many ways shagging a tutor would have been far less shocking than what actually happened, but she doesn't need to know that, not yet. Not ever. Nobody does.

"No, he wasn't. I met him in the bar where I worked. He bought me a drink and we chatted. Shit, how stupid was I?" I ask my sister, but she has no clue what I am really asking her, so I expand. "He told me that he was getting a divorce. That his wife was demanding and was preventing his access to his child. I believed him. I had no reason not to. He came in a few nights a week for about a month, and it was then that I agreed to go out with him. I should have suspected something was off because he either booked a hotel room for us or we went back to my student accommodation, never to his place. Oh, bloody hell."

"What?" Liv asks taking my hand in hers.

"I was so stupid. He always left, afterwards. How did I not realise he was still living with his wife and having sex with her?" I ask myself rather than Liv who is shaking her head.

"No wonder Dec's suggestion hit a raw nerve."

"Hmmm, except it didn't, not on that level. The sex wasn't even that good. Why won't I take what Dec offers when he gives me toe curling and yet with others like my married man and Jack, I have accepted so much less than that?"

She doesn't reply. Neither of us say anything as I absorb my own thoughts and realisation but it's still Liv that speaks.

"Are you reconsidering things with Dec?"

"I dunno, maybe." The truth is that all I can think of is Dec, day and night. Especially at night when I lie in bed alone and all I can think about is lying somewhere, anywhere with him, even if it's only for a short time. "You know before when you said that kissing Mase feels like the difference between a boy and a

77

man?"

She nods and grins, clearly thinking of Mase's kisses.

"I get that now, now that I think about it, really think about it. Others have kissed me and yet when Dec kisses me it's as though he means it."

There, the words are out and honestly if Dec walked in here now, I would be incapable of doing anything other than kissing him, long and deep until we end up naked and lost in the other. Until neither of us could see, think, or feel anything that wasn't each other and what we make together. My thoughts are getting more intensely sexual as I think I can feel his hands on me stroking, touching and caressing and then I hear something that breaks my wandering mind, it's Liv. Turning I see her crying.

"Oh Liv," I say as I pull her in for a hug, unsure why she's crying, especially when I replay my words.

"Sorry. I kind of cry at things now. I'm not really a crier but what you said about Dec kissing you like he means it," and then she's off again. Tears and crying fill the room. "These fucking hormones need to stop this shit."

I laugh at her turn of expression but her repeating my description of Dec's kiss only makes me imagine his kiss once more and I really hope Liv has lined up some double date with an eligible bachelor, although I suppose Dec is technically an eligible bachelor, even as a man whore.

Chapter Ten

Declan

We enter the club, and I must admit it has a nice vibe to it. It's not as big as Dazzler and it is only across one floor but there are two bars, a huge dance floor and a good variety of seating. Mase is still checking his phone and sighing. He'd already told Liv to wait outside because we were literally five minutes away. Liv, as she does, did the opposite and text him to say she was in the club. With his messages and attempts to make contact fruitless, Mase puts his phone away to scan the club. I hear an eighties track come on, maybe a power ballad about needing a hero and then in the middle of the dancefloor we see her at the same second.

"For fuck's sake!" Mase curses while I laugh at him and the captive audience my sister-in-law is holding on the dancefloor.

My brother is already making his way to her, and I am simply following. Nobody dances quite like Liv. I laugh as I recall making her a job offer to be my professional dancefloor filler, an offer she giggled at. The same offer that got me a hard punch to the arm from Mase. Her arms are up in the air as she dances in a series of actions that appear to show her serenading the gathered crowd. She does look bloody phenomenal with her amazing body packed tightly into a pair of skin-tight black trousers and a tiny gold vest style top. Her pregnancy is undetectable in her current state, but I am convinced that even when she is nine months' pregnant, she is still likely to be hot. Mase has reached her now and as pissed off as he looked when he pulled her to him his expression is already softening, especially when she wraps her arms around him before dancing for him.

I think I might as well grab a drink from the bar when something catches my eye, somebody near Liv. A fucking vision in black lace, Anita. She is wearing a very short dress that has a plunging back I see when she twirls on the dancefloor. Her legs look bare meaning that other than the dress she is likely to be wearing just a pair of pants. Her tiny frame as she dances looks as though she needs protecting and her tits and arse are calling to be cupped, held. As I watch, it appears that somebody else agrees because a man is zeroing in on her. His hands are already on her hips as he appears behind her. My look for him is as murderous as my look for her is salacious. I catch Mase's eye, or he's caught mine. Either way he is following my glare, but I am already making my way to where Anita is standing. Briefly, I see Mase say something to Liv who momentarily looks uncomfortable but then smiles as I close the distance.

"Anita." I turn my attention to the man with his hands on my lady's hips still. Fuck, she is not mine, but even so, she certainly isn't this fucker's! "You need to take your hands off her."

He looks at me and smirks. God I am going to wipe that smirk off his fucking face if he doesn't have a word with himself and unhand Anita.

"Now." I insist, taking another step forward and increase the menacing expression on my face.

I feel Mase step alongside me, but I really do not need my big brother to fight this particular battle.

"Okay, okay." The guy laughs but he does remove his hands, then the dumb twat allows his mouth to run. "You clearly have something going on so if you're banging it, I will graciously retreat."

I think he had more words he planned on sharing, but I stop him right there with his banging comment because Anita is not someone you bang. My fist is already colliding with this joker's jaw and my other hand is grabbing Anita's arm to pull her away. Bouncers are already heading towards the dancefloor, and I have no doubt we are all about to be ejected from the place. So much for checking out the competition, although as Anita's hand grips

Family Affair

mine, I figure the night is a greater success than I dared dream.

We are leaving the club and along with the initial pleasure at having Anita's hand in mine, I can feel anger surfacing too, not at the guy I have just punched, but her. For being there, no, not being there because I know for sure that Liv was responsible for that. My anger at her is for being on that dancefloor, allowing another man to put his hands on her and then I am seething about that guy she was seeing, of what they did together. I am unsure if she senses my conflicting emotions but as I turn to face her, she looks wary, apprehensive, but not afraid.

"You!" I snap.

Her response is to bite and nibble her lip rendering me helpless to do anything other than kiss her.

She is pressed against a wall, my weight crushing her as I tilt her head and drop my mouth over hers and am handsomely rewarded by a low moan echoing around us as it escapes her lips. My hand is skimming over her outer thigh to her hip that I am digging my fingers into, pulling her into my body. The sensation of her squirming beneath me spurs me on because I can feel that she is beside herself with the feelings and desires I am bringing to the surface in her, the same ones she evokes in me. Her hands are reaching up, raking my head, tugging my hair as I overpower her tongue that had been attempting to compete with mine but no more, she is compliant and submissive now, whimpering and whining. Then a new sound comes, but from behind me, Mase.

"Anita," he says, looking past me to where a dishevelled but very sexy looking Anita is, still resting against the wall with her eyes wide and her lips swollen. "Are things, okay?" he asks, and I almost feel sorry for him when I take in his mortified expression at finding us kissing, clearly in a *very okay* position.

"Things are fine," I say with a huge grin that quickly disappears when Mase continues.

"Anita," he repeats. "We're going. Courtesy of Rocky here, we were asked to leave too, but you can come with us. If that's what you want."

I am considering how many ways I can tell him to back the fuck off when Anita replies. "Thanks, but I'm fine, with Dec."

She looks across at me and smiles but her smile quickly dwindles leaving only an unsure expression I don't like and then I realise she is giving me a get out. She wants me not to cock this up again by reminding her that she needs to go home once we're done. I will not balls this up again.

"Cupcake, you are more than fine with me," I assure her and immediately reinstate her full smile which in turn makes me reciprocate.

"Aww," Liv suddenly chips in. "He called her Cupcake," she says, and I swear she is actually crying.

"Baby," Mase says as he pulls her close while Anita laughs and then explains to me.

"Hormones, she cries now."

"And then some," Mase mutters but is already preparing to lead his wife away. Not before she's hugged my lady and warned me though.

"Dec, I love you, but don't be a dick and make me have to hurt you."

I can't help but laugh, although I assure her that I intend to do this right. "Scout's honour," I say and salute her.

Anita

Uncertainty is beginning to kick in as we grab a taxi back to Dec's after Mase's intervention regretfully broke the moment. Although I should probably be grateful he did intervene or at least interrupt because without his arrival I would have probably shagged Dec there and then against a wall and most likely been arrested which I am sure would thrill my parents even more than my other recent behaviour. We are both quiet, but I am unsure if doubts are creeping in for us both or whether we're so aware of the electric tension that I'm sure can be heard crackling between us that we can't risk a word or even a glance lighting the touch paper that will see us ripping each other's clothes off in the back of the cab, oblivious to anyone or anything else.

It's no surprise when we pull up in front of a new and quite swanky looking block of apartments located a relatively short distance from Dazzler. I wonder if the location was part of the attraction in choosing his home and then question if he and Mase share their control freak tendencies. That would explain why they both live so close to their work, their businesses, although Mase lives in his office building so maybe he is more controlling than Dec who I realise is helping me out of the cab.

With my hand safely in his, we enter the secure building and head straight to the lift that comes to a standstill in a matter of seconds. We still haven't spoken but as the lift door closes and I plan to speak, I am literally knocked sideways by Dec who has me pressed firmly against the mirrored wall next to the control panel. I have no idea how he has managed it, but the lift is already rising, much like my dress. Dec has one hand in my hair, angling my head so that it is in the perfect position for his mouth to capture it and his other hand is beneath my dress, sliding up my leg until he is cupping my silky covered behind. He squeezes my flesh quite firmly, but his powerful, almost painful kisses stop.

With his eyes firmly fixed on mine he tells me, warns me maybe, "I am very fucking pleased to find you at least have pants on, Cupcake. If you hadn't, I think I might have spanked your sexy fucking arse until it glowed."

I have never been spanked, neither of my parents have ever hit me or my brothers and I think it is unnecessary. I don't understand the message it sends beyond *I am bigger, stronger, and higher ranking than you so do as I say and want, or I will hurt you.* I am especially confused when parents smack their children for hitting or fighting. That baffles me every time. However, now, in this moment I would happily bend over and welcome the feel of Dec's hand on my behind and the breathy gasps and moans I am releasing seem to convey that to him who is still rubbing his hand over my behind, although a finger is slipping beneath the elastic of my underwear now. Instinctively I spread my legs to give him greater access to my body. I think he is going to accept the invitation when the lift comes to a stop and the doors open.

Released by Dec, my hand is now back in his and he is virtually dragging me towards a door that he quickly unlocks. He leads me in and instantly I am pressed against another wall, my third one tonight, but I am hoping we won't be disturbed this time as our lips clash, and we commence battle once more. Dec doesn't disappoint me when he pins me beneath his weight that is almost too much, but not quite and his tongue is already winning the almost familiar dance we partake in every time we do this. I force myself to divert my attention away from the fact that we have started this several times before and have fucked it up each time in spectacular style. Instead, I refocus on his hands that are everywhere, or at least that's how it feels. His lips that are shaping my own, caressing them until they are moulded into the perfect shape for his while his tongue seems to work in perfect unison with mine, like they were made to find each other. Like they belong together. My tongue is submissive to his dominant one that is teasing, taunting and provoking mine to react, it doesn't. It simply absorbs the feelings he evokes in me from my erratic breathing, hot and flushed skin, pebbling nipples and slick arousal between my thighs, taking whatever Dec gives it and it and I am beyond grateful for it. The sharp sensation of teeth grazing and then sinking into my full bottom lip startles me enough that I cry out in shock as much as anything. I am sure I taste the metallic tang of blood but before I have time to consider that further, Dec is drawing my lower lip into his mouth where he simply sucks it.

"Dec," I say when he eventually releases my mouth completely to gaze down at me as he brushes the loose hair back off my face.

"Yes, Cupcake." He grins, his white teeth clearly visible in the darkness of the hall.

"Take me to bed," I shamelessly plead and like that, with no further words, he is leading me down a hallway to the bedroom I know I won't be spending the whole night in, but I am okay with that. Or at least that's what I tell myself.

Chapter Eleven

Declan

The sight of my lady standing before me in my bedroom is almost unbelievable. She is here, with me and so far, we haven't fucked it up. I haven't, and I have no intention of making any mistakes. I am incapable of taking my eyes off her, raking over her body, from her wide eyes that are clearly on board with everything I plan on doing. Her hugely dilated pupils confirm that along with her laboured breaths that are causing her chest to heave wildly, and I can't even allow myself to imagine why she keeps crossing and squeezing her legs.

There had been some thought in my mind of taking this slowly. Really, really slowly, savouring every second of anticipation, but I am unsure if either of us can do that. I certainly can't and the crook of my finger confirms that for me and her. I can't hide the grin that is spreading across my face as she takes two small steps in my direction and then she makes a funny little noise that sounds like something between a kitten's mewl and a growl as I reach for her to pull her close. I refrain from kissing her but have no idea how as I move my mouth to her ear where I lick, nip and suck in between teasing and taunting her with my words.

"Do you have any idea how many times I've imagined this moment?" There is no response beyond her grabbing my shoulders, digging her nails into the muscles there. "I intend to make the reality better than any fucking fantasy. I am going to make you cry, scream, sweat and shout my name, Cupcake." She whimpers as I move my hands up her back and grip the stretchy fabric of her dress, preparing to peel it off. "We are not leaving here until every single person living in this block knows my name. Until you have screamed it for them all to hear."

She clearly likes dialogue because I swear, she is breaking the skin on my shoulders and neck and one of her legs has lifted to wrap around my hip allowing her to press herself against the denim covered firmness there.

"Oh, you like that plan," I whisper with a laugh as I peel the fabric in my hands down her arms, exposing the naked skin beneath it. "You went out almost fucking naked." I hiss, feeling angry at just how accessible her flesh was and the idea of anyone else doing this to her has my blood boiling as the fabric gathers at her hips. "Maybe someone needs her underwear checking before she leaves the house," I threaten, not that I can guarantee I won't be doing just that.

With her leg wrapped around me, her position allows me to stroke her covered sex with my hand that is between her thighs and preparing to remove her dress completely with a little help from my other hand that is sitting at her hip. My dick is lurching to be so close to her as I press firmly against the minimal fabric that is the only barrier between me and her and am rewarded with a groan and the feel of her pressing down against me. I am beyond thrilled and decide to encourage her to simply react to me by slipping a finger beneath the fabric as I issue the threat of underwear checks and find my finger coated with fresh arousal meaning my lady likes my idea.

I laugh against her ear, almost daring her to object to my suggestion as I slide my finger inside her. She doesn't. Quite the opposite. She moans my name.

"I'm going to need my name louder than that for the neighbours, but you'll get there." My confidence causes her to whimper when I remove my finger from her body. I use both hands to push her dress down until it pools around her feet. "Oh, Cupcake." I sigh appreciatively as I stand back and observe the vision that she is in just her pants and shoes.

I would like nothing better than to rip her pants off and bend her over to fuck her, hard and unrelentingly, but not tonight. It is my intention to fuck her for hours, making her come until she thinks she's incapable of more and then I will do it again. She needs to learn a valuable lesson; she is mine and dancing with other men in clubs whilst barely dressed is not an option for her and neither is screwing other men like she has been doing for the last month or so. I ignore my conscience pointing out that I fucked anything with a pulse over the same period because that is different. I was doing it to forget her and just the idea, never mind the image I am now conjuring in my mind is just too much to bear, my lady being touched by anybody else. I really am beyond screwed here with all my Anita thoughts coming back to her being my lady. Yes, she needs to realise she is mine.

Circling her like my prey, I feel a rush, especially when I see her anticipation of what I might do rising so I make another full circuit of her before stopping behind her where I drop to my haunches and peel her pants down her hips and legs until they sit on her shoes. Slowly, I stand, tracing my fingers along the length of the back of her legs, enjoying the way I can feel goosebumps rising to the surface as I cover the expanse of skin on show. Once I get to her behind, I gently touch and stroke the smooth, firm tissue, briefly straying into the warmth and dampness of her arousal. Immediately she spreads her feet, granting me access.

With my mouth a hairs whisper away from her ear I ask, "Who's touching you, Cupcake?" With the last word uttered I gently probe her slick sex.

"You."

"Say my name!" I demand and she complies immediately.

"Dec."

"And who is going to make you come?" She knows what I want, and she gives it to me in a slightly louder voice.

"Dec."

As a reward I skim her clit and am rewarded myself with a low cry as her flesh tenses and trembles beneath my touch.

"And who is going to fuck you, Cupcake?" I slide my thumb inside her and begin to pump it in and out as I stroke her clit again. I actually think she is going to come on the spot. She doesn't, but she does scream her reply.

"Dec!"

"You fucking bet," I almost snarl fighting thoughts of Anita with anyone who isn't me. "I think my immediate neighbours might know my name now but there are more that don't," I tell her before I spin her so that she faces me, and I see some trepidation in her eyes. "Are we doing this?" I ask and am holding my breath as I hope she doesn't say no.

"Yes," she confirms, and I reward her with a smile before moving in for another kiss as I back her towards the bed.

Anita

The sensation of Dec positioning himself between my thighs is new and familiar at the same time. We have never done this, lying down on a bed sex, and I can't deny that it excites and scares me at the same time. It feels as though this is a turning point, that sex against a wall and on a countertop, as great as they were don't and won't compare to this on an emotional level even if it might on a physical one. I have come five times already. Dec is certainly ensuring that tonight is memorable and each of my climaxes so far has been toe curling in the extreme, each one more intense than the last, and the neighbours? Well, I reckon all of them on this floor and the one above and below will be sure of Dec's name by now, but there are at least another twelve below us and one above that might not be too sure yet.

"Cupcake, shall we do this one together?" Dec asks me and gains my full attention once more. "You and me, us?" he adds as if I need some clarification, but his words have the opposite effect, *us*. Does he mean us as in him and me in this moment, the here and now or *us*, meaning the two of us moving forward.

My rambling thoughts centre when I feel his sheathed erection nudging my entrance.

"Dec," I moan as he edges in further, gently stretching me until he is buried to the hilt and then he holds still, his eyes fixed firmly on mine as I utter the one word I still don't understand. "Us."

With that one word he begins to move, slowly at first, gently stroking all my nerve endings back to life and then leans in to kiss me. My hands immediately reach up and lace through his hair, holding him close and then pushing him away as the sensations building in my body threaten to break with the increasing pace Dec is setting. He fixes me with a deep and dark gaze I can't quite decipher.

"Oh God, that feels good."

"Mmm, I love how tight you are, you fit me like a fucking glove," he groans against my neck as he picks up his pace a little. "I really need you to come again. I need to see you come apart for me, because of me," he gasps as his own words clearly excite him.

"I've never come like this before," I admit thinking that all my orgasms with Dec have been with his fingers, mouth, or my own fingers as he's fucked me and before him too.

He kneels up but remains inside me. As he holds himself up on one arm the other reaches between us until he finds my clit that his fingers slide over easily courtesy of my wetness. Wetness I can hear as well as feel. I also hear my own breathing change as the first shocks of a climax begin to quake.

"Come on," he urges me as his thrusts quicken, thrusts that drive me on towards my own release.

"I'm going to come," I tell him hoarsely and roll my head to the side.

"Uh-ho," he chastens. "Your eyes stay on me, always on me when you come. You show me how it feels, what I'm doing to you."

His words are the final straw as far as my control is concerned and staring up at Dec, my eyes firmly on his as I come, hard and loud. My arms find his neck as my legs wrap around his middle while my hips meet him thrust for thrust until I think my climax is waning, but with the feeling of Dec swelling even further inside me and a couple of hard thrusts I am coming undone completely, screaming and shouting his name. I take him there with me until he is frozen in the moment yet still, he doesn't take his eyes off me as I cry, scream, and cling to him in sheer bliss wondering how I can feel sexual pleasure in so many places, from my curling toes to my hair that seems to be experiencing little electric shocks. I am hot, dry, sweating and over sensitive with the sensations I am experiencing.

"Are you okay?" he asks me, concern clear in his voice making me smile.

"Okay? I have surpassed okay and then some."

He smiles too.

Pulling free of me, I wince as my delicate folds attempt to return to *normal* but at this point, I doubt I will ever be normal again and honestly? I'm not sure I want to be.

"Sorry." He kisses my shoulder. "I need to get rid of the condom," he says with a smile as a strange and muffled voice shouts around us.

"Now go to bloody sleep, Dec. Some of us need to get up in the morning!"

We both laugh at the realisation that at least one of his neighbours has heard us.

"Cupcake, there are seventy-one properties in this block so excluding me you only have sixty-nine more neighbours to introduce me to," he says with a cocky grin.

"Hmmm, sixty-nine, eh, Stud?"

"Oh, Cupcake." He grins, leaning in to kiss my shoulder again before leaving the bed and heading to the bathroom.

****

I am wrapped in Dec's arms in his bed and as I don't have spare clothes or an invitation to stay, I disentangle myself and put on last night's clothes while he gently snores and then rolls over. The sight of his back facing me makes me irrationally sad, as if he is closing the door on last night. Quickly, I shake those thoughts from my head, reminding myself of just how humiliated I will feel if I stay and am confronted with his distaste or any awkwardness in the cold light of day. I pick my shoes up before heading out but pause in the kitchen to leave him a quick note that I attach to his fridge door.

Hey Stud (don't want to shout another Dec in case I wake your neighbour),

Last night was great. Maybe see you later at the club,

Cupcake x

It takes me several attempts to write Cupcake but smile once I commit to it.

Chapter Twelve

Declan

When I wake up, I roll over to pull Anita's seriously hot body against mine, but more than anything I want to inhale the glorious scent of her; pineapple, flowers and vanilla which I think is her shampoo. Whatever it is, I love it. Unfortunately, the other side of my bed is empty and cold. I allow myself a few seconds buried in the pillow she lay on and am pleased to find the faint essence of her still there before I get up. I only get as far as the kitchen to realise she has gone, and I regret not waking when she vacated my bed. I didn't expect her to leave, not really, but then I'd told her previously that girls do not stay all night and they don't, so maybe it's for the best. Even I'm not convinced her not being here is for the best.

Reaching for the orange juice I notice a note on the fridge as the door silently closes.

"Oh, Cupcake," I sigh as I read her words then grin at her use of Stud and the reference to my neighbour who seemed relieved when our shagging ended, allowing him to sleep. But this is what I wanted, for us to go to bed together and for her to leave. That is what I always want, so why do I feel like I have missed something?

Knowing Anita will be in the club today makes me happy and nervous at the same time. We still need to iron out the details of us and I also need to make sure that there won't be any unpleasantness or cattiness when she runs into Laura and Lindy because the girls are innocent in this. Well, not innocent in the biblical sense but in so far as they have done nothing wrong in terms of Anita. Maybe when she's back in her own kitchen things will be easier, for us both. When there is no crossover between our working and social lives.

I grab a shower and dress in jeans and a black t-shirt before throwing on boots then head for the door. With ideas of grabbing breakfast on the way, I leave and think about the busy day ahead I have. We are going to start having live bands playing on the slower nights, early, before the club fills and really gets going and today I am going to meet some prospective acts and listen to what they have to offer so I will need breakfast and honestly, I am bloody starving but strangely not tired, even after my lady kept me up for much of the night.

When I enter the club, I'm greeted with near silence. Just the sound of a radio somewhere breaks the quiet and much of the place is in darkness. I gave Nigel a set of keys and the alarm code because I do not want to be out of bed before lunchtime given the choice, especially not when I haven't climbed into it until three or four in the morning which is quite normal for me, and I guess nightclub workers full stop. I follow the sound of some cheesy and bouncy tune all the way to the kitchen where I find Anita, alone. She has her back to the doorway where I stand and enjoy the view of her mixing something in a huge bowl that one arm seems to be wrapped around while her other hand holds a huge wooden spoon that she is using to mix the contents of the bowl. It looks like one hell of a workout she's taking part in and as if to confirm that, she suddenly dumps the bowl down, heavily, with a loud thud and a muttered *bollocks* as she flexes and stretches her mixing arm.

I am about to speak when a different song starts to play on the radio, Spice Up Your Life by the Spice Girls and as she sings louder, really throwing herself into it she begins to dance, a little wildly and quite badly. Clearly her and Liv don't share their dance moves. Walking up behind her I wait until I am almost close enough to kiss her, but I don't. I simply pull her to me, spinning her so that she can see me. She shrieks before looking mortified, right up to the point where I join in with her terrible singing and spin her around the kitchen until the atmosphere between us changes. It intensifies as we come to a standstill, staring at one another, waiting for the other to do something. But who, and what will it be?

"You have a horrible singing voice," I tell her, causing her to laugh as a red blush creeps up her cheeks.

"I have a beautiful voice." She protests, making me laugh too.

"Says who? Helen Keller?"

Her expression turns into one of outrage and then confusion. "Wasn't she blind?"

I laugh again and with a shake of my head reply, "And deaf."

"Oh." Anita seems genuinely surprised by that nugget of information and then smacks my chest before repeating, "I have a beautiful voice. My mum told me."

I am about to dispute this again and maybe even suggest that her mother is biased. Instead, I lower my lips towards hers but before I cover her mouth with mine, say, "I'm sorry I missed you leaving this morning."

The atmosphere thickens again at my words, partly because of the possible meaning behind them. The truth is that what I am really saying is that I am sorry she didn't wake me, so that I might have encouraged her to stay a while longer if not for breakfast, although.

"Dec, it's fine. I know we didn't really discuss things, but you had previously made your feelings on overnight guests crystal clear," she says, and I consider opening up a discussion now, but we are interrupted by the sound of Nigel calling from the corridor, something about needing a hand with stuff from the van.

I move back so as not to cause any kind of confusion to things and then as Nigel appears behind me, I mouth to her, *we'll talk, later* and we will. I need her to know that last night wasn't enough, will never be enough.

Anita

The sight of Dec was more welcome than I thought it might be after last night, not that it hadn't been great. It had been, better than that but I did think that after I left, and he woke up alone that might be it for him. He was going to kiss me when my dad's voice interrupted, kiss and goodness knows what else. I could hazard a guess as to exactly what would have followed a kiss. His words, *we'll talk, later* seemed genuine and I do want to talk to him. Not a full on, what are your intentions kind of talk because I know what his intentions are. Fun, no complications or repercussions. But a talk so that I know what being with him entails.

"Anita," my dad calls as I stand holding a box of fresh salad, daydreaming so I miss him speaking to me.

"Hmm?" I wonder why he is looking so irritated.

"Love, the door."

I look around and see that my position is preventing him closing the van door as he looks ready to collapse beneath a huge amount of flour and dried foods.

"Sorry." I smile and with another flick of his head I finally move and lead him back into the kitchen where we unload the food he has just delivered.

We unpack in relative silence, not an uncomfortable one either. I have worked with him for almost four years and spent multiple years before that helping him in the kitchen, him and my mum. We know how the other works and we work like this, in silence if there is nothing to be said. I am just putting the last of the cream into the fridge when he does speak.

"So, did you have a good night last night? You and Livy?"

I briefly wonder if he is really checking that I did go out with Liv or if he suspects that I was out shagging whoever again, which I kind of was, both, I suppose.

"I was going to call Livy later, maybe invite her and Mase for dinner, or just her if he's busy," Dad says and I wonder just how well that would go down, an invitation to dinner minus Mase.

Then I smirk at just how much my brother-in-law physically bristles when Dad calls Liv Livy. Only he calls her that apparently, but I am unsure if I have heard him call it her with any frequency, just a couple of times, tender moments. I laugh out loud, startling and confusing my father when I realise that's what he calls her when they're being lovey and most likely intimate. No wonder Mase bristles.

"Sorry." He has no clue why I am laughing. "We had a good night. Me and Liv and Mase came too with Dec." I hope I have managed to keep a flatness to my tone so as not to alert him to anything akin to me and Dec.

"What do you make of him?"

"Mase?" I query but answer before he confirms my understanding. "He's just Mase; possessive, protective, loves Liv, friendly enough, what do you mean?" I finally ask with confusion.

"What? No, not Mase, his brother, Dec? He seems a bit flaky to me, a bit of a waster I shouldn't wonder, and definitely a playboy. Yeah, a very poor man's Hugh Heffner." My dad laughs at his own words. Words that stab me, hurting me which is ridiculous considering he's spot on.

"I wouldn't know," is my best retort as I refocus on the cake baking in the oven.

My dad's words play in my head over and over until I have a headache. Not because I think he is being unfair but because he isn't. His summing up of Dec is pretty accurate based on the warnings of my sister, my own observations, and the fact that I left him sleeping in his bed to do the walk of shame in last night's clothes under the cover of night before enduring the knowing smirk and judgemental eyes of the cab driver who dropped me home.

I spend the next couple of hours working quietly alongside my dad who seems oblivious to the whirring of my mind as I think, overthink, and then imagine every possible outcome for me, me and Dec.

With a very specific buffet prepared for some small gallery opening, my dad is ready to load up the van again. I make several trips from the kitchen to the van and back again before finally waving him off. I hope when I return to the club that I will chance upon Dec or that he'll come and find me.

My hopes are dashed when I return indoors. I clean the kitchen and leave it ready for its next use but by the time I am ready to leave there has been no sign of Dec. I reason that he's busy. This is his business, and he must be working. Even if this place is a nightclub, it must require daytime working hours in order for it to run smoothly and it appears to do just that. I don't know the details, but I do know that Mase has money invested and that he would never allow Dec to squander his money nor be lax in his business dealings whilst his money is involved.

By the time I grab my bag and keys I am resigned to not seeing or speaking to Dec, and the truth is I am confused by how that makes me feel. I'm confused, but there's more to it than that. Maybe my confusion is because of all the other feelings, thoughts and emotions flooding through my mind and body; I am happy when I think of Dec, of me and Dec, and I am hopeful, maybe foolishly so, but I can't stop my mind thinking of the two of us together and all the things we might be. I'm sad too though because the voice of reality is intent on dispelling all the positive things I dream of.

I really need to get a hold of this, of it all because I can't bear to think that this is now my mind set, flitting from one extreme feeling to another and all the time having to contend with extreme mood swings too. Currently my mood is dark, and I know it is directly linked to the fact that I haven't seen, spoken, or heard from Dec in the last couple of hours. Only I could end up in this position from something that was supposed to be so simple. Only I would inadvertently hook up with my sister's brother-in-law, several times and despite him being a self-confessed man whore not only be pissed off by it, but imagine being the one to make him better, to make him want more.

"Shit!" Who am I kidding? Not even myself because even if Dec was looking to be rescued and improved it wouldn't be by me, someone like me because a relationship with a man whore who wants strings free sex is all I deserve. Moreover, it might be more than I deserve.

Chapter Thirteen

Declan

From my office window, I have a perfect view of the car park. I watch Anita walk to her car and even from here, I can see that she looks uncomfortable. No, it's not that. She seems upset, worried, and sad. Yes, sad.

I ball my hands into fists at my side, knowing that I've done nothing wrong, I don't think. Yet I know her sadness is somehow down to me. I told her we'd talk later and then avoided going anywhere near the kitchen, avoided going anywhere near her. I tell myself that was because of Nigel. That I didn't want him to pick up on the fact that there is something between us and I didn't want that to cause issues between Anita and her dad. I'm not even convinced by my own reasoning. The truth is that I am shit scared by her and by us if the feelings I have simmering under the surface of my being are anything to go by. Feelings I don't like or want, but they're not listening to me because even now I can feel them intensifying and festering. I should have listened to Mase when he told me not to get involved, not that he said that, not really. But once I knew who she was, I should have moved on and allowed her to do the same. She is a nice girl, a good girl and she is looking for something real and of permanence, both things I can't give and don't want, do I?

I watch her car until it is the tiniest dot on the landscape, my hand roughly pushing through my hair and then force myself away from the window and grab my phone, intent on sending her a message of some sort. After probably the tenth attempt to compose something light, witty, and non-inflammatory I'm relieved to receive a text from Mase, until I open it.

<Any idea why my wife has just called me and bailed on a romantic dinner for 2 in favour of a girly get together with her sister? Please tell me that you fucking her sister isn't fucking with my life already?>

I laugh at his agitation and the fact that his romantic dinner has been put on ice, but my laughter is short lived because I have no clue why Cupcake wants to meet with Liv. My ego is overinflated at the best of times, but it has no bearing in the conclusion that Anita's plans with my sister-in-law are somehow connected to us, to me. Briefly, I wonder if I could get someone to cover for me tonight, allowing me to meet with Mase and by meet with Mase, I mean gate crash the girls' meeting.

"No," I tell myself as I dismiss the idea of not working and reply to my brother.

<No clue why your wife doesn't want a romantic dinner with you…maybe she's bored of you already. Maybe she married the wrong brother>

I know I'm playing with fire by winding Mase up with the inference that Liv is bored of him but also that there might have ever been a Liv and me, a Liv and anyone who isn't Mase. The truth is that I am provoking him deliberately, if only to take my mind off Anita and whatever is on her mind. I don't have to wait long to see how successful my provocation in poking the bear has been.

<Fuck you Dec! My wife has cancelled plans for one reason only, Anita, and for me that means you. If Olivia isn't free tonight, then I'll have to make do with you. I'll see you later and you can tell me what the fuck is going on and how you plan to stop fucking with my life>

"Shit!" That's all I need, Mase, a pissed off Mase coming over later, but it looks as though that is exactly what I'm getting.

It seems that my fucking is fucking with both of our lives but more than anything it is fucking with my head because I am clueless as to what I should and shouldn't do anymore.

****

I don't actually see Mase when he first arrives. By the time I notice him, sitting at the bar, he is about halfway through a bottle of beer. He raises a brow at my smirk for him flying solo, until I remember that the reason he is here with me is because his wife has been summoned to meet with Anita.

I join him at the bar and order more drinks. He opts for a soft drink and explains. "I need to collect my wife and her sister in a while."

"Where have they gone?" I ask, hoping he'll tell me. Maybe I can tag along with him and meet the girls and by girls, I mean hook up with Anita.

He ignores my question.

"How's it going having her around you here?" Mase wears a ridiculously large, smug smile that tells me he knows exactly how it's going.

"Fuck off," is my very mature response.

He laughs at me. "You, little brother, are screwed. You are desperate to go and find her, aren't you? She is under your skin and in your head every second of the day and night. Am I right?"

"Fuck off," I repeat, and he laughs again, louder.

Anita

"You're making a pig's ear of this, that's what you're telling me here?"

I laugh at Liv's choice of words but can't deny their accuracy.

"I mean, Dec is fucking it up with you. You're not alone in this." She laughs herself now. "What do you want from this?"

I shrug. Refusing to admit what I want.

She shakes her head. "When Mase and I began seeing each other properly we knew that we wanted it to work. He wasn't looking for serious and I didn't think I deserved serious, especially not with someone as good as Mase."

I am shocked at her revelations; Mase has never seemed to be anything but serious where Liv's concerned, and she is the best person I know so if anyone deserves a good person it is her, but then aren't her old thoughts regarding Mase the same as mine are in relation to Dec?

"And now?" I don't know if I want reassurance, guarantees or some kind of epiphany with her answer.

"I'm worthy. He made me realise that, but I believe it now, feel it. My childhood was all kinds of fucked up, of that there's no doubt. However, Mase made me see that by being resilient to it and then going on to feel in anyway worthless or less than I should was allowing them to win. They can't win, not ever. And here I am now, happily married and pregnant."

"I am so glad you met him and that you realise how worthy you are."

"Me too, and now we just need to get you to see that you are too, don't we? But does Dec fit into this plan?"

I drop onto her sofa and top up our wine glasses with the non-alcoholic bottle I brought with me. "I'd like Dec to fit into my plans, my future…"

"But?" My sister takes my hand and squeezes it, encouraging me to continue.

"But I don't know if he wants that. He's not exactly long-term plans, is he?"

She shrugs. "Give him a chance. I mean, don't propose, or start talking joint bank accounts or children's names, but take a little time, enjoy what you have.

The wiggling of her eyebrows makes me laugh.

"Let him show you that either you are worth the effort of being monogamous for." She rolls her eyes now and we both laugh. "Or let him prove that he isn't worth the opportunity to love you."

"When and how did you get so wise?"

"When I decided to risk a one-night stand. When Mase shagged me a dozen different ways."

"TMI," comes a call from the now open door.

Dec. He stands with his brother who is grinning broadly at

Liv having heard her words.

"Only a dozen different ways? I apologise for my brother's lack of expertise." Dec grins across at my sister before moaning as the punch to his arm from Mase lands. "Cupcake," he says with a half-smile for me. "Want to kiss my ouchy better?"

"Erm, no," interrupts Liv. "I have a horrible feeling about where the pain of the ouchy is currently settling."

Dec shrugs as Mase leans down and kisses his wife then notices the wine glasses and our near empty bottle.

"Have you been drinking." His voice oozes horror and disapproval.

"Yeah, that's our second bottle," replies Liv, stretching forward to empty the bottle into our glasses.

"Olivia." His tone is flat, but his dark stare and stony expression clearly demonstrate that he is not happy and is going to leave her in no doubt about that.

"Mason," she replies and then seems to take pity on him by showing him the label. "Alcohol free as I am pregnant."

"Oh, good. Coffee, tea, beer?"

Dec nods for a beer and I opt for coffee. Liv goes to help Mase with drinks, leaving me and Dec alone.

"Cupcake. I missed you today."

I nod and struggle to contain a broad grin that is beginning to crack my face. He missed me and God knows I missed him. It's a little ridiculous really that either of us should have missed the other when we were in the same building and yet, we have, both of us.

"I missed you, too. I erm, wasn't expecting you here." I look at my watch and see that it's not even midnight yet.

"No, well, Liv ditched Mase so he came to the club, and it was quiet, and I wanted to see you." He looks awkward at that admission. "So here I am. I thought I could give you a lift home."

"Home?" I have no idea if he means my home or his.

"Yeah, to mine or to yours."

I am panicking because there is no way I can take him back to my parent's home. It would be awkward enough in daylight hours but at this time it will raise some serious questions and that's without considering whether he wants to stay over, expects to.

"I will pay good money to see Nigel's face if you rock up with your toothbrush and pyjamas." Mase is virtually doubled over with laughter.

Liv smacks his arm once he's put the drinks down but laughs too.

"You two are so fucking juvenile," Dec accuses. "I was offering Anita a ride."

Like that, the two of them are laughing like adolescents at the possible implications of Dec's 'ride'. I can't help but join in with them and then Dec does too.

"I pity your child if this is any indication of your maturity," he fires as his parting shot.

They ignore him. Mase has already pulled Liv into his lap and is gently stroking her belly with one hand while the other holds her hip.

Chapter Fourteen

Declan

We hang out with Mase and Liv for a while longer, but saying goodbye to them, or at least the girls saying their goodbyes seems to take longer than the rest of the night combined.

My brother continues to wave at us as the lift doors close while Liv smacks his arm for his obvious teasing of me and Anita. We both laugh once we are alone in the confines of the lift.

"What's it to be then, your place or mine?"

Anita's face morphs into one of abject horror at my question.

"Dec, no, I can't, my parents, my dad—"

Stepping closer, I skim a hand through her hair and lean in as if to kiss her, interrupting, putting her out of her misery. Although, I am curious as to why she went from her parents being an issue to it specifically being her father.

"I know and that's not what I meant. My place clearly means me taking you home with me. Or, your place, meaning I drive you home, possibly kiss you goodnight, but essentially it involves me getting you home safely."

She looks disappointed at my summing up of what me taking her home involves.

"If I go with your place, what does that involve?"

I grin. We both know what that ultimately involves, but I know she likes it when I talk her through it.

"I drive you home with me. When we get in the lift, I am unlikely to be able to keep my hands off you, so will kiss you and touch you. Then, once we get through the door, I am probably going to forgo all social etiquette by not offering to take your coat or make you a drink. What I will do is kiss you some more, and touch you, remove all of your clothes and pleasure you for hours until a few more of my neighbours know my name."

"Oh."

Her big brown eyes are like saucers, but they in no way look opposed to my plan.

"I think my lady likes the sound of that plan."

Her eyes grow even wider when I call her my lady, but I have no intention of back tracking or trying to take it back. She is mine.

"In fact, I think my lady is desperate to get back to mine. Are you desperate, Cupcake?"

"Yes," she whimpers and a cocky grin spreads across my face, a grin that broadens when I notice her squeezing her thighs together.

"So, mine then?"

"Yes."

Thank fuck. If she had opted for a lift back to her parent's I would have ended my night alone in the shower with just my own hand and memories of her to ease the hard ache of my dick and balls.

The lift doors open, and I virtually drag her to my car that's parked on Mase's secure car park.

As I pull out onto the road, I look to my side and see Anita in profile. She is dressed casually in jeans and a long sleeve t-shirt that's partially covered by a denim jacket. Her hair is down and loose and she is wearing zero make-up by the looks of it and looks gorgeous. My usual taste is for something a little more obvious in the womanly and attractive stakes. The opposite of Anita. However, as I take in her natural beauty, I am knocked sideways by her effortless femininity and splendour. I need to stop thinking with my head if these sappy ideas are what I am coming up with. I need to channel thoughts through my other head and start imagining her on all fours while I fuck her.

"Dec."

Her gentle calling of my name to summon me, brings me from my musing.

"Anita."

She smiles.

"I'm sorry about today. I was going to come and find you, but I wasn't sure if I should. If you'd want me to."

I nod. She sounds as confused by things as me. I told her we'd talk later and never went back to find her.

"It's all a bit weird still, isn't it?"

We pull up at my apartment block and together walk over to the lift.

Once inside the lift, the atmosphere between us thickens. I corner her and when I tilt her chin up, her eyes look like sin incarnate.

Fuck! When she looks at me, I am incapable of any thought that isn't depraved and immoral.

"Do you find it weird too?"

I frown, wondering why I might think this is weird and then remember that's what I'd said in the car…that it was weird still.

"Yes. Cupcake," I whisper and bring my forehead to rest against hers. "I don't know what we're doing or how this is going to work out, but let's try."

"Okay."

Her voice quivers and I am sure I feel her physically shake.

"So, when it feels weird, we talk to each other. Not Liv, okay?"

She nods. "Nor Mase."

"Agreed."

I allow my lips to find hers and as our kiss deepens, I find myself pulling her to me, lifting her so her chest is pressed against mine, her legs spread slightly so that somehow one of my thighs ends up wedged between hers. My hands have already made their way beneath her t-shirt and this time I have no issue finding the front fastening on her bra that is now open. I palm one of her breasts and roll and squeeze her already hard and peaking nipple.

The sound of a low moan echoes as it's captured in my mouth. Her arms are tightening around me, and her short nails are beginning to claw my back through the fabric of my clothes as she bears down, pressing her pussy that is radiating heat against my leg.

The lift arrives at my floor not a second too soon because I don't doubt I would have fucked her in the lift had it taken much longer.

I unlock the door and throw it open almost pushing Anita through it, taking a second to gather myself.

"You know where you're going, so get your arse in there. Bedroom. Now."

She looks a little startled, but before I can say anymore, she heads towards my bedroom, possibly sensing that I might just need a moment before joining her.

Anita

He looked almost troubled when we got to the door and when he sent me here, to his bedroom, I was a little startled. I expected to be pinned to a wall or the back of the door. I'd have even thought he might have had me on my knees before the door was shut, but I hadn't expected him to send me to bed, to wait.

I am standing next to the bed, waiting, when I hear his footsteps getting closer. The lights go on and I spin around to find him standing in the open doorway.

He stares at me with such intensity that I feel myself blush and have an urge to cover my still clothed body.

"Take your clothes off."

I swallow hard and look up at the light. I want him. My desire is still there, bubbling beneath the surface, but I am not exactly confident in my own skin and while he has seen me naked, his hands, mouth and penis have travelled my whole body, but like this, me on my own, scares me.

"Cupcake. Take your clothes off," he repeats, but kills the light, just leaving the borrowed light from the hallway and the moonlight shining through the uncovered window to subtly illuminate me and the bedroom.

I am not an exhibitionist and can't remember ever doing this, stripping whilst being watched. The chances are I will bugger it

Family Affair

up one way or another, but he clearly wants this, so, I try.

First, I remove my jacket and toss it aside, then kick off my boots.

Dec leans against the door frame and watches me as I pull off my spotty socks and a small smile curves his lips. When I reach for the bottom of my t-shirt and pull it over my head, his smile disappears, replaced with a much darker and more intense look that suggests he is using all his powers of self-restraint not to rip the remainder of my clothes off himself. Part of me wishes he would, but seeing his desire for me reflecting in his eyes and the way he is balling his hands into fists at his side spurs me on to continue my striptease.

I blink for only a second, but it is long enough for Dec to have cast his own top aside. Looking down, I notice that his feet are bare, so right now, he is closer to naked than I am. Briefly, I drink in his toned chest, abs and torso and feel a grin spreading across my face as I acknowledge the fact that he is mine, kind of. I push the last part from my mind and unfasten the button of my jeans before sliding them down my hips until they drop into pools around my feet. Using my heels, I pull my legs free and stand there, under his scrutiny in a very plain, and highly un-sexy set of white underwear, no satin, no lace, a cotton t-shirt bra, and a co-ordinating, full back cotton bikini brief.

There is a temptation to cover up somehow, but it's too late. He has seen it and no amount of regretting my underwear choice is going to change this to anything sexier and alluring.

"You look fucking amazing." Dec's voice startles me, the interruption of it to my thoughts, but also the conviction in the meaning of the words.

Here I stand in very basic underwear, and it turns him on. I turn him on. I need to remain focused, on what I am doing rather than questioning how that can be.

Staring across at him, I notice that his jeans are flapping open, and he is pushing them down his thighs revealing his lack of underwear and his erection that he strokes the length of.

"Lose some more clothes, Cupcake."

I am almost brought to my knees at the glorious sight of him; toned, confident, sexy and most of all his desire for me.

Reaching behind, I flick open my bra and allow the straps to fall, revealing my breasts that hang slightly, one of the perils of having bigger boobs, they have never been of the tight, perky variety. When my bra falls to the floor, Dec's eyes look down at it briefly and then they lift, settling on me once more. With his glance fixed on my breasts, I cup my own flesh and allow my thumbs to skim across the tight peaks of my nipples causing a groan from both of us and a bite of his lip.

He cocks his head, and his eyes drop to my pants. I have no idea where my raising confidence is coming from but with the thumb of each hand in the side of my waistband, I push my final item of clothing down my body until I am standing there, naked.

Dec says nothing for long, slowly dragging seconds and then he approaches me. I expect him to pounce, to kiss, touch and tease me. He doesn't. He circles me, over and over, then over again.

"Do you have any idea how much I want you? The things I want to do to you?"

He stands behind me and his breath runs across my neck. The coldness of it heats me through to my core. I don't know what to say, so I say nothing.

"I intend to do each and every one of them to you, eventually."

I can hear the hitch in his voice and then feel him moving. He comes to stop in front of me. Looking up I am greeted by his utter and total beauty.

"Do you want me, Cupcake?"

This one I can answer.

"Yes."

"Are you wet already?"

Again, this is easy. I have been damp since I saw him enter my sister's home and now, I am beyond wet.

"Yes."

He grins cockily as he wraps his hand around his erection and with a groan slowly strokes along the length of it twice.

"Get onto the bed. Show me how wet you are. Show me how much you want me, and then I'm going to make you scream my fucking name while you come on my tongue."

Chapter Fifteen

Declan

She is fucking glorious, a sight to behold. The intensity of everything from the second I arrived at Mase's until right now has been overwhelming. That's why I needed her to come in here without me. I needed a little space to just gather my thoughts and calm myself. My desire for her is off the fucking scale and that scares the shit out of me. To watch her remove every item of clothing was better than anything I might ever have seen before, even seeing her wobble as she pulled her spotty socks off. I love her inexperience. The way she hesitates and then, with encouragement she throws herself into it. I have paid handsomely to watch professional strippers and I can honestly say that they had nothing on Anita. Her honestly is something else I admire about her. It's almost as though she is incapable of lying, even about if she wants me, if she's wet…I like to think that she is only ever this honest with me.

I watch her move so that she lies on her back in the middle of my bed, and she knows exactly what I have asked of her. After stroking along the length of my dick a couple of times, I had to stop. If I hadn't, I'd have come by now, possibly right now I think when she pulls her knees up and opens her legs for me. Even without much in the way of light, I can see her glistening before me.

"Oh, Cupcake." I have no clue what else to say, which is unusual for me, but the sight of her opening up and inviting me in is rendering me almost speechless.

"Dec."

Her voice is a whisper, and I can hear her desire for me in her use of my name. This thing between us is off the scale in intensity and desire, for us both. She pauses, her eyes on mine and then one of her hands comes to rest between her spread thighs. I swear that all the air has just been sucked from the room, or at least my lungs as I watch her delicate fingers drop lower and then run along her wet length.

"Dec," she repeats my name, but her voice is a little strained now.

I move closer, but still say nothing. I climb onto the bed and on my knees, I come to rest between her thighs where I have a ringside seat to her arousal. Her fingers move lower again until she is sliding a finger inside herself. I watch as her body clenches around her digit and she releases a low moan. She does this several more times before my hand closes over hers and I lift it up.

We both stare at her finger that is coated in her arousal and I move a little closer, close enough to draw her digit into my mouth where I suck against its length, lapping and licking it until it is clean.

"What did I tell you was going to happen once you were on the bed?"

There is a slightly flat tone to my voice, but I am in no way angry to have seen her touching herself. This woman turns me on a little more every time I am with her.

She stares up at me with wide eyes that look a little wary, but the glimmer behind them leaves me in no doubt that she knows how much I enjoyed watching her touch herself.

"You said I was going to scream your name while I came on your tongue."

I grin down at her. "Yes, I fucking did, and that is exactly what I intend to do."

I dip down, pressing my body against hers and find her lips, wet, warm, and welcoming as I kiss her. The kiss begins to deepen, and her hands begin to knot in my hair that she teases and tugs.

A little reluctantly, I break our kiss and begin to kiss my way down her body, teasing and nipping her skin until I find my face between her thighs. Without any thought, I slide a finger along her wet length, before sliding a finger into a core, one and then a second. A satisfied groan is her response. I pump the length of my fingers, in and out, over and over, until she begins to spasm around my digits. She is so fucking close to coming, but this is not how she is going to come, not the first time any way.

"Dec!" she cries, when I remove my fingers and without even looking at her face, I know she'll be wearing a pout.

"Not yet," I tell her and with my hands cupping her behind to pull her down the bed a little, I allow a small tap of my fingers against her arse cheek.

A little yelp is her response to that, but I can't help but notice her arousal begins to escape her. Interesting.

Before she protests any further, I launch my assault on her with my tongue that takes in the taste of her whole length before circling her clit.

"Shit! Yes!" she calls, her hands already in my hair.

I circle and flick against her clit before drawing it into my mouth, but before she goes over the edge, I withdraw, but only as far as her core that I gently probe and lap. She tastes fucking divine, and I can't ever see me getting enough of her.

The sensation of her rocking her hips against me as she gets closer to release, along with her moans and breathy gasps drive me closer to release myself. I return my mouth to her clit and my fingers to their former position of pumping in and out of her, but this time I reach further inside until I find that special place that sends her wild.

"Fuck! Dec! Don't you dare fucking stop. I'm going to come."

If I wasn't completely absorbed in Anita and her pleasure, I'd laugh at her demands and threatening words, but I am, so continue to drive her closer to the edge of her climax. With my fingers rubbing against her G-spot and my mouth now sucking on her clit, she has nowhere else to go.

On a garbled cry, she comes and as I had said, she calls my name at the top of her voice. Easing her down from her heightened state, I reach up to take her hands that are still in my hair in mine and gently lapped against her core, savouring every last drop of her sweet nectar, my sweet nectar.

Anita

It has been almost a week since Dec came home with Mase and took me back to his place and things are going well between us. I stayed with him all night, but I couldn't really class it as a sleepover because I don't think I got a single wink of sleep that night. The man is an animal, not that I consider that an insult.

I am mixing a pancake batter in Dec's kitchen as I spent last night here too, and now it is breakfast time, well, lunch, but we will be eating breakfast. I allow myself a little chuckle when I remember a few days ago when Dec walked into the kitchen at the club and found me making a batch of blueberry and white chocolate muffins. He stood behind me for a little while and then approached me, telling me that my arse jiggled in a very sexy way when mixing. I flush when I recall that he went on to lift my skirt up, remove my pants and shag me over the countertop about seven seconds before my dad walked in. That was close, maybe too close when I consider that my brothers nor parents know about me and Dec. Liv knows and Mase, but nobody else. My dad is beginning to look suspicious about who my new bloke is, but so far, beyond knowing I am seeing someone, he hasn't pieced any more than that together.

"I swear you only mix things to turn me on."

I turn and see a very sexy Dec sauntering towards me in just a pair of black boxers with his bed head, twinkling eyes and a bit of regrowth across his face making him look like a bloody male model.

With a giggle as he comes up behind me and kisses my neck, I correct him. "No. I mix things for a living, and right now, I am mixing to make us pancakes."

The kisses move across my shoulder, then back up my neck until Dec is tracing a path along my jaw before finding my ear.

"Doesn't mean it doesn't turn me on." He presses his body into mine and I can feel just how turned on he is.

"I really need to walk this week," I tell him deadpan, but I do,

Family Affair

unlike last week after our all-nighter that ran into the next day leaving me sore and struggling to walk normally.

He laughs against my ear and the sound of it along with the vibration of the sound against my skin makes me reconsider the need for mobility.

"Shame," he mutters before landing a single kiss to my cheek. "I am jumping in the shower and then we'll eat before I drop you home."

I turn and watch him walk away, the muscles in his back rippling and his glorious arse daring me not to follow him and then his words register, before I drop you home. He picked me up from a function we catered, meaning my car is at home, which also means my parents or brothers may see him dropping me home.

Dec is devouring his plate full of pancakes that are loaded with syrup and a variety of fruit.

"These might be the best pancakes I have ever eaten," he says between mouthfuls.

I smile across at him. "It's kind of my job, to be able to cook."

He shakes his head. "But this is so much more than being able to cook, Cupcake."

Before I can respond, not that I know how to respond beyond a thank you, Dec begins to laugh.

"What?"

"Have you ever had a pancake made for you by Liv?"

I shake my head. "Should I have?"

He shrugs. "Just be warned that if the opportunity arises, don't. I did, once, only once, and I reckon you could tile a roof with them."

I laugh. "That bad?"

"Worse. Mase bought one of those electric crepe makers or whatever they're called, you must know what my brother is like with gadgets and shit. Liv struggled with it, because anyone who has ever seen her attempt coffee with their coffee machine knows she is not a gadget kind of girl."

We both laugh, partly at Mase's love of a gadget and Liv's hate of them.

Family Affair

"Well, they do say opposites attract, don't they?" I ask, meaning my sister and her husband.

"Yes, yes, they do." Dec replies and suddenly things turn a little strained and I have no clue why. "Finish your breakfast and then we'll go."

Somehow, I manage to finish my food before jumping in the shower and now Dec and I are on our way back to my parent's house where I am hoping to avoid any of them seeing me arrive home with him. At least I am not returning home in last night's clothes which always pleases my father immensely.

We turn into my street and with no cars parked outside our house, I breathe a sigh of relief before Dec parks the car.

"Last night was great," he says, leaning across to brush some loose hair off my face.

"Yeah, it was," I agree.

"And breakfast was amazing."

I laugh that Dec has brought things back round to breakfast.

"What?" he protests. "It was."

"I'm glad you enjoyed it." I mean it.

"I'd like to take you to dinner, but I can't slope out of being at the club tonight."

"It's okay. I understand. We have a function to cater tomorrow. A breakfast thing, so probably best that I get some sleep."

He nods, but looks disappointed, boosting my ego.

"Tomorrow. My mum is having a gathering tomorrow afternoon, for the family. Come with me."

My eyes widen until I can feel them drying, but the truth is that Dec looks more shocked at the invitation than me.

I'm unsure what to say and I think he senses that or sees it as me preparing to decline the invitation. "Liv will be there, her and Mase. Come, please."

I don't know why, but that final word, the note of desperation in it is my undoing. "I'd love to."

Before I can say anything else, he has reached for me and pulled me to him, his lips covering and parting my lips until we are involved in a passionate kiss in broad daylight in front of my parent's house for anyone to see.

Eventually, when we part, we're both breathless.

"I'll call you later with details," he says and with another kiss, a slightly less frantic and fervent one, I get out of his car and wave as he pulls away.

Wearing a huge grin that seems to make my jaw tingle, I turn to walk down the path, although it might be more of a skip than a walk judging by the bubbles popping in my chest when I see that I am not alone. Standing there, having had a bird's eye view of my arrival home is Scott, Liv's brother.

Chapter Sixteen

Declan

"You're taking Anita home? Tomorrow? For one of Mum's, 'it's not a special occasion even though we all know it is' afternoon teas?" Mase's tone is a little disbelieving.

"That's what I said, isn't it? Unless your hearing is failing you in your old age." I sound terse, but his questions and the tone of them is pissing me off. Why wouldn't I take her to my mum's house with me for a family get together? I ignore my own answer that suggests I'm as surprised as Mase by my actions, but when I asked her to come with me, it felt right. I want Anita there with me.

Mase laughs at me, irking me a little more. "Calm your tits." He shakes his head and leans forward in his chair on the opposite side of my desk to me.

I flip him off. Not mature but it's all I have.

"Are you on your period or something, because these mood swings are screaming *manstruation* to me."

I laugh at his play on menstruation that sounds more Liv than Mase. "Fuck off."

"I wasn't saying you shouldn't take Anita with you to Mum's. I was just a little surprised. It's very unlike you not to fly solo at these things."

I nod. Mase's summing up is entirely accurate.

"What did she say when you asked her?"

"She was a little reluctant, but she has agreed to come, and she knows you and Liv will be there, so that probably helped."

"Please pre-warn Mum, you know how she gets when we take a girl home…in fact, pre-warn Anita, you know how Mum gets when we take a girl home."

I really hadn't thought this through. Mum will see this as significant, like marriage and babies significant. It wasn't. I wasn't marriage and babies significant. I couldn't remember the last time I had taken a girl home…that wasn't true, I knew exactly when and I knew precisely who.

My face must morph into one suggesting a bad memory or bitter taste, probably both because Mase is on his feet and standing next to me. He pats me on the back, causing me to look up at him.

"Anita will be fine and the past, well, it's precisely that. Look, I have to go. I promised Liv I wouldn't be too late."

I roll my eyes at my brother who is seriously whipped, but happily so.

"Don't do it, Dec. Not a fucking word or I will be forced to tell you that I have a bath for two and mutual massage on the agenda if I'm not too late."

I feign a distasteful expression, but the truth is, I could go for a bath for two and some massaging, not with Liv because Mase would kill me for the suggestion alone and certainly not with my brother, but with the right person, I can see the attraction of an early finish.

Looking out of the office window, I watch Mase head to his car, talking on his phone, presumably to Liv judging by his grin of shit eating proportions. He really is happy. I mean genuinely ecstatic, like his life couldn't be any more perfect, and it couldn't. He has a successful business that he works hard to maintain. He's married to a beautiful, funny and bright wife who adores him and who is the light of his life and together they're having a baby they are both desperate for. I smile for them both because they deserve all that they have.

My phone is already in my hand and as much as I want to call Anita or drop her a text, I don't. Instead, I call my mum to warn her about me bringing a plus one.

She answers on the second ring. "Declan, darling." She sounds genuinely pleased to hear from me.

"Hey, Mum."

Before I say anything else, she speaks again, suspicious about the reason for my call.

"Declan, please tell me you're not about to make some feeble excuse to avoid my afternoon tea tomorrow. You simply must be here, it's important to me."

I frown down the line, not that she can see it. The truth is if she could see me, I wouldn't frown.

"Mum, calm down. No, I am not making any excuse, quite the opposite. I'd, like to, erm, bring someone with me."

Silence. I wait for her to say something for so long that I pull my phone from my ear to check the call is still connected.

"Mum," I repeat wondering if her silence is a prelude to her denying my request to bring Anita.

"Sorry, darling. Of course you can. Anyone I know? She must be very special if you want to bring her home to meet us all —"

I cut her off. "Don't get carried away, Mum. She's nice, she's called Anita, and we've been seeing each other, but that's all."

I sense her satisfied smirk from the other end of this conversation. "Of course, dear...Anita?" She sounds as though she is trying to place the name. "Declan!"

She's placed it.

"Is that a good idea? I assume this is the same Anita as Olivia's sister? The one you danced with at Mason's wedding. Please, tell me you're not playing with fire—"

Time to cut her off again. "Mum, stop. You really are getting carried away, but yes, the same Anita."

Silence again, but only for a few seconds this time.

"We'll see you tomorrow then, both of you."

"Yes, yes you will," I say to myself after I hang up.

Staring out of the window again, I can't help but wonder if this is going to prove to be a mistake of epic proportions to take Anita home when up to now neither of us have really acknowledged that we're even seeing each other.

Family Affair

Anita

I'm like a cat on a hot tin roof, waiting for Scott to say something about what he saw. I don't know what he saw. Did he see me and Dec kissing in his car, or did he only see him drop me off?

We passed on the path, him leaving the house and me entering it. He offered me a nod and then he was gone.

Now I am waiting for him to return as I have already decided that if he doesn't say anything, I will because I need not to have this hanging over my head. I don't know Scott very well, although he's been here some months, but he's a bit of a closed book really. He was brought up in the weird and abusive church with Liv where bad things happened, not that I know the details of what Scott was subjected to but knowing what happened to Liv it's likely to have been pretty awful. I do know they had lots of rules and if they were broken, they were punished harshly. Because of this, I have no clue how he might react to having seen me with Dec. Will he see it as breaking rules on my part or just deceitful? If he does, will he feel obliged to tell our dad what he witnessed?

My mind is awash with all these thoughts and worries, meaning I will need to clear the air with Scott at the earliest opportunity and certainly before I go with Dec to his mother's house. If I go with him.

****

I'm still worrying about the fallout from things when the front door opens. My family have all come home at the same time. They appear to have formed an orderly line judging by how they walk into the living room where I am sitting nervously. First comes my mum, then dad, both of my brothers and finally Scott who looks at me, without a single word besides his nod of greeting and acknowledgement.

Immediately, Dad begins chatting about the function we're catering the following morning. He has already planned a trip to Dec's kitchen early the following morning to collect the things in the fridges there, but tonight, between us, we will prep a few things before making a very early start to ensure everything is fresh.

After a brief discussion on the plan for dinner, I watch as Scott goes upstairs. I make my excuses and follow him.

When Scott moved in, we had to move things around a little. My parents, me and each of my brothers had our own bedroom and the other room upstairs was an office for the catering business. Scott slept on the sofa for a few nights, but I think Dad thought he was getting itchy feet and was likely to move on, possibly without leaving a forwarding address, so the office got relocated to the conservatory downstairs. The office space was then transformed into a bedroom for Scott. It's not the biggest space, but he seems to like it.

I tap on his door that is shut. His door is always shut whether he is in there or not. I guess he values his privacy and I respect that. With my brothers, I would have knocked the door, but already been opening it, hoping not to catch them doing anything that brothers might do behind closed doors. Scott and I don't have that familiarity, so I knock and wait.

After a few seconds, the door opens and he retreats to his bed where he sits and watches me, I presume inviting me in.

"Hi." I have no clue what to say. What I want to say.

He studies me for a few seconds. "Hi." He smiles what looks like a sympathetic smile. He knows why I am here, meaning he knows about me and Dec.

"Do you mind if I close the door?" The last thing I need is for my parents, especially my dad to find out about me and Dec by overhearing a conversation between me and Scott.

"If you want to."

I do.

With the door closed, I awkwardly shuffle from one foot to the other and then come out with a few garbled words. "I don't know what you know, what you saw…me and Dec, well there's not a me and Dec, not really, not like serious…"

He laughs, but unlike some occasions when I feel he is laughing at us, this is different. I'd never really noticed how attractive he is, but he is usually brooding and scowling. Now with his brilliant smile lighting up his whole face, I can't help but see just how handsome he is.

"Look, whatever you and Dec are doing is between the two of you. It's none of my business. So, if you are asking me to keep my mouth shut, I can do that, however, what I won't do is lie for you. I don't like lies and deceit. In my experience they have a habit of coming back and biting you on the arse…biting me on the arse, so as I say, I won't lie for you. If anyone asks me if I have seen you and Dec together or kissing, I'll tell the truth, but so long as you are discreet, there's no likelihood of anyone asking that, is there?"

I shake my head, unsure what else there is to say.

"If it's serious, you should be the one to tell the old man." Scott laughs. "He won't like it, but then it's not his choice."

I shrug, unsure what to say now. I'm unsure if it is serious, for Dec anyway. "I'm not sure Dad would see it as not being his choice."

We both laugh.

"The time isn't right," I say, hoping Scott will leave it there.

"For you or Dec?"

"Maybe both of us." I feel slightly guilty now, thinking that I have agreed to visit Dec's mum with him and am now protesting that the time isn't right to tell my parents that we're involved.

"You have to do what you think is right, but please don't let someone else be the one to tell Dad when the time is right."

Scott's right.

"Does Liv know?" he suddenly asks and one look at my face seems to confirm that. "Even more reason for you to be the one to tell him then or you'll drop us all in it, and like me, Liv has been bitten by other people's lies."

I take his warning if that's what it is and after a nod of agreement, I leave.

Chapter Seventeen

Declan

"I am not sulking." My protest is weak. I am sulking.

Liv laughs at me while Mase shakes his head in the rear-view mirror of his car.

"I don't see why we need chaperoning."

Liv spins in the front passenger seat to face me. "Because our dad doesn't know about you and Anita, and she wants to keep it that way."

"Great, so now she's ashamed of me!" I snap at my sister-in-law, knowing I'm being an arsehole.

"Maybe she thinks you're ashamed of her as you run as fast as you can whenever our dad is around."

I like Liv, love her, but she's pissing me off and I am already in a foul mood.

"What the fuck has it got to do with anyone else? He isn't even her real dad."

Liv is ballsy and not one to back down from confrontation, not that she courts it, but she looks taken aback by my tone and I imagine the words themselves. She quickly recovers but it's my brother who speaks first.

"Declan, watch your mouth. You do not speak to Liv that way, ever, not even when you're pissed off that Anita would only allow you to pick her up if we came too. This is your doing, yours and hers, not ours, and whether you consider their dad to be hers or not, she considers him to be precisely that and so does he."

I sulk a little more but know he's right and I owe Liv an apology. Before I can voice it, she reaches over, taking her arm from beneath the seatbelt and gives Mase a peck on the cheek.

"Babe, thank you for defending me, but there is no need, really."

Mase looks sceptical. "Livy, put your arm back under the seatbelt."

Liv complies then turns her attention back to me again. "Dec, I love you, please remember that, but know that if I wasn't pregnant and on my best behaviour, I would come back there and punch you really fucking hard. You chose to shag some nameless caterer, not knowing she was the nearest thing I had to a sister at our engagement party and when you discovered who she was, ignored her. Then, you decided to go back for seconds at our wedding, in our honeymoon suite no less."

She leaves that hanging there, the fact that she knows that. Mase spins to look at her, shocked at her knowledge of that fact. She looks between us and rolls her eyes.

"I am not a fucking idiot. So, back to my point; you shagged her and fucked it up several times over and then decided you were going to make a go of it or whatever you're both doing, so if people don't know or she tries to keep it a secret, that is on you, not me. So, sort yourself out, stop with the pouting and sulking routine and bitching at me or pregnant or not, you will be going to visit your mother whipped."

I stare at her, knowing she can throw a punch. Remembering when she punched Mase and almost broke her hand.

"You are scary, Liv," I accuse while she simply shrugs as we turn into the road where Anita lives.

Liv has barely made it out of the car when Mase's seatbelt is flying off and he is turning towards me.

"What the fuck is the matter with you? I warned you not to bring this to my doorstep or to fuck with my life, mine and Livy's, and here we are."

I'm unsure if he expects me to answer, apologise or offer some kind of explanation. I do none of those things, but just sit there and stare at him.

He shakes his head, roughly runs a hand through his hair and then frowns, looking scarily like our dad.

"And if you ever take that sullen tone with my wife again, I will be the one punching you, not her."

I know what's expected now and without reservation I do it. "Sorry."

He nods. "Just sort your shit, both of you and if you're taking her to meet the family, you might want to consider breaking the news to Nigel about the two of you."

I'm the one nodding now. "What if he forbids her to see me. I don't think he likes me."

Mase laughs. "Of course he doesn't. He can see what you're like and as a man he gets it. I don't think he likes me very much either, but that's where I have the advantage because he had to accept me and Livy when he came back into her life."

"Thanks. Don't tell Liv I said this, but I think he sees Anita as a little girl still. His little girl."

"I think you're probably right, but the girls are here now, so let's play nicely."

Anita climbs in next to me and waves towards the door, almost ignoring my presence. Liv and Mase wave too, and when I look, I see the parents standing to wave us off, to wave the girls off. Anita's mum is wearing a big grin and looks genuinely friendly and warm at the sight of us going out together. Then I shift my gaze to Nigel who is glaring at me with a huge scowl for good measure. Maybe it's too soon to go public with Anita.

The sound of Liv's phone going off distracts everyone as Mase pulls away from the house.

She laughs. "Your dad has messaged to say he wants to meet up next week."

Mase shrugs but neither me nor Liv are taken in by his innocent reaction. "All of us?"

"I'm surprised you don't already know," she accuses but there is still humour in her voice. "He wants, and I quote, *to discuss security around the baby.*"

I hold back a snigger as I realise, like a little boy in the playground that Anita's dad isn't going to scare or intimidate me because not only is my dad bigger, but my dad could snap her dad in a dozen different ways.

Anita is looking between me, Mase and Liv. "Security around the baby?" She's confused.

"He's very security conscious," I tell her.

She nods but is still a little clueless. Mase laughs.

"Mason…" Liv's tone is serious. "I won't be fucking tagged or chipped."

I can hold my laughter in no longer and Mase joins in with me.

Liv glares between the two of us while Anita looks at me with a look of total horror and confusion.

"Cupcake," I say, pulling her hand into mine. "I'll explain later."

She nods and moves closer towards me while Liv continues to stare at Mase, repeating her objections.

Anita

I have no clue what the hell has just gone on between Mase, Olivia, Declan and Mr Harding senior who isn't even here. To be honest, I'm not really that bothered by it either because I am far too preoccupied with the frosty atmosphere between me and my dad.

When I told them I was going out with Liv to visit her mother-in-law, he was suspicious, although my mum said several times, *how lovely*. When he found out that not only Mason, but Declan was going too and it was a bit of a family get together, his suspicion heightened to the point that the hour before I left the house felt like an interrogation. He actually followed me around the house to continue discussing why I was going.

When I didn't commit to anything beyond Liv suggesting that Mrs Harding, although she's no longer Mrs Harding I realise as she is no longer married to Dec and Mase's dad, might be in line for some catering, he turned his comments and questions to Declan. He doesn't like Dec, that much is clear, but then, I guess he doesn't need to, not really. Before I left, he had gone so far as to suggest that Dec was likely to ply me with alcohol and take advantage of me before moving on to his next victim. That is the term my dad used, *victim*. I assumed that someone like Dec would be a father's worst nightmare, but when I was with him the one thing I never felt like was a victim.

"You'll love Charlotte, she is so sweet and is absolutely besotted with her boys." Liv laughs with the last two words.

"And why wouldn't she be? She's our mother, and we, well at least I am, I am a blessing." Mase sounds slightly affronted at Liv's laughter at his mother's apparent adoration of him and his brother, but mainly him.

"Hey, I am a blessing too, and was a far more attractive baby than you."

Liv rolls her eyes at Dec who is deadly serious in his own belief of how attractive a baby he had been.

"I look forward to meeting her, regardless of who was the most attractive," I say, genuinely looking forward to meeting the woman who had managed to raise these two attractive, strong willed and very confident men again, not that our brief introduction and my sister's engagement party and then her wedding counted as meeting properly.

"Well, now is your chance, Cupcake," Dec says, pointing out of his window.

I am agog at the sight of the huge house and grounds we are pulling up in front of.

"This is your home?" I whisper for no reason beyond the fact that I am in a state of shock at this mansion I have been invited to. I know Mase is rich but assumed that was from his business rather than him having been born into it. That thinking has always been confirmed in my mind by the knowledge that whilst Dec wasn't living hand to mouth, his brother had invested money in the club to allow Dec to run his own business.

"No," Dec says as the car comes to a standstill and Mase is already out and rounding the car to help Olivia out.

I turn to Dec, and he continues. "This wasn't our family home. Mum lives here with her current husband, Tommy."

I nod, remembering that his mother has been married several times since her first marriage to Mase and Dec's dad, Jimmy.

My door flies open and Mase stands there with an arm around Liv. "Come on you two, Mum's on the prowl.

We both follow Mason's gaze to find Charlotte looking perfect in every way heading towards us.

****

Once in the house, any initial nerves I felt are gone. Charlotte is lovely and her husband, Tommy is funny and very friendly, immediately putting me at ease. There are a few other people there and from what I can gather they are stepchildren and grandchildren of Charlotte's. Everyone seems to love her, and I can see why as I watch her interactions with the children and adults.

The sound of voices from the hall is followed by a couple, the man is carrying a toddler and the woman is clearly pregnant and with them is a girl, an older girl of maybe eleven or twelve years.

"Uncle Mase," she squeals, hurtling towards Mase.

"Oi, never mind Uncle Mase, we all know I am the cool uncle and your favourite," Dec calls wearing a big grin for the little girl who possibly hasn't seen him.

She releases Mase and hurls herself towards Dec who is already bracing himself for the impact of her hug.

"What are you doing here? I didn't know you were coming. Mum said you might not turn up."

Dec turns towards the little girl's mum who I remember is Bethy, his sister. "Cheers, sis, you know I struggle to turn down one of Mum's afternoon teas."

Bethy smirks but does roll her eyes while Mia remains attached to Dec's side and Charlotte is positively beaming at her youngest son.

"Anita," Charlotte calls to me. "Would you like to see the sunroom? Olivia, you should come too as you designed it and literally changed my life."

Liv is already on her feet. I have heard the story of the sunroom but have never seen it so am happy to go and take a look. Plus, with all of the people in this room viewing me with interest as they perceive me to be Dec's plus one, I am glad of the opportunity to leave the room for a while.

Dec smiles as his mother reaches for me and with one arm already linked with Liv's, she repeats the move with the other arm that links with mine and we are off to the sunroom.

The room that Liv renovated is beautiful and although I may not know Charlotte very well, at all even, it is very her; simple, classic, elegant and clean cut. She doesn't stop singing Liv's praises as she tells me how much she loves this room, although her description of the old room is beyond hideous, and I assume she is exaggerating.

"Tommy has some photos on his phone…" she begins as we are joined by Tommy who has overheard what his wife has said judging by how quickly he gets his phone out to show me hideous images of bright oranges, reds and strange shades of yellow.

"Wow!" I have no other words to convey how awful the room that is barely recognisable as the one I am standing in is shown to me in a series of images.

"Well, that's one word for it." Tommy laughs then turns to his wife. "Imelda and her clan have just arrived."

"Oh, I am pleased. Maybe it's time to build a few bridges, hey, Olivia?" Charlotte says to a nervous looking Liv.

I have no idea who Imelda is or why there is beef between her and my sister. Charlotte is already leading Liv back towards the large lounge where everyone is assembled.

Tommy looks across at me and offers a genuinely friendly looking smile. "Shall we?" He gestures to the doors that lead back to the house.

I am unsure why, but I feel as though I need a moment. "I, erm, bathroom," I stammer.

With another smile, Tommy directs me to a nearby bathroom that doesn't require me to go back to the lounge just yet.

Chapter Eighteen

Declan

I am sitting talking to my niece, well, she is talking at me and by talking at me I mean interrogating me.

"So, who is Anita again?"

I stare down at her, having already answered this question numerous times, plus she already knows who she is.

"Liv's sister," I repeat.

Mia looks back at me and shakes her head before quirking an eyebrow that is essentially her calling me out on my bullshit.

"But *who* is she? Like really?"

I look across to my sister who quickly turns away, refusing to get stuck in the middle of this, unlike Mase who is now sitting the other side of our niece.

"Yes, Dec, who is Anita, like really?"

I fight off the near overpowering urge to tell him to fuck off and address Mia. "I don't understand your question."

Mase sniggers while Mia rolls her eyes. "Who is she to you? Why have you brought her here?" She turns to my brother. "Uncle Mase, doesn't Liv have some brothers?"

He nods his head. "She does."

"So why aren't they here too, Uncle Dec?"

And now there is nowhere to hide. I have just had my arse handed to me by my almost teenage niece and I have no clue what to say. Fortunately, Mase chooses this moment to come good and save me.

"She was at a loose end, so Liv and I invited her to come to ours, but then Grandma reminded us we were coming over, so, we asked if Anita could come with us, and as Uncle Dec is really unpopular and has no friends, Anita is keeping him company."

Mia laughs at the last bit but seems to buy what Mase is saying.

We are all distracted by the sight of one of our stepsister's, Imelda entering the room with her children and husband, Christian.

"Great," mutters Mase at the sight of Olivia's former boss who is still a dick to her, Christian, who is already making a beeline for us.

"If it's not the Chuckle Brothers." He laughs, taking a seat next to me which if he insists on sitting with us, it's better next to me rather than Mase who is more likely to punch him, especially if he starts hurling shitty comments and insults Liv's way.

I look across and see a group of children, including Christian's, chatting and playing together.

"The kids look well," I say, hoping to strike up a safe conversation.

He shrugs and heads into territory that is anything but safe, although I am unsure if he realises just how potentially unsafe it might be.

"I hear we have another waif and stray interloper in our midst."

I frown my confusion at him, unlike my brother who physically bristles.

"And rumour has it that she is of the Carrington variety." The contempt with which he says Olivia's maiden name is shocking and unmistakable.

I resent his derogatory tone when referring to Anita, and I don't know why, but I have an overwhelming urge to point out that Anita is not a Carrington but assume his issue with Anita is her connection to Olivia.

"Back the fuck off," Mase says in a hushed tone. "You start your shit today, Christian, and I swear to everything I hold dear that I will put you on your arse before throwing you out of this house and you won't be coming back."

Mase gets to his feet just as Olivia returns with our mother and strides over to stand between them, one arm draped around each of them.

Christian openly sneers at Olivia before scanning the rest of the room. "Where is she then, the other Carrington slapper?"

I am scanning the room myself, looking for Anita, focusing on Tommy returning without her when my brain deciphers what Christian has just said and my fury rises in an instant.

"Watch your mouth," I snap, not as quietly as my brother judging by the eyes in the room focusing on me. "You don't even know her, so wind your neck in or it will be me rather than Mase putting you on your arse."

He looks slightly taken aback, not that I can blame him for that. I am a little taken aback by my reaction. Mase is the fiery one not me and yet, where Anita is concerned, I will fight for her. I will defend her against any insults or threats because she is mine and I love her.

"Fuck!"

This is not what I planned or expected. This was not supposed to happen, not to me. Not ever and yet, here I am! This is not what we agreed and while I was warning her that I wasn't looking for more, I am the one to fall for her and I hadn't even realised until this very second.

Christian looks startled by my final, one word outburst, and why wouldn't he be? I am startled by it. My expletive clearly came out a lot louder than I thought as I notice my brother frown at me but looks across at Christian accusingly, so I assume he thinks he has said something else.

I shake my head at Mase and walk over to Tommy. "Anita?"

He smiles at me, presumably seeing through my façade of Anita being here as anything other than my plus one. My lady. My Cupcake.

"Went to find the downstairs bathroom."

I nod at him and without another word, I am off to find her.

Loitering in the hallway, I smile when the bathroom door opens, and Anita appears. She really does look amazing and I regret not fully taking that in earlier. When she looks up and sees me, she flashes me the brightest of smiles.

"I thought you'd run out on me," I tell her and she laughs.

"Not yet."

"You're going nowhere without me today, Cupcake." My firm tone confirms I mean every word. "I haven't even kissed you today." I am already pulling her towards me, oblivious of our public location.

"Dec," she warns, more aware of where we are. "Someone might see."

"I don't care."

She looks startled, but it's true.

"Come on." I take her hand and lead her to the kitchen where we can grab a drink and I can kiss her.

We have barely crossed the threshold to the kitchen when I pounce. I have her pinned between my body and the island that sits in the middle of the room and am kissing her hard. She offers no resistance and responds to me immediately, her body softening against mine as her arms wind around my neck so she can pull me in even closer.

I capture her moans and mewls in my mouth, both of us oblivious to anything or anyone that isn't us and the closeness we're sharing and that lasts right up to the point that a cough signals we are no longer alone. The cough is quickly followed by a laugh.

"Busted."

We both turn to see Liv grinning in our direction.

Anita flushes while I return my sister-in-law's grin with one of my own.

"No judgement from me," she assures us, maybe Anita more than me. "Mase and I have been caught in compromising positions on multiple occasions, most of them by Dec."

I shrug, unable to dispute what she is saying.

"Right, you need to go and guard my husband who is ready to announce my pregnancy," she says to me before turning to Anita. "But you can stay while I find something my baby wants to eat."

I give Anita a single kiss to her lips before moving over to where Liv stands and drop a quick peck to the cheek that she swats away but smiles at me warmly as I leave the girls alone.

Anita

Watching on as Liv mooches around the kitchen, I wonder what is going on with Dec. He seems different. Different to his slightly offhand and awkward self who was in the car when Mase picked me up, and even more different to his usual cocky routine. This one seems a little more serious, and yet not serious…perhaps more intense, either way, he is different, and I have no clue why.

"Brownie?" Liv's offer of one of the trays of sweet treats she has found interrupts my thoughts about Dec's mood.

I laugh as she takes another couple before passing me the tray.

"Charlotte bakes the best brownies, ever."

I quirk a disbelieving brow and my sister seems to remember that I am a baker.

"Ah, well, you've never made me any, but I am happy to do the comparison test."

With a brownie entering my mouth, my response about her trying to get herself double brownies is muffled.

"What's up with Dec?" she asks when her own mouth is empty.

"I don't know what you mean."

She rolls her eyes. "He seems weird, more weird than usual. He was a bit arsy when we picked you up."

I give her a look that I hope will encourage her to expand on that. It doesn't.

"I threatened to punch him."

"What?"

She waves her hand at me, dismissing my question.

"Anyway, he went from that, to back to normal and then, you and him in here…" Her voice trails off.

"What? Me and him in here, what?" I don't understand what she means by that because as she said herself, her and Mase are no strangers to being caught out and Mase has caught us in various stages of undress.

Liv looks awkward. "I dunno. I mean, you were kissing and whatever else you were doing, but it was weird."

"Weird?" I am unsure if I am beginning to feel a sense of judgement from her or whether I am simply becoming offended by the aforementioned judgement.

"Yeah. Don't look at me like that! Not bad weird, just weird as in, clingy."

"Clingy?" I am definitely leaning towards offended at the inference that I am clingy.

"Yes, bloody clingy. Dec doesn't do clingy, and yet when I walked in, he seemed clingy and needy." She shudders. "This is not a side of Declan I am familiar with, and I just don't know what to do with that."

I laugh, no longer offended when I realise that she has noticed the change in Dec and is in no way judging me or my relationship with him. The only one she is judging and not in a negative way is Declan.

"I thought I was imagining it, but he is different, isn't he?"

She nods, another brownie disappearing into her mouth.

"Girls, here you are?" Charlotte appears behind us and immediately spots Liv with possibly only half a tray of brownies now. "Hungry?" she asks but wears a huge smile.

Liv looks uncomfortable, then I remember that her pregnancy is still a secret, so maybe she doesn't want to fake hunger when she had earlier blamed her baby's need for food.

Charlotte moves closer and pulls Liv in for a huge hug. "I am guessing this is a secret, but I knew the second I saw you today and this..." she points towards the tray of brownies, "This just confirms it. That and the fact that Mason is fit to burst."

Liv laughs. "I hope you don't mind that we didn't tell you first."

Charlotte looks towards me, then back to Liv. "I assume Auntie Anita is in on the secret, and Uncle Dec?"

Liv nods looking guilty.

"Of course I don't mind. I'm just thrilled for you both and to be having another grandbaby on the way." She hugs Liv more tightly before grabbing my hand and pulling me in to join their little hug fest. "But unless we want Mason to have some kind of episode, I won't ask you to carry anything out there for me."

Charlotte is already gathering trays of drinks and snacks.

"Let me," I offer, happy to help and glad to have a distraction from Dec's change in mood.

"Thank you." Charlotte replies with a grin for me and then pauses. "Declan likes you."

I am like a rabbit caught in the headlights, unsure what Dec has told her about us, if anything, and more unsure what to say in response.

"Come on then, before they all follow us in here."

Clearly, I don't need to say anything then.

I follow Charlotte with a tray in each hand as Liv mutters something about needing a wee again.

Dec grabs the trays from me as soon as I appear with his mother, looking slightly irritated.

"You are not waiting staff," he mutters.

"I know, and neither is your mother. I was helping and as she has guessed about Liv being pregnant, she wouldn't let her carry anything."

"Ah. Sorry. I want you to feel comfortable here, not like you've catered the afternoon."

I nod, reach up and stroke his cheek. "Thank you."

He smiles, a warm and gentle smile that melts my heart and heats me up as I realise, I don't think I have ever seen him wear that smile before.

Suddenly, there is nobody else present, it's just us and I swear he is leaning in to kiss me when Mase appears, oblivious to our moment.

"Where's Liv?" Before I can answer, he checks out the trays Dec is holding. "No brownies, so I am guessing if I find the brownies, I will find my wife."

I laugh as I give him an affirming nod.

"Mason." We all turn to see Bethy summoning her oldest brother. "Come here, we need to talk."

Charlotte is standing next to her daughter wearing a slightly guilty expression making me think that Liv and Mase's baby secret is even less of a secret than it was.

"Go," I tell him. "You go and get grilled, and I'll retrieve Liv from the brownies." I smile up at Dec and take in just how gorgeous he is.

"What?" He frowns a little awkwardly.

"Nothing, just you make a very handsome waiter."

He laughs. "Jeez, your pickup lines are cheesy, but I'm glad you appreciate my waiting skills, because later, I intend to be at your beck and call."

I flush, knowing he is talking sex.

"Yup! Your every wish is going to be catered for."

I flush a little deeper but seem to have lost the power of speech.

He laughs. "Go and save the brownies before Liv eats them all."

****

I am about to re-enter the kitchen when I hear voices; one man and one woman. Liv is the woman and the man's voice is familiar, too.

"So, whoring yourself to Mase is working out well for you!"

The venom in the man's voice is shocking to me. It sounds as if this person holds real hatred for Liv, something I didn't think was possible from anyone.

"Christian, this really is unnecessary. For whatever reason, you don't like me, never have, but whether you like it or not we are going to be thrown together at these types of occasions."

"I don't like it and if I have my way those opportunities will be limited in number and time."

I move closer, but don't quite enter the kitchen. I can see Liv standing near the island in the middle of the room.

"Whatever. You keep being a dick to me and see how that works out for you." Liv sounds exasperated even with her flat tone.

I watch as she seems to step away, preparing to leave I assume. I physically jump when I watch a hand grab her wrist, the owner of the hand still out of sight.

"Take your hand off me." Liv's voice is still flat, but I can hear the determination in her voice.

Briefly, I wonder if I am about to see her punch someone first-hand.

"How is my company?" he spits.

"Doing considerably better than when you had any involvement."

"You little bitch!"

There sounds to be real menace in his voice, and I am genuinely concerned for Liv's safety. This is her former boss who with no reason disliked her, his dislike turning to vitriol contempt once she became involved with Mase and he in turn involved himself in her career.

I do cross the threshold now in order to somehow protect Liv, but when I do, I am rendered immobile and speechless at the sight before me. Liv looks angry rather than scared and is shaking herself free. My gaze moves from her wrist to the other person's hand, up his arm until my eyes come to rest on a face I unfortunately know. No wonder his voice sounded familiar.

He turns to see the source of the interruption and the hatred his face morphed into for Liv, is nothing compared to the look of loathing when he takes in my face and the penny of who I am drops.

The others, including Liv had called her former boss Christian. I had no idea if that was his name, but assumed it was. I had known him as Tristan.

I am still rooted to the spot as Liv passes me by with a muttering of, "Come on, he really isn't worth our time."

With a slack jaw and feet of lead, I remain, unlike Christian or Tristan, whoever the fuck he is. He closes the gap in no time and as he glares at me, he laughs.

"I couldn't have dreamed this up. You, and her? You're the sister? The apple doesn't fall far from the tree with you Carrington girls, does it?"

He steps closer still and my breathing hitches, seeming to please him.

"If the rumour mill out there is to be believed, our Dec is smitten with you." His face forms a scowl, and his mouth contorts into an evil looking grimace. "I wonder if he'll feel the same way when he discovers what you are and the depths you've sunk to? The fact that my dick was inside you long before his?"

I feel sick, like, really, vomit down myself sick, but somehow, I hold it down. Not that what Tristan is saying doesn't scare me shitless because it would completely blow me and Dec out of the water if everything comes out and I know everything will come out if he follows through with his threat.

Somehow, I manage a reply and act far braver than I feel. "Maybe we should return to everyone else…perhaps you could introduce me to your wife and children."

Chapter Nineteen

Declan

There is no disguising my smirk as, from a safe distance, I watch my brother undergoing an interrogation from our sister. I assume the 'Liv's pregnant' cat is well and truly out of the bag now.

I'm still lost in my smug enjoyment of my brother's discomfort when I catch Liv in my peripheral vision coming alongside me. She looks flustered and a little upset.

"You okay?"

"Fucking arsehole dickhead twat in there." Her thumb is thrown back towards the kitchen.

I skim the room. She can only mean one person, Christian.

"What did he say?" I know it will be vile, but nothing prepares me for the fact that not only did he say shitty things, but he actually lay his hands on her, grabbing her. "Are you okay? Should I get Mase?"

"Fuck no!" She looks horrified. "The last thing any of us need is for Mase to lose his shit with Christian, so, thanks, but no thanks."

"Fair point, but you're okay?" I am genuinely concerned for her wellbeing.

"Yeah, Anita kind of came to my rescue," she says and then looks around. "I am sure she was with me when I left."

I look around, following Liv's gaze, neither of us finding Anita.

"Well, I don't see her, so you go and lend your husband some support and I will go and find Cupcake."

She grins up at me and my term of endearment for her sister and I swear she looks ready to cry.

"Go, shoo," I tell her before spinning her in the direction of my brother while I head for the kitchen to find Anita.

****

I hear Christian's voice as I get to the kitchen but don't quite catch what he says. Anita's voice takes over now.

"Maybe we should return to everyone else…perhaps you could introduce me to your wife and children."

Whilst her words sound reasonable enough there is something off in her tone and it makes me incredibly uncomfortable. I can't quite put my finger on what her voice is laced with, but whatever it is, it's heavy and loaded. Is it contempt I detect? Maybe not, but it's not positive and yet somehow familiar.

I hear a hiss that is definitely Christian's meaning he is picking up on the negativity my Cupcake's voice is aiming at him.

I've heard enough.

"Anita," I call, walking in, hoping my face doesn't divulge my irritation and concern at whatever is going on between them. "Oh, Christian. I didn't realise you'd escaped the circus." I offer him my best fake laugh. "Anita, Bethy wants to pick your brains on catering."

Anita looks a little stunned, but relieved more than anything. She steps back from Christian making me realise just how close to each other they were. I am getting more and more pissed off with every passing second I stand here so am relieved when Anita comes alongside me and takes the hand I offer.

We return to the others, and I keep Anita close by for the remainder of the afternoon, ensuring Christian keeps his distance. Mase keeps checking in with me meaning he knows something is off with me, as does Liv who says nothing, but her gaze is constantly flitting between me and her sister. Eventually, a couple of others make noises about leaving and Mase quickly jumps on that bandwagon. Thank fuck because I feel ready to explode with pent up rage at the niggling feeling in my head that there is something between Christian and Anita I am unaware of, but I won't be unaware for much longer if I get my way and I always get my way.

****

We have barely left my mother's property when Mase launches into his own version of the Spanish Inquisition for Liv about Christian.

"So, what did he have to say?"

"Nothing really."

I avoid looking at either of them because he did far more than nothing really and I don't want to get dragged into this, especially not when I am more interested in what was going on between him and Anita.

"You're lying!" Mase accuses with an angry snap in his voice.

"Mason!" Liv hisses. "He doesn't like me and is generally unpleasant, we all know this, so, he didn't really have anything new to say. Happy now?"

"Fucking ecstatic," Mase grinds out between gritted teeth.

I briefly move my glance from an uncomfortable looking Anita to the woods we are driving past, but my attention quickly snaps back, much like my head when Anita speaks.

"Why doesn't he like you, Tristan?"

With the use of the wrong name, she has all of our attention.

"Christian," Liv corrects.

Anita flushes at her mistake and if that doesn't piss me off and increase my suspicion a little more.

"I mean he's not exactly a super friendly people person with anyone," Liv continues.

Mase nods his agreement. I maintain my silence.

"But I think he only really attempts to be civil professionally or if the person he's dealing with is somehow advantageous to him. I am not and have never been advantageous to him and in terms of having been employed by him, well, he very much had me pigeonholed as his receptionist and no more."

Liv was pretty much spot on in her summing up but wasn't done yet.

"He wasn't unpleasant to you, was he? I assumed you were on my heels when I left the kitchen."

My rapt attention is now fully on Anita, looking for any sign of, well, anything that might offer some answers to my unanswered questions about her and Christian.

"No, no," she mutters. "I mean why would he be? I doubt he knew who I was or most likely he must have thought I was something to do with catering, the food…" her voice trails off, possibly because she can hear how flustered she is becoming, and if she can't, I certainly can and that convinces me even more that there is something off with her and Christian, or Tristan as she earlier called him.

My mood is darkening with every breath I take. I need this conversation to end before I lose my shit completely. Not that there won't be a conversation about this, but it will be private—between me and Anita and it will be happening the second we leave this car if I have any say in it.

Anita

My stomach hasn't stop churning since I saw Tristan…I still can't get my head around him being called Christian. My slip up, calling him by the name I'd known him go by has caused raised eyebrows and smirks if not suspicion from Liv and Mase—Declan? Well, that is a different story because as much as he has held my hand and kept me close, he is antsy and agitated with everything, but I suspect mainly me. Did he hear something when he came to the kitchen? Something I said, or God forbid, what Tristan said? I am certain he didn't hear anything about me having sex with the other man or he'd have said something, of that, I am sure.

"So, where are you two going? Home, Dec's, ours?"

Liv spins in her seat to face us. I remain silent, deferring to Dec to make the decision for us both. My preference is to go home and not face the conversation I feel sure is impending with Dec, a conversation I neither want nor have any clue what it might involve. At least going back to my sister's home will allow me to avoid whatever awaits me a while longer or possibly even gain some insight into what that conversation might involve.

"Mine," Dec replies, blowing all alternatives out of the water. "I have work later and Anita and I have things to sort out before then."

Liv frowns as her glance lands on me. My response is a shrug. Dec says no more while Mase remains silent but takes a turn that confirms we are going to his brother's home.

****

Dec is pacing the floor of his flat while I sit on the sofa, watching him, waiting. Seconds turn into minutes and the minutes seem to last for hours.

I get to my feet. "Maybe I should go—"

"You are going nowhere!" Dec roars, turning until he stands before me. "I don't even know where the fuck to start here. There is something going on between you and Christian…I don't know what or why but there is something and I don't fucking like it."

I stare at him, unable to deny any of what he is saying. I wish I could.

"Say something!" he barks at me, his grip on all things good seems to be hanging by a thread.

"What? What do you want me to say? You have got something of a bee in your bonnet about me and a member of your family and you expect me to say something? But what? Why? I don't know what you want from me, Dec. You have said it yourself; you don't know what *it* is or why you think it, but somehow this is my problem rather than yours."

Dec steps away, his fingers running through his hair, tugging the ends, hard judging by the pained expression on his face.

I move towards him and feel nothing but guilt now. Not because I think I owe Dec anything in the way of an explanation about my past any more than he owes me one, but because I know I am lying to him, or about to if pushed. His reaction to discovering me in his mother's kitchen, talking, regardless of what he heard, to the man I now know is his stepsister's husband, has convinced me that telling him the truth would be a bad idea. Until I must. If I must.

I briefly acknowledge to myself that there is plenty that I do feel guilty about but none of that is something I intend to discuss or divulge to him…to anyone.

"Dec. I don't know what's going on here. If I have done something, tell me. If you're pissed off with me, tell me, but I am not staying here to put up with your mood swings based on whatever is in your head. So, if you want to talk about it, we can, but I mean talk with actual words, not sulking."

Silence is his only response for a few seconds as he seems to consider what I am saying.

"Sorry," he eventually says. "I don't know why it bothered me so much, but when I came to find you in the kitchen, you seemed familiar with Christian. Too familiar."

"Familiar?" I am doing everything I can to hide the panic that I hear in my voice.

"Yes, familiar." He sighs loudly. "I don't know what it was, but…for fuck's sake. Sorry. Look, there's something I need to tell you and maybe that is what's wrong with me. Why I got myself in such a fucking state hearing you talking to another man."

He sounds disgusted with himself that me speaking to Christian, regardless of what he heard, got under his skin. I do briefly smile before remembering that my conversation in the kitchen, whilst innocent on this occasion has less than innocent origins.

"Dec, maybe I should go—" I repeat my earlier offer. Maybe it would be better for us both to have some time to think. Dec to think through whatever is bothering him and me to think about what I am going to tell him because despite my earlier thoughts on telling him nothing. Lying. I won't do that, not that I plan on telling him the whole truth.

"No, please, stay. I told you, there's something I need to tell you and I think that something is fucking with my head."

"O—k—ay." I feel nervous now. What could possibly be fucking with his head like this and as it is clearly related to me, maybe he would be better off removing me and it from his life.

"This afternoon, I was thinking and then I came to a realisation, and I was okay with it, or so I thought." He looks awkward. "I am okay with it, kind of, but it's a shock and not what I planned on any level—"

I cut him off, hoping to somehow stop his ramblings. "Dec, you're worrying me."

"Sorry." He takes a very deep breath. "Although maybe you should be worried. "Anita…" Another deep breath follows. "I love you, okay? I. Bloody. Love. You."

Chapter Twenty

Declan

I love her. The words are out and there's no taking them back, even if I want to.

Watching her, I see a small grin already spreading across her face. All thoughts of anyone who isn't me and her are gone for now. In this moment, this magical moment, it is just the two of us and I won't let anything, or anyone spoil it.

"Please say something," I mutter, but this time my words are a plea laced with fear rather than anger.

"You love me."

I stare at her and with a half-smile, shake my head. "I was hoping for something different to that, but yes, I love you."

"You love me," she repeats, her grin broadening.

"We have established that several times already."

Suddenly, her smile drops.

"What?" Panic is in my voice now as I wonder if she has realised that my feelings are in no way reciprocated.

"Does loving me make you sad or angry?"

I think back to my strange mood of just minutes before and know that is what is behind this question.

"Of course not." I step closer and reach for her wrist, pulling her towards me. "I mean, it wasn't something I planned, and it confuses me in many ways."

She nods. "Confuses you?"

I nod back at her.

"It scares me, Dec, my feelings…" her voice trails off.

Maybe I should say something, give a little here to reassure her in some way that I share her fears and probably those of everyone who has ever fallen in love.

She continues before I can say anything. "We don't know each other, not really, and what if we hurt each other, or ourselves?"

"Oh, Cupcake, you're not saying anything I haven't already thought. We can get to know each other…talk."

We both laugh knowing that our conversations have so often turned into banter and sexual innuendo that has inevitably turned into sex. Hot sex, but still sex. And this is why I have avoided serious relationships with feelings and all the associated shit that comes with it.

"I am shit scared of hurting you. I am more scared of being hurt, to be honest, so, as much as it would hurt for you to opt out now—" I stop, unsure what I am saying or how this will turn out.

"Go on, please."

I take a deep breath and blow it out slowly before continuing. "If you don't feel the same or don't want to run the risk of getting hurt, I respect it. In fact, I would much rather you pull the plaster off now than for it to be done six months down the road."

She looks stunned. I am stunned. I had no idea any of that was going to get spewed by me, but now that it has, well, it really can't be taken back.

"I don't doubt that the sensible thing to do would be to call it quits, or even revert back to no strings sex."

She knows as well as I do, we can't do that. I say nothing but shake my head. Now that I have these fucking feelings involved it must be all or nothing for me. I don't do anything else.

"Okay, so we either call it quits or jump in with both feet?"

"Yeah."

Her grin is back, and I feel as though the breath I have just exhaled has been held in for far too long.

With my hand still holding her wrist, her free hand reaches up and she tilts my head to look down at the ground between us. I'm confused as to what there is to see until she does the tiniest of two footed jumps.

"Both feet, Stud."

My eyes are back on hers now, the reality of what we have just agreed to kicking in for real now.

I instinctively lean in to kiss her but before my lips find hers, she speaks. "I. Bloody. Love. You. Too."

Her use of my own punctuated declaration of bloody love fills my heart with joy and I feel as though I am soaring off the ground. Her arms wrap around me, and she pulls me closer.

"Now, kiss me."

"With fucking pleasure."

I need no further encouragement and before either of us can do or say anything else, I am taking her in my arms, kissing her, worshipping her, counting my lucky stars for her, and loving her.

****

It's a couple of hours later, as we sit in the kitchen eating omelettes that I broach the subject of Christian, and hope that I am not about to burst the happy little bubble we've built around ourselves.

"Christian—"

She cuts me off, but I can see by her face that there's something between them. My suspicions were clearly correct.

"We were involved."

I don't know what I expected, but it wasn't fucking that.

"Involved?" I am verbally and physically bristling.

"Yes, involved, like you and the temptress twins and goodness knows who else."

Her reprimand is delivered calmly and her point hits home. Whatever was between them is in the past and is no more than my own previous *involvements*.

"Sorry. Go on."

She looks nervous, scared almost and that causes my anger to rise again, but it's not aimed at her. My wrath is firmly directed at Christian.

"When I was at university, I worked in a bar. This man came in and we chatted, flirted and started seeing each other. I thought we were embarking on an actual relationship, and he allowed me to believe that."

"He didn't see it as an actual relationship?"

She shakes her head and I have a strong urge to punch Christian, although, my conscience points out that I have been in that position on multiple occasions where a girl has seen things between us far more seriously than I have, not that I have ever encouraged that.

"I thought he did and as I say, he allowed me to continue in that belief. Long story short—he was married with kids. I had no clue about that until the end and felt awful to have been the other woman, even if I thought I was the only woman."

"Fuck!" I hadn't thought the voices in my head this far through, having somehow assumed Anita and Christian must have known each other before he became involved with my stepsister, but then, the maths didn't exactly work out when I considered it now.

"Needless to say, he wasn't very happy to see me in your mum's kitchen."

"Motherfucker! Did he do anything? Threaten you?" I am certain he will have said plenty of unpleasant things to her and having seen how openly hostile he is to Liv, her relationship to Anita is only likely to have made him worse.

She shrugs, confirming he was an arsehole. "I'm not what you might call his favourite person. It was unpleasant at the time and it's still that way."

I reach across the counter we're on opposite sides of and pick her hand up, gently landing a kiss to her knuckles. "We don't have much to do with him, especially not since he turned on Liv, but I won't sit silently by if he treats you badly."

"You don't need to rescue me."

"Maybe not." I grin across at her. "But I will. Always."

She stretches up on the stool she's sitting on, leaning over until her lips are almost against mine and then she pauses. "For a man whore you are incredibly romantic."

I grab her head, pulling her closer until our lips mesh. "Let's see how romantic you think I am when I make you scream my fucking name as you come."

Family Affair

Anita

The weeks since Dec and I admitted our feelings passed by smoothly and there have been zero interactions with Christian, who I now know without doubt was not and had never been called Tristan. That had just been another layer of his deception.

I pace the floor, waiting for Dec to finish getting ready for our night out. We are meeting with my family to break the news of us. I am clueless about how my family will react. Liv will be there and undoubtedly soften any blows that come my way and will intervene to lighten things up if our dad gets a little terse about things. Of course, with Liv and her now obvious pregnant belly, comes Mase who will certainly have Dec's back if things become unpleasant. I am overthinking things with thoughts of unpleasantness.

"You all set, Cupcake," Dec says, coming up behind me to pull me in for a warm embrace.

I spin and smile at the sight of him in well fitted black suit trousers and a white shirt that has the top couple of buttons undone. God, he looks amazing and so effortlessly stylish too.

"You look like you should be on the cover of a magazine."

He rolls his eyes. "And this dress." He tugs at the tie of the dark denim wrap dress I am wearing. "Looks like it should be on the bedroom floor."

"Cheesy."

My accusation is greeted with a shrug.

"Okay, let me try again. You would look better on the end of my dick."

I smack his chest this time.

"Fuck me! I will never understand women. I give you cheesy, you don't like it. I give you romance and that's wrong!"

I roar with laughter. "That was many things, but none of them were romance."

"We need to go, or we'll be the last to arrive and Mase will be getting all tetchy at trying to keep a secret."

I laugh, knowing he is right, especially when I consider how he outed Liv's pregnancy in the middle of dad making a birthday toast for my mum.

****

I feel nervous for us both as we stand at the entrance to the restaurant. My breathing is heavy, and I am trying not to hyperventilate. I have no idea why I am this nervous, apart from the fact that my dad openly disapproves of Dec and what he perceives as his poor man's Hugh Hefner lifestyle, oh, and because I have never brought a boyfriend home. Not unless you count Matthew Mitchell when I was fourteen-years-old. That might be a good reason for my nervousness because my brothers were dickheads to him and my dad was embarrassingly threatening, ridiculously so considering he was the same age as me.

"Let's do this." Dec is already leading me through the door and across the restaurant to where my family are.

The raised eyebrows and knowing glances confirm that everyone except for my dad has got the message that us arriving together, my hand in Dec's, means he is the boyfriend I am introducing them all to. My dad seems to be holding court, gesturing and laughing as he tells some story.

We come to stand alongside my mum who smiles up at us while Mase gets to his feet to greet us, unlike my brothers who grin at us. My stepbrother, Scott, looks uncomfortable as he nods in our direction. Liv springs to her feet and rushes to hug me before kissing Dec, and that seems to be when Dad notices who I am with.

He scowls silently, then, a little reluctantly, accepts the hand Dec offers him.

"Sit down, everyone. Lovely to see you again, Declan," my mum says, setting about easing the obvious tension.

The vacant seats for us are situated next to Liv and Scott. Dec takes the seat next to my sister and just one place away from his brother while I settle between Dec and Scott.

The whole experience is a little surreal and although everyone makes conversation, my dad's relatively quiet and when I look up, I find his attention is on me or Dec.

My mum is aware of it too, and she keeps trying to distract my dad with conversation, but her attempts aren't what you could call successful.

"Are you going to find out the gender of the baby?" Is one of her attempts to deflect attention from us.

Mase looks at Liv, who shrugs. "We haven't really decided. Neither of us mind if it's a boy or a girl so there's no real need to know."

Mum nods.

"What about a baby shower?" Dad asks. "They're all the rage."

I stifle a giggle, unsure if he was a fan of such occasions, although we have catered a few.

"What?" He looks affronted when my brothers and Scott laugh, especially when the latter makes a guffaw noise.

"A baby shower, really? They're just an excuse for people to get extra gifts and to show all of their friends on social media how great their life is, even if it is going to shit behind the scenes."

His final comment silences everyone, except for Mase. "I take your point and respect your opinion."

Dec and I exchange a glance knowing that he probably doesn't respect his opinion and there is a *but* on the way.

"But..."

Dec and I smile at each other now.

"Neither Liv nor I are big on social media and even if we were, our life would be great, on there and behind the scenes."

Scott shakes his head, unbothered by Mase getting huffy and in fairness to him, his words weren't really directed at Liv and Mase, of that, I am sure.

"Oh, and we don't need anyone to buy things for our child, now or in the future."

"That's a no to the baby shower then," says Dec with a huge, cheeky grin.

Everyone laughs, even Mase.

We're onto dessert when my dad can hold it in no more and addresses the subject of me and Dec. "You two, are together then, seeing each other?"

I nod and smile.

Dec smiles too. "Yes, very much together."

"And how long has this been going on?" Dad sounds a little

terse now.

I could kiss Dec now as he looks to me, deferring to me, allowing me to dictate the information being shared with my family, and I suspect he's happy to let me lie and say we are new, if that's what I want. I don't want that.

"It's been a few months. Quite a few months. We started talking when Mase and Liv got engaged."

Dec looks hot under the collar at my reference to that meeting, and we did talk even if it was mainly Dec and his dirty talk.

"What?" Dad is raising his voice and drawing some attention from nearby diners. "Is he the one that was sending you home in the previous night's clothes at all hours."

I am shocked at just how angry he is about us being together at all, but his tone at the memory of my walk of shame brings out his most severe annoyance. I feel Dec stiffen beside me and know he is pissed off, possibly more because it wasn't him.

"No, I was not the one sending her home at all hours," Dec snaps. "She said we started talking then, not that we started sleeping together."

My dad is now a very strange shade of red and my mum looks awkward. I see Liv nudge Mase as if encouraging him to say or do something. He shakes his head and seems to have no intention of involving himself. My brothers look between my boyfriend and my dad as they bat the conversation back and forth. Scott looks down into his lap and shakes his head, if only to himself.

"It took us a little while to realise we were serious about each other, but as Cupc— Anita," he corrects himself. "As Anita said, we have been involved for a few months."

My dad, who is being a bit of a dick now, rolls his eyes then looks around the table. "I assume you two knew." He points at Liv and Mase.

They nod, making no apologies or anything else.

Dad looks around the table again. "Anybody else?"

My brothers and mum shake their heads while Scott says nothing.

"Scott?" Dad is now on his feet, and I swear he's about to

lose his shit.

"Leave me out of it," Scott replies. "She is an adult. They both are, so let them make adult decisions."

My dad looks confused. "Anita doesn't understand…she was sheltered…she needs help and guidance—"

Scott stands too. He laughs, but it's hard and full of hurt and sadness. "No wonder Raymond wanted you out of the way. There can only ever be enough room for one abusive, asshole, dictator."

I look to Liv, wanting her to stop this. Raymond was hers and Scott's stepfather who was the head of the weird church and in different ways he abused them both.

"Scott." Liv reaches across and takes his hand.

"What?" he asks. "Tell me he doesn't sound like him with his opinions being more important than anyone else's and his need to help and guide the rest of us, Anita, because she clearly isn't capable of making her own choices, especially not if he doesn't approve of them."

Everyone falls silent until Dec speaks again. "We didn't come here to ask for permission or approval. We're together. It would be nice if you supported it, but if you don't the only people you'll hurt will be yourself and Anita."

"Nigel, sit down." My mum looks well pissed off with Dad now. "Dec's right and although I would never compare you to that awful man, I can understand why Scott may have said what he did." She turns to Scott who is still standing, his hand still in Liv's. "Please, Scott, sit down."

He does.

"So, no baby shower, in case there was any doubt." Mase's dry delivery makes everyone laugh, albeit briefly.

Chapter Twenty-One

Declan

My mood is still out of kilter by the time dinner ends. Liv and Anita's dad's attitude towards me pisses me off. I don't need him to like me, and he doesn't. He has made that crystal clear, although, I think it is more his perception of who and what I am that he dislikes. I may not be a parent, but I get that, after all, he still views her as his little girl, but fuck me, he hasn't given me a chance yet.

Having Mase and Liv in my corner had been a blessing, their support and diffusion of some of the tension had been very much appreciated. The real advocate for Nigel treating his daughter like an adult, if not for our relationship was Scott. The way he had taken his dad to task had been impressive, but again, that was more about Nigel's spouting of needing to guide Anita.

"You okay?" Liv asks, leaning in to whisper to me.

I turn and smile. "Yeah, even better when we can leave."

She laughs, drawing some attention from the others including Anita who is getting to her feet along with her parents. Presumably, Liv and I have missed that the evening is ending.

I stand too and watch on as they all start exchanging kisses before preparing to leave. Liv takes Mase's hand and once standing does a bit of a strange jig from one foot to the other.

"I need a wee," she announces.

"I'll come with you." Anita is already grabbing her sister's arm and dragging her off to the ladies.

"We'll leave you both to wait for them then," Nigel tells us, preparing to leave with his family. He pauses before me. "Should I expect my daughter home tonight?" He's wearing an expression that suggests he has a bad taste in his mouth.

"Maybe you should ask your daughter that," I reply, snapping a little.

No more words are exchanged as Nigel turns and follows the rest of his family out.

"What a complete and utter cockwomble he is!"

Mase laughs. "He loves her."

"And if he said that to you about Liv?"

He shakes his head. "I'd be calling him far worse than a cockwomble. I've told you before, with Liv he had no choice but to accept I was there if he was going to enter her life again. But with you...you're the one entering her life, not the other way round."

"He's still a cockwomble."

"And I am sure he speaks as highly about you."

Mase is right. I know that. I am the big bad wolf coming along to take advantage of Little Red Riding Hood and Nigel is the woodcutter, ready to split me open or chop my head off. I smirk rather immaturely as I decide it's my balls he is ready to chop off.

"He'll come round," Mase assures me. "You just need to show him that you're not the man he believes you are."

Again, my brother is right.

He laughs. "Do you remember what Dad was like whenever Bethy brought a boy home for him to meet?"

I howl because I remember it all too well. "How many did he scare off before she stopped telling him?"

Mase grins. "You know he knew about each and every one of them, and I think Bethy suspected he did too."

"Did he tag her?"

Mase laughs now, knowing that Liv is obsessed with our dad being intent on tagging or tracking her.

"How is security on junior?"

He shrugs. "Covert."

I feel my eyebrows arch. "Really? He hasn't implanted anything without her knowledge, has he?" This is another of

Liv's suspicions.

Mase rolls his eyes. "No, he hasn't, but he needs to stop dropping that into conversation with Liv and then telling her it's illegal because that just makes her think even more that he's done it without her knowledge."

Our dad loves to wind people up and with Liv having already decided he's James Bond, she is very easy to wind up.

"I'm not convinced he hasn't done it at your request and your kid is going to look like something from a weird sci-fi movie, surrounded by security gadgets."

"And you don't need to say that to her either or she'll be sure he has, and as for my kid, her safety will be my main priority."

I stare across at my brother. He hasn't even realised the cat he has let out of the bag. "*Her* safety?"

"Fuck. Don't say a fucking word to Liv! She will have my balls if she finds out I've told anyone we're having a girl."

I laugh at him. "You'd have made a shit spy."

"I get that from Mum." He laughs.

"Oh, and your balls…I believe your wife is currently wearing them as earrings."

He flips me the middle finger before an older woman waves across the restaurant to us.

"Shit! Mase, we need to make this short and sweet, okay. Anita does not need to walk back into this."

"You haven't told her?"

"No."

He looks concerned and slightly disapprovingly.

"I know, but the time hasn't been right and it's in the past. Nothing to do with her."

The woman, Audrey, is almost in front of us now.

"From experience, I will guarantee that Anita won't see it that way."

"Declan." Audrey, with kind eyes and a genuinely warm smile reaches up and kisses my cheek. She turns to Mase. "And Mason, how are you both?"

"Good, thanks. You?" I ask feeling slightly guilty that I don't already know the answer to that question.

"Fine, darling, you know me." She looks to Mase again.

"I'm well, thank you," he tells her. "Married." He holds up his ring finger.

I look at him with a wry smile as I roll my eyes and silently mouth the word *wanker* at him.

He ignores me and continues speaking. "And a baby on the way."

"How lovely," she gushes. "And you, Declan?"

My level of discomfort is through the fucking roof with that question. I need to shut this down and get out of here, quickly.

"Gosh, no! You know me, Audrey. I'll leave all of that to Mason."

Mason frowns at me, clearly disapproving of my dishonest response, but he still has my back. "Audrey, it's been lovely to see you, but we have to get going or we'll be late."

"Of course." She leans in and Mase lowers his cheek for her to kiss before she turns her attention back to me. "I'm glad you're well, Declan, and please, don't be a stranger." Her voice carries an emotional wobble now, as she pulls me in for a hug I didn't know I needed, but I did.

The burn in my jaw and stinging in my eyes confirms just how much I needed that hug.

"Take care, Audrey," Mase tells her, already leading me to the exit while texting on his phone. "I'll tell the girls to meet us outside."

Anita

"What the fuck?" I have literally just walked out of the ladies and am greeted by Mase and Dec standing with an older lady who is kissing Dec. Not a snog kiss, but a very warm and familiar looking kiss on his cheek.

"Man whore," Liv says, seeing what I am seeing. She's joking. Her laugh confirms that, but for some reason, I'm not amused. Something about the interaction I am witnessing seems too friendly...intimate almost, not that I think she and Dec have been intimate.

Liv is staring at me, clearly confused by my reaction and behaviour.

"I was joking," she says.

"I know."

"He adores you and you may have achieved the impossible and tamed the man whore."

With a shake of my head, refusing to fully accept that Dec is entirely tamed, I decide to diffuse the atmosphere I'm creating. "You might want to stop calling him that or in a few years you'll have to endure him being called Uncle Man Whore by your daughter."

"Ssh," she hisses. "I wasn't supposed to tell anyone, so you need to lose the word daughter, niece, she and her from your vocabulary."

I laugh at her now. "Why is it a secret again?"

"Not sure, but we decided we wanted to know but for it to be something nobody else knows...and it has been for the last couple of weeks."

I don't pretend to understand hers and Mase's logic in this, but then, I don't need to. Looking back over to the boys, I see they're leaving, just as Liv receives a message.

"They're waiting outside for us."

I am even more suspicious about who this woman is. Who she is to Dec but walk aside Liv until we reach the boys outside. Mase and Dec turn together and almost in synchronicity they each put an arm around us.

"You okay?" Dec asks, leaning in to kiss the top of my head. "With how things went with your parents?" he adds.

"Kind of. It could have gone better, but it could have been worse I suppose."

That is the truth of it really. I knew my dad wouldn't be thrilled about me and Dec but hopefully, over time, he will see what I see. Suddenly, I feel less sure of things when I think back to the woman he and Mase were with in the restaurant, prompting me to broach the subject of her.

"Who was your friend?" I look between Dec and his brother as we walk towards the car park together.

"Friend?" Dec sounds nervous.

I look at Mase more closely and he looks shifty.

Liv laughs. "Unless you two are in the habit of locking lips

Family Affair

with older ladies who take care of themselves."

Mase looks even more uncomfortable now and Dec looks like he might vomit.

Liv frowns up at her husband. "If you are about to tell me she was a former cougar of yours, we might have a problem, and by problem, I mean a broken hand for me and a rattling jaw for you."

Mase looks horrified now. "No, she is not a former cougar. I don't have any former cougars."

"She was a former business associate of Mason's," Dec tells us now, drawing my focus to him again.

It's plausible and yet, it doesn't quite ring true and when I look back at Mase, I know it's a lie. Who the fuck is that woman and why is Dec so reluctant to tell me the truth about her?

"Are you two going straight home?" Mase asks his brother rather than me.

I expect him to reply with a simple yes because that had been my understanding of our plans. That is not what I hear.

"I need to pop into the club for a while. It's a busy night and if it gets too busy, they might be short staffed."

Liv looks at me and seeing my confused and hurt expression, stops dead, and frowns across at Dec. "Are you dropping Anita off home first, or shall we?"

He shrugs.

Stepping back, I glare up at him and shake my head. "Don't you dare shrug and apparently not give a shit about how I am getting home!" I am fuming.

"Liv," Mase interrupts. "I have some business. Club business to deal with, so why don't you take Anita and when Dec and I are done, he'll drop me home."

This is bullshit. I know it, Liv knows and so do both men. This was never part of tonight's plan, so why has that changed? The woman in the restaurant.

"You are talking bollocks here, Mase. Total and utter crap, but, whatever. Keys!" Liv's final word is a demand and there is no doubting how angry she is.

"Baby—"

She cuts him off. "Keys or I'm taking Anita to catch the all-

161

night bus. Your choice."

"Like fuck you are!" He gives her his keys. "We'll talk when I get home."

"You bet we will."

I turn to Dec who appears to be in turmoil, something between anxious and sorry.

"Go home with Liv and I can pick you up later when I drop Mase back."

It's at moments like this I wish I was more like Liv. She wouldn't leave here until Dec was in no doubt that he was in deep shit and that she would be getting answers from him one way or another. Shit! Mase has somehow managed to get himself in deeper shit with Liv than Dec is with me and in my heart, I know that woman in the restaurant who was at the centre of this was connected to Dec, not Mase.

With a desire to be more Liv like, I shake my head and take a few steps back.

"Whatever, Dec." I begin to walk away then glance over my shoulder to fix him with my gaze. "You never know, I might even be at Liv's when you deem me worthy of knowing what the fuck is going on…or I might not."

I turn back and continue walking, hoping Liv is hot on my heels.

"Cupcake. It really isn't what you think." His voice is filled with desperation and part of me wants to turn back and comfort him, offer him some kind of sign that it's okay.

I don't. Just. Instead, I don't look back at all but do shout back to him over the sound of Liv's steps catching up with me. "You have no clue what I think, because you didn't bother to ask."

Chapter Twenty-Two

Declan

"Fuck!" Mase roars as he watches his car disappear and then he turns to me.

"I know, sorry." I try to calm his wrath, but that only seems to encourage it.

"Sorry? You're sorry? You're a fucking idiot is what you are, Declan." He stands perfectly still, his stony glare fixed on me. "I warned you about you and Anita and how it shouldn't affect me and Livy, and yet here we are."

"Sorry," I repeat and then think about me and Anita. She looked seriously pissed off, however, more than that she looked hurt and that makes me feel worse still.

"Stop fucking apologising, or even better stop dragging me and my wife into your drama."

I don't point out that as he and I are close and that his wife is my lady's sister, so somehow, I think he and Liv will always be dragged into it. Mase is angry, really angry, like changing through darker and darker shades of red until steam is coming out of his ears angry. He can be pissy and antsy about stuff he isn't comfortable with, and business can rile him, but nothing sends him raging like Liv. Like something that is likely to hurt her or get under her skin. Like things that will make her angry, especially when that anger is directed at him and that is exactly what I have done, again.

"You have to tell her about Audrey." His shoulders have dropped slightly, and his hands are no longer balled into fists, so he's softening and calming down a little.

I nod. He's right. "What do I tell her though?"

His hands are clenching I notice. He's getting cross again. "Oh, I don't know…maybe you could act like a fucking adult and tell her the truth!"

I shake my head. "I'm not ready to do that."

"Then get ready, little brother, because when I tell Liv, she is unlikely to be willing to keep your secrets for you."

"No! Don't tell Liv, please."

There's a low wall near where we're standing, and I feel guilty as I watch Mase move closer and drop down onto it.

He reaches up to his head where he roughly runs his hand through his hair and then, with his eyes closed, pinches the bridge of his nose as if he has a headache.

"Dec, I love you, even if you are a fucking idiot." His eyes are open and he is looking up at me.

I know what's coming next and to be honest, it's no more than I'm expecting. If anything, if he said anything different, I'd be disappointed.

"I don't lie to Liv. Assuming she's speaking to me, I know that as soon as I get home, she is going to hurl swear words at me, possibly throw a punch if she's close enough…" A wry smile curls his lips ever so slightly and I can't help but reciprocate because as much as we joke about Liv throwing punches, it really isn't her typical reaction. She's one of the gentlest, least violent people I have ever met. "And then she is going to ask me what is going on and exactly who Audrey is because she in no way bought that she was a former business associate."

I nod. I knew that and I respect him and Liv.

"You could ask her not to tell Anita."

His face is back to angry, and he is on his feet and pacing. "And here we are again, your actual fucking, fucking with my life."

Suddenly, my own anger rises, aimed at Mase, but I am angrier with myself for being in this position than at him for not trying to fix it by coercing his wife in some way.

"Fucking? My fucking! Anita and I do not fuck—I mean we

do, but it's not fucking, not like before with other people. She is different and she deserves more respect than your comment demonstrates."

I find myself flying towards my larger brother, ready to fight, but I'm unsure who I am really fighting.

Punches fly and a few kicks that wouldn't look out of place on a school playground follow before Mase, who appears to have seen me coming, has me pinned against a wall by my throat.

"Calm the fuck down!"

I am still thrashing a little.

"Declan, stop!"

I feel myself slump in his grip.

He looks down at me and shakes his head. "Sorry, about the fucking comment. The only way Liv will agree to keep quiet is if you are going to tell Anita."

A nod is my only response.

"So, you are on a clock."

Another nod follows.

"You are also fucked beyond belief if the suggestion of you fucking her gets you all hot and bothered."

I frown, which makes a change from nodding.

"Dec, when the idea of someone else referring to your girl as being the one you're fucking sends you into shitty fight moves, it's love. The real thing."

He releases me. I straighten my clothes and take his former place on the wall while he continues to speak.

"Don't fuck this up if it's real because you won't ever find it again."

I know he is right. I believe every word he is saying, and yet, I don't want to accept that because that means I have to tell Anita about Audrey and I'm not ashamed of it. It happened and I learned from it, but what I learned is the opposite of what I want with Anita.

Mase is right.

"I am fucked."

He laughs. "Yup, well and truly. Come on, assuming you don't really need to go to the club, let's find a bar, grab one drink and you can make a plan of how this is going to work. Then, hopefully, the girls will have calmed down enough for me to go home to my wife who will make good on the promise I was previously on, and you can take Anita home and do whatever you've planned on doing."

He offers me a hand and pulls me to my feet before back slapping me.

"Thanks, Mase."

"No problem. That's what big brothers are for, but stop dropping me in the shit, please."

"Sorry. I'll try."

"Hmmm." He doesn't sound convinced. "And it's a good job your work life comes with bouncers because you still can't fucking fight for shit."

Anita

"Anita." Liv is staring at me expectantly, waiting for an answer.

"Home. Mum and Dad's home, not Declan's home."

She nods and immediately turns the car in that direction.

Neither of us speak for several long seconds and then it's her that opens conversation.

"Dec won't be happy when he gets to mine and finds you're not there."

"Good. Do you know what Liv, I don't want to be a doormat anymore—"

She cuts in. "You're not—"

It's my turn to interrupt her now. "I am, always have been, especially with men. From Adam Ashton in year one right up to now with Dec. I am just so fucking grateful that they have deemed me worthy of their attention that I put up with every bit of shit going and keep coming back for more. I am not perfect, and I've done things I am not proud of, but for once I want to be a choice not an option and for the person I am with to be proud to have me and be willing to do anything to keep me."

The first of my tears rolls down my cheek.

"And that is no more than you deserve, and I think Dec might be that person."

"Yet here we are, Declan with Mase, presumably getting their stories straight and me with you, crying."

She pulls over and parks at the roadside a few streets from home and in seconds I find myself wrapped in her arms being squeezed tightly under the guise of a hug. "I promise, there will be no getting their story straight and when Mase gets home, I will know the truth, the whole truth."

I can't help myself, I laugh at her. "You are fucking scary."

"So I've been told." She grins.

"I need to be more like you."

She shakes her head. "No, you need to be more like you and as for you being an option…" She releases a long exhale. "Never. Don't let anyone use you, not ever. I have been there." She takes a deep breath and I know she means her abusive stepfather.

I am about to speak, to offer her words of comfort, but she waves it away and continues.

"I know, I had no choice in the matter, and I was a child, yada yada, but I have been there and the feelings of being powerless and worthless are the worst."

I nod and feel several tears hot on my cheeks.

"You sure you want to go home?"

"Yeah, I think I need to take some time away from Dec, or at least show him that he made a mistake in not telling me who that woman was."

She stares at me.

"What?"

"Nothing, just…look, he should have told you who she was tonight, but you know, whoever she is, there will be other people and I don't know that you, or any of us, have the right to know everything about everyone if it's the past and not important to the future."

She's right and I absolutely agree with her. I don't want to know everything. I would probably be scarred if I did with Dec's past.

She shrugs and rolls her eyes making me smile.

"I don't want to know everything and everyone, maybe just

the things and people who will make him lie when confronted by them."

"Sounds fair."

"What?" I ask again, seeing an expression cross her face that suggests she has more to say.

"That has to cut both ways, like Christian."

"Christian doesn't impact on my present or future, well, he didn't until he turned out to be related to the Hardings."

"Exactly," Liv says with a knowing glimmer in her eyes that suggests she knows there's more to me and Christian than I have let on. "I'm always here to talk to and to listen."

"I know." An emotional wobble enters my voice because as much as I would like to share with my sister, I can't because she will then be conflicted as to where her loyalties lie. "But you're a Harding, too, and I wouldn't ever want to put you in a position of needing to lie or at least keep secrets from Mase."

"I know." She looks conflicted already and I haven't even told her anything yet which proves to me that I shouldn't. "You're sure about going home?" she asks, our conversation having come full circle.

"Absolutely."

When we pull up outside my parent's house, I hesitate.

"There's still time for us to head back to mine."

I laugh. "No, I just know Dad will say something or give me knowing looks."

Liv is already out of the car and opening my door. "Come on, then, let's do this together."

As she hits the remote locking button, she is already pulling me towards the house.

With the front door closing behind us, she calls out as my nerves begin to kick in, desperately trying to find an explanation for my return home so early, possibly even at all tonight and definitely minus Dec.

"Hi."

We enter the lounge and find my parents sat in front of the TV. They both turn and while my mum frowns, Dad seems to be searching behind us.

"Just the two of you?" I think that's his tactful way of asking where Dec is. His expression changes to one of suspicion.

Here we go.

"Yeah." Liv doesn't seem to miss a beat. "There was some problem at the club, so Mase has gone with Dec to sort it out."

"Is everything okay?" Mum asks.

"Yeah, nothing major. Some problem with a customer having a go at a member of staff, and the police being involved or something, but Dec was in a hurry, so we didn't get details. We offered to tag along, but you know what Mase is like, especially with a baby on board." She points to her belly. "Anyway, Dec wasn't sure how long he'd be…"

"Which is why I thought I may as well come home."

Mum and Dad both nod, buying Liv's story completely and my few words of explanation for being home.

"You staying for a cup of tea, Liv?" Mum is already on her feet and preparing to put the kettle on.

Chapter Twenty-Three

Declan

Mase stares at me across the roof as he gets out of my car and stands to his full height when we arrive at his home. "You ready to sort things out with Anita?"

I nod. "What do I say to her?"

"The truth."

"But—"

Mase spins on his heels as we make our way towards the lift that will take us to the home he shares with Liv.

"Declan! I thought we'd agreed that you were going to tell her the truth."

"I am."

"Then do that. No half-truths or omissions because they're essentially lies. In fact, they're worse than lies, and not only will they come back and bite you on the arse. They will hurt Anita and I know that's the last thing you want."

"Thanks, Mase."

"No problem. What else are big brothers for? Come on, time to face the music."

When we walk into the flat on the top floor of Mase's work building, that is essentially a penthouse apartment, we are greeted by the sound of silence.

"Where are they?" I whisper, somehow encouraged to match the quiet of my surroundings.

Mase shrugs. "My car was downstairs, so Liv made it home."

"Maybe they've gone on somewhere..." my voice trails off

when I see the murderous expression spreading across his face.

"They fucking better not have. In case you'd forgotten, my wife is pregnant."

"As if anyone could forget that fact."

Looking around, I wait for something to confirm that the words I had planned to keep in my head have been spoken. I quickly realise that my words had remained in my head and the words were Liv's as she comes into view in the dimly lit, open plan lounge.

"Baby." Mase is already heading for his wife who stands against the wall of the corridor that leads to their bedroom.

I notice that she is wearing a pair of soft shorts and a baggy T-shirt. Sleepwear, begging the question if Liv was in bed, where is Anita?

"Don't baby me." She side steps him. "We need to talk."

"I know and we will."

She looks across at him and as pissed off as she is with him, there's still a softness to her that shows that she loves him and they will be okay, no matter what.

I want that with Anita.

That thought prompts me to speak as I watch Liv make her way into the kitchen.

"Drink?" She stands with the fridge door open.

"I'll do it," Mase says, taking some milk from her hand.

She rolls her eyes at him then she looks at me. "Dec, do you want a drink?"

"Where's Anita?" I ignore her question but have found my voice at least.

"Home."

I absorb her reply before a frown mars my brow. "She doesn't have a key. How long ago did you drop her off? I don't want her hanging around for me."

I get the roll of Liv's eyes now.

"You men are so conceited and cocksure! I said she has gone *home*." She overemphasises the word home as if she is trying to convey some other meaning, but it is wasted on me.

I stare at her, silently fuming that I am no closer to knowing where my lady is, but silently accept that although she is being a bit of an arse about it, this is a situation of my own making, not Liv's.

A very small, but unamused laugh leaves Liv's mouth. "She has a key to *her* home. She has gone home."

"Why?" My question doesn't need an answer and I am relieved when Liv doesn't offer one. "You took her there instead of here!" My tone is accusatory and that was my intention.

"Declan," Mase warns.

Liv steps closer. "Declan, I am a grown-up and another grown-up asked me to take her home. I knew you wouldn't be happy, said as much to her, but it was her choice, just like it was yours and Mase's to lie to our faces. Now, normally, you'd be welcome to stay, but assuming you don't want the drink that was offered, Mase and I have an argument to have before I go to bed to sleep because my baby considers two in the morning the time to lie on my bladder and then I struggle to get back to sleep."

She rubs her belly and smiles softly.

"Yeah. Sorry. Mase, I'll catch you tomorrow, and Liv, I don't need to know when you are peeing." I lean in and land a kiss to her cheek before rushing back to the lift.

Before the doors have closed, I hear Liv speak. "Who the fuck is Audrey and why have you lied to me?"

I swallow down my guilt and will the lift to travel quicker so I can go and explain myself to Anita, not that I have actually thought that plan through because it is now after midnight, and I assume her and her parents are all in bed.

Pulling up outside her family home that is in darkness, I briefly question if this is a mistake. I push that thought down and am out of my car and heading to the front door. Pausing, I look at the doorbell and the darkened house again. Maybe I should wait. Or not. I pull my phone from my pocket and type a message.

<Cupcake, open the window, please. x>

Anita

I've tossed and turned from the second I got into bed which was about half an hour after Liv left. However, I am struggling to get to sleep. I have so many questions in my head. Questions for Dec and for the first time since returning home, I begin to wonder if I should have waited for him. No. If I'd waited, we would have ended up arguing because I am angry as well as hurt.

My mind turns to that woman, Audrey. Who is she and what could be so awful that Dec felt the need to lie about her identity and drag his brother into it? I brush off any guilt I feel emerging for Mase. He's a big boy and although I know their intentions are well meant, Mase and Liv think nothing of offering opinions on my relationship with Dec. I love that Liv cares so much and I do acknowledge that Mase is a little more reluctant to be involved, but they are.

The sound of my message alert breaks my thoughts and then I hear something else. A tapping sound but without any regular pattern or rhythm. I hear it again as I sit up and reach for my phone to find a message from Dec.

<Cupcake, open the window, please. x>

Then the tapping sounds again. Shit! It's something hitting the window. Dec.

I rush to the window before he wakes anyone else. Pulling the curtains back I see him standing beneath my window and as I open it something hits me, a small piece of gravel, the sort we have on the ground around the path. At least I know what he was throwing at my window.

Dec drops his hand, presumably releasing more stones.

"Window's open," I whisper down. "You can go now."

Dec holds my stare. "I want to talk."

"Oh, well in that case, I will of course drop everything." This could go really badly because he is pissing me off.

"You're angry?"

Fucking hell! There are moments when his stupidity shocks

me. "No shit, Sherlock."

"Let me in."

"No! My parents are in bed and we do not need to wake them to share this."

He nods. "Yeah, your dad already hates me. So…"

I watch, aghast as I realise he is climbing the lower of the branches on the tree to the front of the house. He makes short work of the height until he is within a couple of feet of my open window.

"You might need to step back."

My face is screwed up into a confused frown. "This is not an 80s movie."

He laughs. "No. If it was, I'd have been blasting tunes from the ground before climbing up here. Cupcake, step back, please."

I consider refusing but the chances are, him climbing back down the tree will make more noise than letting him in.

He lands with something of a thud a few seconds later. Getting to his full height he looks down at me and I can see now that he looks sad.

"I went to Mase's and you weren't there."

"I came home." Clearly my explanation is unnecessary as we are both standing in my bedroom.

Dec scans my room. "Your bedroom?"

"Yeah. Good job you got the right one."

"Yeah…I hadn't even considered that when I started throwing stones."

"Liv told me you were here…at home. She's great and somehow a pain in the arse at the same time."

I smile, imagining the grief she may have given him.

He reaches for me and gently brushes his thumb over my cheek. "If you really want me to, I'll leave, but I want to explain about Audrey."

Part of me wants to tell him to go. To show him that I can be tough too. Someone who won't take his shit indefinitely. Someone more like Liv, but then I am not Liv, I'm me, and he is here and ready to tell me what I want to know.

"You'd better come in properly then," I whisper. The last

thing I need to do is to wake my parents.

I close the window and indicate for him to take a seat at my dressing table while I sit on the edge of my bed.

"I have never slept with Audrey." He laughs a little. "That is not a claim I ever imagined making. I was involved with her daughter, Amber."

Looking across at Dec, I absolutely believe every word he says, and yet, it still doesn't make sense for him to have lied about who Audrey is. He could have told me this, so there must be more.

"Involved?"

"Yes, seriously involved."

"How seriously?" My heart is thumping against my chest as I consider all the possible responses I might get.

"Really seriously, like engaged serious."

I get to my feet and pace a little before finding myself standing before Dec, looking down at him still at my dressing table.

"You were engaged," I state more than ask in a flat tone that I hope doesn't give the impression of anger or apathy because whilst I am not angry, I care, I care deeply. I hate the idea of him ever having felt strongly enough about another woman to have been engaged.

He reaches for my hand and brushes a thumb over my knuckles, and it is one of the most understanding and comforting things I have ever been on the receiving end of. He understands how I feel.

"Yeah. She erm…she jilted me."

My jaw drops as I absorb what he is telling me. "Jilted you?" I just need to be sure.

"Yup, at the altar. Me and Mase stood there in our Sunday best, waiting for the arrival of the bride along with the rest of the congregation and she didn't show."

He laughs but it's hard and a little cold.

"Shit!" I'm unsure what else I can say.

"Yup." He laughs again, but this time it does at least carry some warmth and a little amusement. "So eloquently put, Cupcake."

"Sorry."

"No, don't be."

He reaches for me and pulls me down until I am in his lap, straddling him, but this is not sexual. This is comforting, open and somehow feels real and meaningful. My face immediately and instinctively comes to rest in his neck while I feel his in my hair, inhaling my scent.

"Anita," he says just as there's a loud knock on my door, followed by it opening to reveal my dad filling the space while my mum stands a few steps behind him.

My mum doesn't look in anyway surprised to discover us here, unlike my dad who might have steam coming out of his ears.

Chapter Twenty-Four

Declan

I still can't believe how angry Nigel was to find his daughter in an embrace with me. Well, I can because I'm sure it looked sexual more than anything, even if that is the last thing it was. It was loving and intimate but on a deeper level. Nigel didn't see that. I did think at one point that he was going to burst a blood vessel or something. Her mum was cool though and I think could see there was more than possibly met the eye going on.

Looking around my office in the empty club, I thank my lucky stars that Nigel's business is no longer operating from my kitchen, or it would be really quite awkward today. Part of me regrets Anita no longer working here but then I also appreciate having my own space without the distraction of her ever-tempting self and frosting.

My phone dances across the desk and I immediately smile when I see Anita's name lighting up the screen. I text her first thing and am relieved to see a reply.

<Morning, Stud. My dad is still refusing to speak to me... probably for the best. My mum still thinks you looked incredibly athletic climbing out of the window and back down the tree x>

I laugh and compose my reply.

<As it's after 12 it's technically afternoon but am glad to

hear from you no matter what time of the day it is. Your dad probably used all of his words up on me last night! And I am so pleased your mother got something from my descent from your window x>

Her reply is immediate.

<I still can't believe he did that to you. Yeah, she reckons it was incredibly romantic, like something out of a romance novel x>

<I still can't believe he did that to me. But his house, his rules and I guess he had a point that I should leave his house the way I'd entered it x>

I hear a lorry pulling into the back yard. Moving to the window I see it's a delivery of beer.

<Sorry, got to go. A delivery has just arrived. I'll call you later and arrange tonight's plans x>

I slip my phone into my pocket and head downstairs to open the cellar up.

I have just seen the back of the delivery guys when I notice another vehicle pulling into the yard. *Shit.* Nigel, and he still doesn't look happy.

"A word," he calls, already out of his van and heading for me.

I nod and can only dream that he will stop at one word but know he won't.

He follows me into the club where I hold up a cup and offer him coffee from behind the bar. I'd prefer something much stronger if I am about to be subjected to a lecture of some kind, but I am hoping to create a good impression.

A nod confirms he's having coffee and is clearly here for more than just the one word.

With two cups of coffee, I round the bar and take a stool, indicating for Nigel to take one too.

He accepts the drink and fixes me with a stare that I can't decipher. Silence hangs between us before he finally breaks it.

"You had no right being in my house last night."

I actually thought we'd discussed this already, just before he made me climb back down that bloody tree.

"As I have already said, I am sorry that I was there without your knowledge, and I am, but there really wasn't anything untoward going on."

He scowls at me.

"And whilst I may not have had your permission, it's not like I broke in."

His face contorts through a variety of emotions, most of them linked to annoyance. "She's my daughter. My little girl and I found her draped all over you in her bedroom, in my house."

I'd like to dispute the description of her draped all over me, if only because he makes it sound sordid. I don't. I let it go.

"I can appreciate that, but there was something we needed to discuss, and it couldn't wait til the morning."

"And what was that?"

"Sorry, Nigel, not to be rude, but that's none of your business. It's between me and Anita."

He offers no protest, but he doesn't look thrilled.

"You are going to hurt her."

"I have no intention of hurting her. I love her."

He looks slightly startled at that revelation.

"That may be so, but it doesn't mean you won't hurt her. She's not like your usual types."

I can only imagine what he considers my usual type to be.

He continues. "She's a good girl. Never been the sort to have lots of boyfriends or sleep around."

He shudders. I nod, confirming what he's saying, although I would put everything I own on the fact he has no clue about Christian. I shouldn't have thought about that because now I am fighting against images of him touching her and kissing her and that is without me considering his marriage to my stepsister.

"She's not like Liv…" his voice trails off and I stare at him, wondering if he has just called his other daughter a slapper and thank all things holy that Mase isn't here to hear it.

"I don't think..." I allow my own voice to trail off, wondering just how I am going to deal with this because Liv is many things, none of them a slapper.

"What? No!" He looks alarmed when he figures what I'd taken from his comment. "Livy is a good girl, too, but she wasn't sheltered and protected like Anita. Liv met bad people... Anita never did."

I accept what he's saying and believe completely that his meaning is precisely what he claims it to be.

"When I met Carol, I had lost my own children."

I say nothing but can see that fact saddens him and makes him feel guilty in equal parts. Part of me wants to point out that he didn't lose them. He knew exactly where they were, so technically he left them.

"She had three fatherless children and I was a childless father."

Again, I choose not to correct him. He was not childless as far as I was concerned, and I knew that was something Mase and I agreed on. We were children of divorce and had watched our mother remarry four times and yet, none of those men were ever our fathers. They were our mother's husbands, but never our dad because we had one of those already. A loving, attentive and present father.

This conversation was beginning to irk me. "Nigel, I get it. You made a new family and loved the children as if they were your own, but those children, Anita, is no longer a child. She is a grown woman."

He fidgets in his seat; he's getting pissed off again.

"I will apologise again for the way I entered your house and for the position you believe you found me in with your daughter, but I won't apologise for being with her. I love her and she loves me. We are together and plan on remaining that way."

"You're not good enough for her," he snaps.

I fight the smile threatening to curl my lips. "You will get no argument from me on that score."

He looks startled by my response. "I don't like you."

I do laugh now. "Can't say as I blame you, but Anita does."

He gets to his feet and offers me a single nod. "Don't hurt

her."

Before I can respond he has turned away and is heading towards the exit.

I release a long, loud breath and decide that went much better than I might have hoped.

Anita

"He'll get over it." My mum leans against the countertop near to where I am mixing frosting.

"Will he? He didn't look like it was something he'd get over too soon."

She shrugs. "Anita, it was a shock for him. He knows you're an adult, but he doesn't like it so when he sees you and Dec all wrapped up together, he has no choice but to face that fact head on."

What she's saying makes sense. He has always been protective. Overprotective, but he needs to accept my status as a fully-fledged adult.

"Where is he, anyway?" The silence of my mother's reply makes me suspicious. Turning to face her, I use her name in question. "Mum?"

"He didn't want you to know."

"Mum!" My voice is more insistent and filled with more than a little angst.

"Fine! He's gone to see Dec—to talk to him—man to man."

I don't whether to laugh or cry at the notion of either of them being capable of acting like a man rather than a boy.

"Un-bloody-believable! When is he going to accept that I am a grown woman?"

"When you stop sneaking boys into the house." The sound of my father's voice draws my attention to him entering the kitchen. "And in case you were wondering there were no punches thrown or insults hurled."

I look across at him slightly disbelievingly but before I can say anything my phone buzzes on the kitchen counter I am standing next to. Dec.

<Just to give you the heads up, your dad paid me a visit earlier…I'm still not his favourite person, but I think we're okay. Call me when you're free and we can do dinner and catch-up x>

Our plans turn out to be me going to Dec's for dinner and a plan for me to stay over. He meets me at the door and unlike his usual reaction of dragging me in and devouring me is replaced with a gentler approach that consists of a warm embrace and a gentle kiss to my lips.

"Come in, dinner is almost done."

We sit together in a comfortable silence eating pasta with peppers and cheese. I take a sip of the wine Dec has poured and look across at him. He suddenly looks nervous.

"Are you okay there, Stud?"

He smiles and I reciprocate, loving that he still enjoys my use of his nickname.

"There's something I need to tell you…" As his voice trails off, he moves his remaining pasta around the bowl.

"Is this something to do with my dad?"

We haven't actually discussed my dad's visit to him.

"No, not at all. I think we may have reached an understanding of sorts."

I nod, believing what he says. "If not that, then what?"

"I told you about Amber and our wedding that never was." He takes a slug of his wine and with a long exhale prepares to continue. "There was more to it than that. Afterwards, she disappeared, not even Audrey knew where she was. She offered no explanation to any of us as to why she had changed her mind about getting married." Dec laughs. "I didn't even want to get married, not really. It wasn't something I wanted or needed and with how many marriages I'd seen fail, I knew there were no guarantees of a happy ending."

"She, Amber did?"

"Yup! I don't know why. Maybe because her friends were all getting married."

I scowl. "You must have had feelings, both of you."

"Of course. We were a good match, well, I thought we were,

and we did love each other, but maybe we were in love with the idea of being in love a little more."

I watch on silently as he pushes his hands through his hair.

"I went off the rails a little bit and was beginning to get my man whore reputation and needed some focus. Mase suggested as I was spending so much time in clubs, I should run one. He invested and it got me back on track. About eighteen months after the wedding day, Amber came back."

"Just like that?"

"Yup, just like that. Completely out of the blue and with no warning. She tried to talk, wanted to explain, but it all sounded like excuses and bullshit to me. I was done the second she jilted me without so much as a backwards look."

I'm not entirely surprised by the bitterness and hard edge to Dec's voice, and yet, it unnerves me slightly.

"Mase and my parents were concerned by her reappearance and the effect it was having on me, so, my dad decided to look into where Amber had been as that was a subject she absolutely refused to be drawn on, suspiciously so."

"Dec, what is it your dad does?" While I was sure this probably wasn't where my attention should be drawn, I couldn't help it. Between how enigmatic Jimmy seemed to be, the references to him tagging Liv with implants and the sense of mystery that shrouded him and his 'work', I was intrigued.

Dec chuckled, pulling my hand to his lips where he kissed my knuckles. "I could tell you, but then he'd have to kill you."

"Oh."

He laughs again at my single word response and continues with his story. "Dad found out where she'd been, somewhere near Manchester, and while she was there, she had a baby."

Silence hangs between us for long, heavy seconds.

"Yours?"

He nods sadly.

"You have a child with her?"

I can feel fight or flight instinct kicking in. He had a child. A child I have never even heard him mention. Nobody has mentioned this child, ever. I can't believe Liv wouldn't have mentioned this to me.

"No!" he protests and then corrects himself. "I mean, yes, kind of."

"Dec, I don't understand."

"Sorry, I'm not being clear." His voice breaks and I can see tears beginning to shine in his eyes.

This is hard for him, and that fact makes me strangely happy and honoured that he is choosing to share this with me. I wait expectantly, anticipating the word abortion or termination to follow.

"The baby, my daughter, was adopted."

"Adopted?" I feel sick. In fact, I might be sick with all the feelings and emotions washing over me and infiltrating every fibre of my being.

"Yeah, and there was fuck all I could do about it and God knows, I tried."

I am stunned. What the hell am I supposed to say to this. I had no right to be part of this. It was private and personal to him and Amber and I felt as though I was intruding now.

"I'm sorry," I decide on saying, reaching for him, to pull him closer. "I'm sorry," I repeat, not really knowing what else to say. "I'm sure they found her a wonderful home, so you and Amber have nothing to feel bad about."

In an instant, Dec has pulled away and is storming in the opposite direction to me. "Her home should have been here, with me, with her family, and I do feel bad. Bad that I trusted Amber enough that she was able to do this to me. Oh, and as for her—" The venom in that one word, *her*, stuns me. "She deserves to feel bad about it all. She made the choices, the decisions she had no right to make without me and I hope she feels guilty for what she did for the rest of her life because that is what she deserves. So, you see, Anita, we might have to agree to disagree on this because for me she has everything to feel bad about."

I am rooted to my seat and have no idea what I should or shouldn't say or do to avoid making things worse.

"I need to get out for a while," Dec announces, reaching for his phone. "I just need some space, sorry."

He heads for the door and then turns to look at me.

"Cupcake, this is not your fault, and I am sorry that I can't stay here right now, but please, don't go. I don't talk about this often…like ever, so I just need some space and air, alone."

I nod, silently begging him to leave so I can fall apart in private.

Chapter Twenty-Five

Declan

Standing in the doorway, I smile a truly contented smile. Anita is in the kitchen at my mother's home, putting the final touches to a cake for Liv's baby shower. The same baby shower neither she nor Mase wanted, but after our mother began to plan one anyway, they gave in gracefully.

"I am getting a strong sense of déjà vu, Cupcake."

Anita spins and giggles at me. "Yeah, well, it might be wise for you to keep your hands, lips and everything else to yourself here, Stud."

I laugh, remembering our first encounter in the kitchen at Dazzler. "You're probably right. My mother does not need to walk in on that."

"Agreed." She turns back to the cake.

I close the distance and once I am close enough, slide an arm around her middle where she willingly allows me to pull her backwards to rest against my front. Leaning in, I inhale her glorious scent before lowering my lips to gently kiss her neck. She relaxes into my touch and kiss, and in this split second, I have never been happier. I love that her immediate, her reflex action is to soften into me and embrace everything I have to offer.

Life with Anita is as near to perfect as I have ever known. Since we put all our cards on the table a couple of months ago, life has just got better and better. Even her dad doesn't seem to entirely hate me, well maybe a little, but I can live with that.

Family Affair

A loud cough pulls us both up short. Mase.

Turning, I smile while Anita blushes a little and if that doesn't make her look even more adorable.

"I know we have had this conversation before, Dec, but please, don't contaminate the cakes my wife is going to eat. Technically, my baby is going to eat those cakes too, so doubly don't contaminate them."

Anita and I share a roll of our eyes and laugh. Mase doesn't.

"Can I have a word? Business," he says and although I see Anita raise a slightly disbelieving brow, my brother may well want to talk business.

He has money invested in the club and we have talked about adding more bars and clubs to form a chain. Also, Mase knows his shit when it comes to investments and often makes recommendations or shares information with me.

I lean down and land a single, almost chaste kiss to my lady's cheek and prepare to leave with Mase, but not before dipping a finger into the frosting on the top of the cake.

"Declan!" Mase says through gritted teeth. "What have I just said? I don't know where those fingers have been!"

Anita and I both laugh, knowing exactly where my fingers have been.

"I don't want to know!" Mase calls but does throw in a token laugh as he leaves with me following behind.

Once we're out of the kitchen, Mase heads towards the sunroom and takes a seat near the open door.

"Have you thought any more about the clubs?"

"Yeah. It's a good idea to expand and I think it might be useful to have different places for different tastes rather than focusing all our efforts on one portion of the market."

He smiles and quirks a brow.

"What?"

"You. You sound all grown-up when you talk so seriously about diversification and marketing plans."

"Fuck you, Mase." The words are harsh, but my smirk says it's not serious because he is right. This is grown-up and I don't really do that.

"Back at you, Dec." He smiles again, but this one is a little more thoughtful.

"What?" I ask again.

"It suits you, being a grown-up. And Anita, she suits you, too."

"Okay..." I draw the word out. "Stop that mushy shit now or before we know it, we'll be all cuddly in a menbrace."

"A menbrace?"

"Yeah, it's like a hug for men."

He laughs and it is definitely at me. "I got it, but fuck me, you're making words up now for the mushy shit. It really must be true love."

"Whatever." I wave his fun poking off. "I remember when Liv first landed in your life, so you have zero room to piss take."

He smiles warmly, clearly remembering Liv's arrival and then he frowns. "She was a complete and utter pain in the arse. Did my head in on a daily basis and fuck me if she didn't give me the greatest mind fucks ever."

I watch him and say nothing.

"And it was amazing and perfect, just like my wife."

I make a little gesture as if to be sick, but we both know I don't mean it. I love Liv and even the mind fuck stuff and grief she caused Mase was never, ever intentional or through manipulation, it was just that she had never really met anyone like him or been loved and treated like fine art.

"Are my ears burning?"

Liv appears and after ruffling my hair makes her way to Mase and takes up her place in his lap.

"This furniture might not be up to the three of us sitting in one space," she says, rubbing a loving and protective hand over her very swollen belly.

Mase pulls her closer, ignoring her words.

I smile at them, not just because I love them both and are happy for them, but because when I watch them together, I know this is what I want, and it is almost what I have with Anita.

"How long do we have until mini-me arrives now?"

"About five and a half weeks," Liv tells me.

"You still working?" I kind of know she is, and I also know

this is a bone of contention for Mase.

"Yeah."

"Not for much longer," Mase mutters, earning himself a sideways glance from his wife, although I notice she calms him by putting his hand onto her bump that he immediately begins to rub and physically calms.

"Would you come and look at a couple of places with me?" I shock myself with that question, unsure if I am moving too fast. "You know Mase and I have talked about expanding and I have found a couple of possible places, but I'd like your opinion and ideas on design."

"Of course." She grins and I can already see the cogs whirring in her mind.

"Great, I'll call you later or tomorrow and arrange something."

Mase looks wary, looking just like our dad. "Dec, do not part with money, or even shake on a deal without all of the appropriate surveys and legal work done."

I laugh at his over cautious big brother routine. "Of course not, plus, Liv is going to keep my feet on the ground."

She grins across at me as I get to my feet. Mase rolls his eyes. Clearly, he doesn't trust either of us not to get carried away.

I look at my watch. "Dad should be arriving anytime now, so, I will leave Anita with the cake and find the old man."

I walk away and can already hear Mase giving Liv orders on not encouraging anything rash from me, while she is already airing plans to find her sister and hopefully something to eat.

Anita

The afternoon has been amazing. I loved every second of being here with Dec and feeling part of his family. They are lovely people and so warm in their interactions with me. There are children and babies everywhere and it is truly amazing to see the way Charlotte and Tommy welcome and embrace them all into their home, especially when you consider that most of the people present are no blood relation to either.

When Jimmy arrived, I was unsure if it was going to become

awkward as he was entering the home of his ex-wife and her husband, but all parties were relaxed and seemed genuinely happy to be there, sharing the time together and the celebration of another grandchild due to enter the family in a matter of weeks.

I feel the scowl form on my brow as I look down at the lemon frosted cake I am cutting for everyone to take home. Christian. He is the only blot on the landscape, but even that hasn't detracted from the positive experience of the day, not that he even acknowledged me, which suits me just fine. Liv was here, helping me, which essentially means, I cut the cake and she consumes anything that drops off. She needed a wee though, possibly about her tenth of the afternoon, so has left me to it.

The sound of footsteps coming up behind me in the kitchen as I am wrapping the cake makes me smile. I assume it is Dec until I feel an unwelcome but slightly familiar scent wash over me. Maybe Christian has decided he's going to acknowledge my presence after all.

"I must admit, I'm a little impressed that you are still around, but I doubt it will be for much longer. Dec has, how shall I put this, *a short attention span.*"

His voice carries nothing but contempt for me.

"And hopefully Mase will get bored of your sister around the same time and all the trash can be taken out together."

I am in no way amused by him or his comments, but laugh as I spin to face him and wonder what I ever saw him in.

"In case you'd missed the point of today, it is to celebrate the fact that Liv and her husband, Mase, are having a baby in a matter of a few weeks, so, whether you like it or not, Liv is going nowhere."

He looks like he has a bad taste in his mouth and the sneer curling his lips confirms his distaste. There is a small glimmer in his eyes that suggests he knows I am right and that gives me a huge sense of satisfaction.

The look is soon replaced by a cockier one that is accompanied by a shrug. "You win some you lose some, so I'll just have to settle for Dec kicking you to the kerb."

What the fuck is his problem here, besides me and my sister?

"Christian, what happened, happened. You went back to play the faithful husband and father while I moved on." My voice sounds calm and steady, but inside I am quivering.

He takes a step closer so I can feel his breath on my face, making me nervous that he is going to try and kiss me. He doesn't. Instead, he laughs.

"Maybe I should catch up with Dec, chew the fat as it were. He can tell me all about how the two of you got together."

My jaw drops. I can't believe he would do that, although we both know his idea of chewing the fat translates to being an intention to out me as someone he used to sleep with and then I remember. Dec knows.

I'm the one moving closer now, almost daring him to follow through on his very obvious threat.

"Dec knows about us, so, go ahead, catch up, but then he might decide it's time to catch up with your wife."

With a huge sense of satisfaction, I watch as Christian steps back from me with a very nervous expression spreading across his face.

"Dec knows?" he asks, seeming to regain his composure.

"Yes."

And then he seizes upon the one thing Dec doesn't know, something nobody knows except for me and Christian.

"He knows everything?"

My face is all the answer he needs.

"As I thought."

He turns to walk away, and I know I should let him, but I don't. I am absolutely livid with him, for his attitude towards me now, but for all he ever did that wronged me.

"And I assume your wife knows none of it, least of all the fact that you got me pregnant."

He spins back and with his face the image of fury, he is striding towards me looking murderous.

"You little bitch!" he hisses as he reaches me. "According to you it was mine, but who knows with a whore like you."

The bastard! How dare he suggest it could have been anyone else's. I am not a whore and would never have gone near him had I known he was married. I was lonely and sad, and he showed me attention and affection. Unfortunately, I was stupid enough to fall for it. With my anger matching his, before I know what I am doing, my hand is raised and landing across his arrogant, smug face.

The slap echoes around us and in the blink of an eye, Christian's hand is on my face, tightly gripping my chin and jaw.

"If you even hint at your bastard child being mine, I won't hesitate in telling the whole family that I knew you, that a married associate of mine was the one fucking you and when he abandoned you, pregnant with goodness knows whose baby, I very kindly gave you some money to help you out and as you don't have a child, I can only assume you used it for an abortion."

Tears sting my eyes as his grip tightens, but it's his words that sting.

"And trust me, I will be convincing."

"Dec will believe me." I truly believe that.

Christian laughs. "Maybe, but do you really think with his past that a woman who screws a married man, gets pregnant and then aborts the baby will last long?"

The first of my tears escapes my eyes and rolls down my cheek. He is right, we both know it.

"Thought so."

"What the fuck?"

We both turn to find Liv standing in the doorway, staring at the scene of me and Christian before us not knowing how long she has been there or just how much she has heard.

"Just what we're missing, the other sister."

"Take your hands off her," Liv demands, ignoring Christian's reference to her.

"With pleasure." He releases me and rubs his hands down his jeans, looking as though he is wiping something truly unpleasant from his skin.

Liv moves closer while Christian steps away, making for the door but does shout over his shoulder.

"Remember what I said."

Liv stares at me, reaching forward to stroke the sore skin that has previously been squeezed by the man who despises us both.

"What the fuck? Are you okay? Obviously not," she answers for herself. "I'll fetch Dec, or Mase…maybe Jimmy would be better because Mase is desperate for an excuse to punch Christian, and I think Dec will beat him to it if he knows he had his hands on you—"

I cut her off. "No, none of them, please."

"Anita," she begins in her best pleading voice.

"No," I insist.

"Okay." She's not happy.

I move, preparing to take some cake through to everyone but Liv is not done yet.

"What did he mean about a woman who screws a married man, gets pregnant and aborts the baby?"

Fuck! Well, I suppose that answers how much she heard.

Chapter Twenty-Six

Declan

Today has to be the weirdest Monday ever. Not the hardest or worst, but the *weirdest*.

I am checking out possible places for a new bar with Liv and she is in a very strange mood. I can't put my finger on it, but she is sombre, a little too quiet and every time I look at her, I find her watching me with an expression akin to sympathy. Initially I wondered if she and Mase had had some kind of argument, but he called her earlier in the day and they were clearly on good terms, very good terms.

We are just leaving a warehouse on the docks that would be an amazing location and the possibilities for making it a unique venue are limitless when I start questioning if there is something going on in the Carrington family because Anita was in a strange mood from the second we left the baby shower. In fact, even leaving there was an odd experience. Anita and Liv returned from the kitchen, but now that I think about it, Liv seemed to be in pursuit of Anita as they reappeared in the lounge where the rest of us were. Liv was empty handed, despite going into the kitchen to collect cake. Anita had a tray piled high with cake and once it was distributed, she had suggested we leave. We did and before we had reached the end of the drive, she was all over me, not that I objected to that in any way. I lived for that, but now, with hindsight paired with Liv's weird mood, there is something fishy going on, of that, I am sure.

Maybe I would have smelled a rat sooner had Anita not been

naked for the remainder of the weekend. By the time we'd gotten back to mine, she had already given me the best blow job of my life and before the front door closed, I was rock hard at the sight of her shedding her clothes. That is how the rest of the weekend had gone. Again, I had no objection to my lady being horny and seeking out pleasure from and with me, but now, her dedication to shagging me into oblivion seems like it may have been some kind of distraction and fuck me if it didn't work.

"You and Mase enjoy the baby shower?"

"What?" Liv spins to face me and looks alarmed by my very innocent question.

My suspicion is rising.

She seems to take stock. "Sorry, miles away. We didn't want one in the first place, but yes, it was nice to see everyone."

"Even Christian?" My question is light-hearted, and I expect Liv to laugh at the idea that she would ever be pleased to see him.

Her reaction, like her face is one of horror and I would almost go as far as to suggest fear. She stops dead and stares up at me looking nervous. Shit! Did he do something or say something to really upset her?

"Liv, are you okay? Did something happen?" I am as nervous as her now because if it did, I will tell Mase, and he will lose his shit big style.

"What? No!" She almost shrieks the last word, and the addition of a very strange and high-pitched laugh confirms she is lying about something.

"Liv…"

Her phone rings, interrupting us. I stand by, leaning against my car as she agrees to find somewhere for lunch and to sit down and relax for at least an hour before looking at any more locations with me. She giggles and laughs with Mase and looks like she usually does, so whatever is making her act strange, along with her sister is nothing to do with her and my brother, leading me to the conclusion that her mood and behaviour is down to one thing. One person.

Sitting in a nearby pub, Liv and I eat lunch. She has her computer out and is already putting together a list of pros and cons for the three places we've already seen. I watch on as she grabs a notepad and pencil and begins to quickly sketch ideas for each of the possible locations keeping the general theme from Dazzler.

She is incredibly focused, so much so that she doesn't seem to notice me studying her, engrossed as she is in her drawing. She is no longer preoccupied or nervous in any way. It's like this, work, and when she's with Mase are her natural environments. I can't help but smile, my smile only broadening when she subconsciously reaches down to gently stroke her belly.

"How is the next Harding generation?"

She looks up and grins across at me and for the first time I can see that the pregnancy glow is a very real thing. I am beginning to wonder what Anita would look like, her belly swollen with my baby and her whole being aglow.

"Sitting on my bladder if you really want to know."

I laugh, back in the moment with my sister-in-law rather than with her non pregnant sister as she staggers to her feet, clutching her side and wincing.

"You okay there, tubs?"

She scowls at me but doesn't really rise to my sizeist comment. "Aside from the fact that if I don't leave right now for the bathroom, I'm going to leave a puddle and your shoes are in the splash zone."

"Wow! Mase is beyond blessed to have you with lines like that…I have no more words."

She giggles and makes her way to the bathroom, looking very much like a cross between a duck and a penguin.

I pick up my phone and roll it in my hand before dropping Anita a quick text, all earlier suspicions and thoughts of her weird mood gone.

<Hey, Cupcake, how's my beautiful lady doing today? In case I didn't mention it, I thoroughly enjoyed the weekend with you x>

<You and me both, Stud. In fact, I missed you so much

Family Affair

today, I think this could be a 3 day weekend! X>

Anita

I am still managing to avoid Liv, despite her calling and texting every day in the week or so since she walked in on me and Christian. It's becoming increasingly difficult to do as she and Dec speak most days about the extension of the Dazzler chain.

Tonight is date night, so I know I can evade her for at least one more day, but beyond that I am on borrowed time because Dec has already asked me if I've had a fight with her and that she keeps asking him if I am okay.

"Hey, where's my sexy lady?" Dec's voice is getting louder meaning he is moving closer to the bedroom.

I am slipping on heeled shoes as the finishing touch to the red stretchy dress I'm not convinced isn't too short as I tug on the hem that sits on my thighs, just.

"Going out on date night is optional, right?"

I laugh as Dec appears behind me and I watch our reflections in the mirror as an arm snakes around my middle.

"I think the use of the word *out* might mean it's *not* optional."

"Shame," he whispers against my ear, the feel of his breath causing goosebumps to rise across my skin.

"Yeah, but the plus side of date night out is the unwritten but clearly obvious rule that when we get home, you get lucky."

I laugh as I watch Dec's face morph into a happy, expectant and slightly horny expression.

"Well, in that case, let's get this date on the road."

With a single spank to my behind, Dec is already taking my hand in his and pulling me to the door.

As far as I knew, tonight was a regular date night; dinner and a few glasses of wine, then back home where sex would be on the agenda. Arriving at the restaurant blows that thought out of the water.

The restaurant is high end. Somewhere I have been once before when Liv first came into our family. Mase took us all out,

Family Affair

brought us here for dinner. The food is to die for but is so expensive they don't put prices on the menu. Dec really is pulling out all the stops tonight, but why?

We're shown through to the back of the restaurant and that's when I see them, already sitting at the table with two empty seats. My family including Liv, Mase and Scott, plus Dec's parents and his stepdad.

We take our seats and to say I am confused is an understatement.

"Am I missing something?" I ask Dec in a hushed tone, leaning closer to him.

"All will be revealed, Cupcake."

Everyone looks as confused as me, well, almost everyone, Mase seems to know exactly what's going on here. The penny drops. This is clearly an announcement about the expansion of the business. I wonder why Liv looks perplexed, but reason that she was helping to scope out locations and that is where her role ended, so maybe she doesn't know what's happening with the new place going forward.

Talk begins and my thoughts on the night disappear, I should just enjoy the company, the food and amazing cocktail menu I'd like to work my way through.

The main courses are just being finished off when my dad begins to look between me and Liv. "You're both quiet tonight."

I was hoping the remaining tension between us had gone unnoticed. No such luck. I try to nip this line of conversation in the bud and avoid offering anything inflammatory. "You should be thankful for that rather than complaining…you usually tell us we talk too much." I laugh and hope everyone joins in with me, most do. Not Liv.

My father's attention falls to her. "Livy?"

Mase bristles next to his wife at Dad calling her Livy.

"What?" she asks. "It just seems that we have little to say to each other tonight."

I feel as though I stop breathing for a second as I expect everyone to jump on her suggestion that we have nothing to say to each other.

The waiter returns and clears the table, interrupting things. I

Family Affair

turn to say something to my mum but before I say more than a couple of words, I notice her startled expression as she looks just beyond me.

I turn back and nothing could have prepared me for the sight that greets me. Initially, I wonder why I can't see Dec, and then I realise he is no longer in his seat but kneeling on the floor. What the hell! Has he fallen or dropped something? He makes no attempt to move and for a few, very long seconds, I have no idea what to make of it.

"Anita." Dec says my name and my eyes fix on his.

He looks at me with a happy and excited expression, but his eyes look a little nervous. Suddenly it's like nobody else is here, it's just the two of us, and then I realise what is going on; why we're at this restaurant, why our families are present and why he is on his knees, specifically down on one knee. Fuck! This is huge and I have no idea how to process it or how to respond.

"Anita," he repeats. "I never thought this would happen to me...but it has." He takes a deep, and I suspect, calming breath. "From the second I laid eyes on you, my world was shook, rocked to the core and although it was a shock and I fought it..."

I hear light laughter around us, but I don't respond in any way. My focus is on Dec and only Dec.

"...it is the best thing to ever happen. You are the best thing to ever happen to me and now I've had a taste of life with you, I am unprepared to live it without you. Anita, will you marry me?"

I knew it was coming, or at least suspected that's where this was going and somehow, it was still a shock when those final four words registered in my mind.

He is still on one knee, his expression becoming more concerned as the seconds of silence stretch out before us when I notice the most beautiful ring in his hand. A cluster of diamonds around the most perfect ruby.

I have no clue how long the silence has lasted, but I know I need to say something. What do I say? What do I want to say?

Family Affair

Chapter Twenty-Seven

Declan

Here I am kneeling on the floor in the restaurant, surrounded by our closest family members with an engagement ring in my hand while Anita simply stares down at me. I am hot, sweating and that is partly down to the heat of the room but more to do with the panic that she has yet to answer me.

My heart is hammering away in my chest, and I swear if she doesn't put me out of my misery soon with a response, I am going to vomit. Panic is beginning to surge within me, causing me to take a succession of deep breaths.

Why the fuck did I choose to do it this way? I should have made this a private moment to allow her to say no. Instead, I invited everyone here to witness the magical moment of my proposal and Anita's subsequent acceptance and desire to be my wife. Briefly, my mind goes to Amber, my last proposal—that worked out so well for me, didn't it? I can't believe that I have put myself in this position and opened myself up to another rejection. The last one was bad enough, so much so that I barely survived it and I know that my feelings for Anita and the future I want with her are far more than those I had for Amber. If she says no—if she rejects me, I won't survive it, not this time. The truth there is that if she rejects me, I won't want to survive.

The knee I am down on is going to sleep and the other leg feels as though it is seizing up, and that along with what I am sure is the sound of tumbleweed blowing around me is enough for me to prepare to stand up and end this painfully long moment for all of us. With a final glance up at Anita, I see tears welling in her eyes while her lip begins to quiver. Is she sad? Has my proposal saddened her or is this one of those moments were what we associate with sadness is the opposite? My gaze is fixed on hers and in that moment, I am frozen to the spot, all thoughts of getting up gone.

I watch on as her lips begin to move and as I see them making the shapes of sounds, I hear nothing. This is what I imagine it feels like when you have been subjected to an unprotected loud noise, like a rocket taking off or a bomb exploding. Then, as if rain clouds lifting to make way for the sunshine, her voice breaks through the fuzziness of my mind.

"Yes."

I stare and although I think I heard correctly, I'm not sure. I need confirmation. "What?"

She laughs as do others around the table. I hear Mase mutter something about me being a dickhead.

"Yes," Anita repeats.

There is no planning or thought that goes into the next seconds. I am sliding the ring on her finger and rather than getting to my feet and pulling her to hers, I am reaching for her to pull her into my lap where I hold her tight, then allow her to sit back slightly, allowing me to brush her hair back before tenderly cupping her face and pulling it back in to kiss her. Gently, unrushed and loving rather than passionate.

Eventually, we are on our feet and receiving the congratulations of everyone around us. The whole family seem genuinely pleased for us, even Nigel, although that might be because I asked his permission a few days before. I thought he might like the idea of me deferring to him and somehow letting him think he had any say in this. The truth is that I hadn't fully thought that idea through until I was telling Mase who had asked what I would do if Nigel said no. I hadn't even considered that despite him still not being overly keen on me being his daughter's boyfriend. If he had said no my proposal would not have been as public and possibly not tonight, but there is no doubt in my mind that I would still have proposed to Anita and now I am even more certain that she would have said yes.

Liv leans in and kisses me, congratulates me but it sounds less than happy, almost sympathetic. She stretches across me to look at Anita's hand. She gushes over the ring, but that's as far as it goes and then she sits back down. What the fuck is her problem? Before I debate asking her just that, Mase is giving me a hug and a back slap as he repeats his earlier dickhead comment and something about thinking Anita was going to say no. We both laugh until I make a dig about the fact that Liv turned down his proposal first time. At that point I am the only one laughing but I couldn't give a fuck because this is the best night of my life and only the beginning of my life with Anita as my fiancée and then my wife.

Scott, Liv's brother shakes my hand and mutters words of congratulations, but it sounds a little lacklustre. Soon enough, he takes the seat next to Liv and watching them together, I can see they each look uncomfortable. It's then I decide that their reactions are down to the fact they're both Carringtons and as such were in that freaky church, so it must be that causing their underwhelmed behaviour.

With greetings and words of happiness all exchanged, we take our seats again where mine and Anita's mothers waste no time in discussing plans. dresses, flowers, colour schemes, venues and dates. All things I hadn't really considered. I look towards my brother who seems to know this judging by the grin he is aiming at me. His attention only leaves me when Liv releases a low grumble whilst rubbing a hand across her belly.

"You okay there?" Mase sounds concerned.

"Yeah. The baby is just lying in an awkward position I think."

"You're sure?" My mother is preparing to get up from her seat. To do what, I'm not too sure.

Liv waves her concerns away. "Absolutely. It's those practice contraction things too."

"Braxton Hicks," my sister, Bethy, throws in.

"Yeah, that's them. They're worse at night and have been breaking my sleep a little." She yawns. "In fact, it's about an hour past my bedtime."

Mase is already on his feet, congratulating me again, before offering Anita his genuine and heartfelt commiserations. Yet, I am the dickhead.

I smile at his teasing before he turns back to his wife. "Right then, Mrs Harding, let's get you and junior home to bed before you fall asleep at the table."

"How weird is that? You two—" I point between Anita and Liv, "are not blood sisters and yet, once we marry, you'll have the same name."

Everyone laughs at my observation, everyone except Liv. She looks uncomfortable and in a weird way, I'm hoping that's because she is suffering with pregnancy aches and pains.

Anita

My mind is actually blown and not just because of Dec's proposal. I am lying sprawled out beneath him, panting heavily as he pushes me towards my release. We have been all over each other since we left the restaurant.

There had been a moment at the restaurant where I considered saying no, but then I realised that I wanted to say yes more than anything in the world. Still the only blot on the landscape is Christian. I know that I need to explain everything to Dec, to make him understand everything that went on, but that scares me shitless because as much as he wants me and loves me, the details I need to share might be the thing that makes him change his mind and leave me, never to return.

I also need to face Liv. Whilst it wasn't either of our faults that she walked in on Christian's cruel comments, I have done an amazing job of avoiding her since then. It's not so much that I feel I can't speak to her, I know I can, but she will be compromised. Compromised more than she already is. I look at it from her point of view and she really is stuck between a rock and a hard place. On one hand she has me, her sister who is keeping a secret from her boyfriend, fiancé. I allow myself a small smile at that title. The complication for Liv is that on the other side is the boyfriend, her brother-in-law who she loves but worse than that, she is being forced to keep a secret from her own husband because with all the unknowns in this sorry mess, Mase telling Dec is a certainty.

"Cupcake."

Dec's calling to me brings me back to the moment we are in. I reach up and gently stroke his face before sliding my fingers through his hair just as he slams into me again and hits something deep inside that is beyond sensitive.

"Fuck!" I cry as my fingers tighten on the strands of his hair and I give them a hard tug.

"Oww." He laughs as my fingers loosen their grip on his hair. "You like that then."

"God, yes. Again," I plead, already feeling my orgasm building once more and can only hope that this time Dec will let me explore and ride it out fully.

He hits that spot again, then a third and a fourth time and I know the fifth will be my undoing.

"Declan, baby," I pant out and am rewarded with the fifth strike that sees me crying, thrashing, and reaching for anything I can get my hands on as the world spins off its axis, and everything turns shimmery through my unshed tear glazed vision.

This is perfect, he is perfect, we are perfect, and I need not to fuck this up. I need to make everything right.

Dec's lips crash against mine and in that second, as intense as our pleasure is, we are making love, the kiss, the way his body worships mine and finally the second our eyes lock as he releases inside me.

****

Breakfast proves to be easy and relaxed. We flirt and kiss at every opportunity between eating the French toast and crispy bacon Dec has cooked. I can't keep the soppy smirk off my face as I realise that this could be my life. That thought sours my mood. I need to sort things out and I am going to start today. Enough is enough. It's time to be honest and move on. I make a mental list of people to clear the air with, Christian, Liv and then Dec. I choose Dec last, not because he isn't my priority, he is, but because I need to tell Christian that he doesn't scare me and I won't be chased off by him, and Liv because she deserves to hear the truth from me and not to have to keep my secrets. Once I have done that, I will return to Dec and tell him everything, right down to the tiniest detail, and then nothing and nobody can throw a spanner in the works of our future.

"You got much on today?"

I look across at Dec and offer him a short nod. "I thought I might check in with Liv, see how she's doing."

"Sounds like a good idea. She has been a bit off."

I nod. She has, but unlike my boyfriend, I know why.

"What about you?"

"I am meeting Liv and Mase later to discuss money and designs."

"Nice. Exciting times."

Dec laughs. "Cupcake, that is some serious understatement you have going on there. I am going to be the captain of an empire!"

I laugh loudly at his excitement and phrasing. He moves to the side of the breakfast bar I am sitting on and tilts my head so I am looking up into his beautiful eyes.

"And you are going to be the captain's wife."

I feel a burn in my jaw as my emotions at such a simple declaration tugs at my heartstrings.

"Yes, I am." My voice wobbles.

"Hey, that's supposed to make you smile and be happy, not cry."

He brushes away the single rogue tear that has escaped my eyes.

"I am happy," I tell him as several more tears fall.

In the blink of an eye, I am on my feet and being engulfed in Dec's embrace. I feel safe here and hope that never changes.

"I love you," I manage to splutter.

"I love you, too, even if you are an emotional conundrum."

Before I can respond, not that I really know what to say to that, Dec continues.

"But then why wouldn't you be. You have every right to be overwhelmed. You hit the jackpot when you snagged me…I can hear the sound of a million other women's hearts breaking.

And like that with a friendly smack to his chest, my cocky, arrogant stud has me grounded and laughing.

****

I drop a text to Liv and also to Christian, inviting them to meet me. The invitation to Christian was more of a demand than anything and for all his holier than though threats, he has as much to lose as I do if he doesn't meet with me.

Liv's reply is short and sweet, agreeing to the time and location. Christian's takes a while longer to land and is curt to say the least, but as I suspected, he agrees.

All I need to do now is sort things with them before the hardest part, telling Dec.

Chapter Twenty-Eight

Declan

I am technically on my second breakfast of the day as I sit in Mase's kitchen tucking into a full English he has prepared for us both. Accepting a refill of my cup, I look around.

"No Liv?"

He shakes his head. "She didn't sleep very well..."

I smirk.

"Get your mind out of the gutter and stop thinking about my wife having sex."

I laugh at the warning I've heard several times before.

"The baby is keeping her up most of the night. Between peeing and shoving arms and legs into her ribs and shit, neither of us are getting much sleep."

He does look a little jaded around the eyes, but he is still smiling.

"Good practice for night feeds and dirty nappies."

"It certainly is. I'm just hoping we get a baby that likes to sleep at night, or we might need to get a nanny."

"You are so fucking pretentious with a live-in nanny to cover your sleepless nights."

I feel sad suddenly as I imagine my own child waking in the night and being tended to by someone who is neither of her natural parents. Mase sees my change in demeanour, reaches across and gives my shoulder something between a rub and a pat.

"We are not having a live-in nanny." Liv appears and does

look tired but also glowing and gorgeous as usual. She rubs her hand across her belly and makes her way to Mase's side. "We have discussed this. No nanny." She stretches up and kisses his cheek.

"Fine," Mase replies with a pout. "I am more than happy for you to be a full-time stay at home mum."

The look on my sister-in-law's face suggests this is a discussion they have also had several times and she doesn't seem in favour of having it again.

She turns to me. "Any more thoughts on the places we've seen so far, Dec?"

"A few. Dad is meeting us here to discuss the properties—"

She cuts me off. "Why is Jimmy discussing the properties?"

"He always does," Mase explains. "He looks into the property, previous owners and whether they were dodgy and if they were, how likely that is to have an effect on us going forward."

"Ah, okay."

I can't hide my smile. Liv just accepts that explanation, which sounds a bit dodgy even if it is the truth. But then again, Liv has been tagged and traced by our old man before now.

"And here he is," Mase announces, already heading for the lift to meet our dad.

Liv takes his seat and seems to be silently studying me. When she sees that I've noticed she reverts conversation back to the buildings we've viewed. "When double 0 Jimmy has given you the lowdown on local gangsters, let me know which ones you're interested in, and we can go back for another viewing and more brainstorming."

She gets up, goes over, and kisses my dad on the cheek before he leans down to talk to his unborn grandchild and then she disappears.

Me, my dad and brother are going through details when Liv returns with a couple of sketch pads that she places next to us. "Some ideas for you to think about and if you boys don't need me here, I am heading over to Dazzler to meet Anita."

We all nod, although I'm a little confused until I remember that Anita was using my kitchen today for some huge cake she's baking.

"Let Cupcake know I'll be expecting cake with her own special frosting on top," I call as Liv prepares to kiss Mase before leaving.

Her face turns into a sour expression. "There is no way in hell I am passing that message on and you and her and your special frosting, well, I don't want to know." She shudders.

I'm a bit confused and then the penny drops. "Good God, no! Jeez, what is the matter with you? You really think frosting is a euphemism?"

I know me and Anita are rather fond of sharing frosting, but as if I would discuss that in front of Dad and Mase, never mind sending a message about it to her!

"Oh." Liv blushes a beautiful shade of scarlet, looking awkward as hell.

"Yeah, well, maybe forget the message."

****

Some of the information my dad has dug up is comedy gold and other bits are scary as hell. By the time he has finished, we are down to three possible choices; the warehouse on the docks that would be amazing as a club venue, a disused old cinema that would work as well and a small shop with original features and character that could work as a coffee shop come bistro.

Dad is already preparing his retreat once the talk turns to cash. He isn't short of money but has a healthy dislike of it based on the fact that he doesn't know enough about it. That is Mase's speciality which is why both me and our dad take financial and investment advice from my brother.

"Your call ultimately," Mase tells me. "We'd need to do some negotiation on the price of the warehouse on the docks, plus, your insurance premiums would be higher with the location."

"So, your vote would go to the cinema?"

He shrugs. "I don't have a vote, Dec. Your business, you choose. They're both highly viable options and I'll be happy with my return on either."

"I loved the docks, and the possibilities were endless, but it didn't have the same character as the cinema."

He nods.

"Okay. Cinema."

"Just like that?" Mase laughs.

"Yeah, although it's not just like that because I have been dreaming about that place."

He doesn't laugh at that comment, just nods. "That's a good indication."

I go to speak, then stop, a couple of times before he rolls his eyes, knowing there's something else I want to say. "What about the shop? Could we do that too?"

"Fucking hell! I thought I was the one who tried to bite off more than I could chew in business."

"Is that a no?"

"No. It's not a no. I'll look at the figures but with the lower cost of the cinema it could be an option. You'd really need to think about what you were doing with each property and when though."

"Thanks, Mase."

"No problem, now sod off and do whatever it is you do while I go and sit through a three-hour conference call before looking at your figures."

I am up on my feet and already know where I am going from here. Who I am going to. Anita. I have missed my lady and am hoping that by the time I reach her Olivia will be long gone and I can sample her special frosting. I laugh again at the idea of my earlier, innocent use of frosting. This time, it might not be quite so innocent.

Anita

As I am working from Dec's kitchen today and he is meeting with Mase on the other side of town, it seems the safest option to meet Liv and Christian here. My sister is due any second and I am crapping myself to reveal all to her. If she disapproves, she could tell Mase before I get the chance to tell Dec and that would be the worst outcome for him to hear the details from anyone who isn't me.

"Hi," she calls, heading towards me if the sound of her increasingly loud footsteps is anything to go by.

"Hi," I repeat back when I turn and find her standing in the doorway while I mix some frosting.

She is almost sneering as she looks at the huge bowl I'm mixing in.

"What?"

She shudders. "Just something Dec said about special frosting."

I laugh and am relieved when she joins in.

"Sorry," I begin.

"Sorry? For what?" I hear and see her bristling.

"For avoiding you. For not explaining sooner."

She rubs a hand across her belly that I am sure has grown since she entered the kitchen. She looks concerned for me, but she also looks tired. I grab a high stool for her and once she has struggled onto it, I scoot up onto the work top, so we are pretty much eye to eye.

"Why did you, avoid me?"

It's a simple enough question, I just hope my response doesn't offend her.

"I was ashamed of what happened, what I did. When you walked in on me and Christian at Charlotte's, I reacted out of fear."

"Fear? Of me?" She kind of sounds offended already.

"Yes," I admit a little warily and fortunately she gives me a half-smile and rub of the knee. "I was scared that you would hate me, but more than that, I was scared you'd tell Mase, and —"

"And he'd tell Dec," she finishes for me.

"Yes."

"You were probably justified in that fear. I mean, he may have given you a time limit to do it, or even got Jimmy digging on you, but there is no way he would have sat tight on you having been pregnant with Christian's baby."

We stare at each other, and it feels as though in some ways a weight has been lifted from me. She understands why I didn't tell her sooner and more than that, she doesn't appear to hate me or be judging me.

She is suddenly on her feet and pulling me in for a close hug, well, as close as we can be considering she's about eight and a half months pregnant.

"So, should I assume you've told Dec yourself?"

She pulls back and one look at my face confirms that I haven't.

Before she starts firing questions at me, I explain. "I'll tell him later. I wanted to tell you, and to let Christian know that I'm not scared of him or his threats. He has as much to lose as me, more maybe."

Another voice speaks rather than Liv.

"Look at what we have here; the ugly sisters or sisters Grimm." Christian laughs, immediately moving across the room and taking Liv's vacant seat. "So, you're not scared of me and my threats…great, let's invite Dec to join us."

I wasn't expecting that. His phone is out and whether he's bluffing or not, I can't allow him to tell Dec instead of me. I snatch his phone and lock it.

"As I thought. So, let me explain how this is going down."

I stare at this odious little man and wonder how I had ever found him likeable never mind attractive. I wish I had never met him and more than that, if I had to, I wish I had never let him touch me.

"I hear Declan is expanding his little empire, so, you are going to tell him that he should let me do the redesigns on his new place."

I watch as Liv rolls her eyes.

He cuts her a look. "It's not like you need the cash now you're carrying a Harding, assuming it has Harding blood in its veins."

"Fuck off, Christian. She is not going to send Dec your way for work. Even if she could, Dec wouldn't do it. He is his own man and makes his own choices."

"You stupid fucking bitch!" he spits at Liv; real venom being aimed at her. He reaches for her and grabs her arm, pulling her closer.

Liv releases a scream of shock rather than fear I think, her free arm automatically going to her unborn child in some attempt to protect them both.

I feel as though I am watching some kind of movie as events unfold before me. Christian still has a hold of Liv's arm and is still pulling her by it. I watch in horror as she seems to stumble and falls to the hard kitchen floor.

"You fucking idiot," I scream as I go to where Liv is moving into a sitting position, preparing to stand. "Even if I had been prepared to do your bidding with Dec before, which I wasn't, I certainly wouldn't be doing it now you've thrown my pregnant sister to the floor."

"Fine, then let's call Declan and tell him how you aborted my baby. Flushed it away without a second thought. I'm sure he'll be only too happy to have you stick around after that bombshell! Oh, and if your *sister*," he sneers the word sister knowing Liv and I are not actually related. "If she wants to keep her relationship, she'll have to choose Dec as the wronged party and kick you to the curb. Mase wouldn't accept any less than that."

Tears begin to prick at my eyes, the first escaping when I lock eyes with Liv and can see that she believes the last bit about Mase.

"We all know Dec isn't fussy about who he fucks, well," Christian gestures to me. "But as I hear congratulations are in order, he may be a little pickier in a fiancée or a wife, don't you think? So, you play ball with me, and he won't ever need to hear that you're a dirty slut who picks up married men, coerces them into giving you money in exchange for your silence, only to deliberately get pregnant to trap me and when I called time and told you to do your worst, you aborted an innocent baby."

I actually want to punch him. Christian looks so smug. I almost forget about Liv until I hear her release a little groan as she adjusts her position still sitting on the floor. She looks pale and shaken.

Instead of helping Liv up, I stand, stretching to my full height to face Christian. He is a bully, always has been, with me and Liv from all I have heard. I briefly think of his wife and assume if he isn't this arsehole with her, which I find hard to believe, it's because her dad is loaded and was beneficial to his career.

"I didn't abort an innocent baby."

Christian smirks and again I want to punch him but settle for wiping the arrogant smirk from his face with my words instead.

"I could never have aborted my own child. I gave her up for adoption."

And then the world comes crashing down with a single word.

"Cupcake."

Chapter Twenty-Nine

Declan

The sound of voices drift from the kitchen, Anita, and another I recognise, but it's not Liv's. Christian. Mase's meeting call got cancelled so he decided to come and retrieve Liv for lunch and a relaxing afternoon. I didn't delve into how he planned on relaxing her but can feel him walking behind me.

We come to a standstill near the kitchen and everything blurs. Time stands still and flashes by at the same time. Christian is doing all the talking about someone coercing married men and getting pregnant…Anita. I know they were involved, but this can't be right. She couldn't have got pregnant. She would have told me, wouldn't she? An abortion? I wouldn't have judged her for that. Not in the circumstances, so why didn't she tell me? I told her everything about me and Amber and the child we should have had.

My whirring mind and attempts to understand and reason the thoughts in my head stop dead when I hear Anita's words. Words from her own mouth.

"I could never have aborted my own child. I gave her up for adoption."

She had been pregnant, like Amber, and just like Amber she gave the child up for adoption. It now seems that the thing that broke me almost to the point of complete and utter destruction, obliterating my trust in anyone outside of my family, in women until Anita, is back to finish the job off.

Why didn't she tell me when I told her about Amber? Surely

that would have been the ideal time to explain her own situation. To make me understand why she did that. She didn't. I am crushed at the realisation that she didn't even value me and our relationship enough to tell me to my face. This is how I discover the truth, by accident. There's a sour taste in my mouth at the realisation that she never intended to tell me.

I hurt everywhere; my heart is broken.

"Cupcake." One word, my pet name for her, the last time I will say it.

I push the hurt aside and allow anger to rise within me. Somehow Mase and I stand together in the doorway and take in the scene; Anita and Christian, the former looking horrified and the latter looking scared. Then I hear Mase call Liv's name before I see her struggling to get to her feet from the floor.

Christian chooses now to speak, but to Mase rather than me. "It was an accident."

He doesn't have time to utter another sound before Mase has made short work of the distance between them and his fist is colliding with Christian's jaw sending him to the floor where Liv had been.

"You fucking piece of shit. You do not, ever, speak to her, look at her, or anything else within fifty feet of her, and I swear if you even consider putting a finger on her, I will kill you, do you understand?"

Mase pulls Christian, who is nodding frantically to his feet before hitting him again.

"Mason," Liv's voice breaks through my brother's red mist of fury.

He immediately goes to her, checking her over for any sign of injury.

It's my turn to look at Christian now. "Get the fuck out. Don't ever come back or speak to me or anything…and keep away from her, for good." I point in Anita's direction.

Christian mutters something about a misunderstanding, his wife, his children, and fuck knows what else. I have stopped listening and I really don't care what he's got to say.

"Out!" I roar and he has the good sense to leave.

Turning back, I see Mase holding Liv tightly.

"Did you know?"

Mase shakes his head, so I turn my attention to Liv. She shakes her head too. "Not everything."

I roughly run my hands over my face and through my hair as I try to order the chaotic thoughts in my mind before having to speak to Anita.

"Dec, do you want us to stay, or go, or whatever?" Mase looks seriously concerned for me. I notice that he hasn't spoken or looked at Anita either.

"No. I need to do this alone. Thanks."

Mase nods and begins to lead Liv away. She turns back, a little reluctant to leave.

"Dec, don't do anything rash, please. Listen to her—"

I neither want nor need her advice so shut her down quickly. "Liv, I don't want to say nasty shit to you, but I am struggling here. You need to go with Mase. This is fuck all to do with anyone who isn't me or her."

She looks as though she is about to come back at me, and I need her not to.

I hold up a halting hand. "No. Go. Now. I don't even know if I believe that you were oblivious to everything, so, please, leave."

She is clearly upset, but right now, it's my own upset concerning me more.

I half expect Mase to take me to task, he doesn't. Instead, he takes Liv's arm a little more firmly to direct her through the kitchen door and away from this fucking war zone I feel my life has become.

"Dec," Anita begins and that's as far as she gets.

I need answers, not excuses so I ignore her plead of my name. "He got you pregnant."

She nods, tears begin to run down her face. I fight the urge to reach across and brush them away, to comfort her because I am hurting as much as her, maybe more so.

"You told him, and I assume he didn't want to know."

Another nod and more tears.

"Whose idea was it to get rid of the baby?"

"His. He told me I couldn't have it, that I would be alone,

and he wouldn't help financially."

It's my turn to nod now. I can hear Christian telling her that.

"You agreed?"

"I didn't think I had a choice."

"Of course you had a fucking choice!" I am incensed at her pathetic response. "Everyone has a choice. You chose to sleep with him. You contributed to getting pregnant by a married man —"

She cuts me off, her words a jumble of sounds through her sobs. "I didn't know he was married."

I laugh, a cold and heartless laugh, which is ironic considering my heart is currently being torn from my chest. "Well, that's okay then! So long as you didn't realise you were fucking a married man the moral high ground is clearly yours!"

"Dec."

"No, I've heard enough unless you can tell me that you didn't give your own child up for adoption without the courtesy of advising the father beforehand."

And there it is, my real issue with this. As much as Christian is a creepy, cheating arsehole, he has had done to him what was done to me. I know he's unlikely to lose any sleep over that unless he thinks his dirty secret is about to be discovered, but the fact remains that Anita did to him what Amber did to me. I clearly have a type, but no more. I am done.

With my shoulders pushed back, I wait. Anita says nothing. There is nothing left for her to say.

I look around the kitchen at her bowls and utensils.

"You have until the club opens tonight to remove your things from my kitchen. You and your company are no longer welcome here."

I hear the sobs catch in her throat, but I am not prepared to look at her or allow my feelings to be manipulated into feeling anything but anger and contempt for her, so continue making my way as far from her as possible.

"Your belongings at mine will be back at yours within the hour. Goodbye, Anita."

The sound of her cries, howling from the confines of the kitchen follow me all the way home. The ringing of them in my ears cutting me like a knife, but this is the right decision. She is not the girl for me. She is not the girl I thought she was, and it is better that I found out now.

I need something to dull the pain and anguish coursing through my body. Whiskey is a good start, but where do I go from there?

Anita

When I gave up my baby, it was the right decision, maybe not for me, but certainly for her. She needed and deserved what I alone couldn't give her, and I do not regret that decision. What I do regret is not being honest from the start, with my parents and Liv possibly, but definitely with Dec.

It is because of my dishonestly rather than the actual adoption that led to him breaking things off between us and cutting ties completely.

It's been almost three weeks and he hasn't once made contact and having spoken to Liv most days; I know she's not spoken to Dec directly, but Mase has, I know Dec is in a bad way and drinking too much. I can only imagine how many women he has got through in order to block me out. Maybe blocking me out was the easy bit and I was never as important to him as he professed, or I believed. I dismiss that. What we had was real and special. I was the one who ruined it, not him.

My dad was fuming and assumed it was all Dec's fault. I explained it wasn't, but he refused to accept that until I opened and told him and my mum the whole truth, including Christian and the baby.

I barely sleep with thoughts of Dec and what could have been, but those same thoughts make me cry, a lot. After a chat with Scott, who told me how brave I was to have made a decision for my child rather than myself, I have decided that I am going away. I don't entirely know how long for or where to, but my bag is packed and I am going to see Liv before heading to the airport to jump on a plane somewhere, hopefully somewhere hot.

Apart from Christian, this is the biggest risk I have ever

taken. I just hope it works out better than it did with him. I have no clue what has happened with him and his wife if anything because Liv won't even discuss him beyond saying Mase has been desperate to punch him for years and him laying a hand on her was the final straw.

I look around my room before skipping downstairs, ready to leave having already done all my goodbyes. The cab is already outside and waiting, I just need to take this final step.

The lift to Mase and Liv's home is quick and before I really register being in it, the doors are opening to reveal my sister waddling towards me. She is huge and looks ready to burst.

"Not a bloody word," she says, already pulling me into her warm embrace.

With my hand in hers she takes me to the sofa where we sit opposite one another. From her position, Liv eyes my suitcase near the lift doors.

"Are you going somewhere?"

I nod. "I think it's for the best. For me and all of you."

She looks sad. "What about the baby. I'm already two days over."

I shake my head, refusing to cry so soon. We haven't even said goodbye yet.

"I don't want you to go." Liv allows a couple of stray tears to fall.

"I have to. This situation is impossible. I love Dec and I had no idea not having him could hurt so badly, but it does. I am barely surviving, and he is Mase's brother so I can't pretend he doesn't exist or avoid him forever, can I?"

She gives a slow shake of her head.

"We both need some time and space before we can be in your life and not each other's."

"Why are you being so mature and sensible?" she asks with a short laugh.

"I dunno. Maybe I grew up. I felt so guilty about my baby and so, so ashamed, but now, I can see that I did the right thing. I was brave and selfless and letting her go is the only thing that hurt me more than losing Dec. I didn't know you or Mase or Dec when I made that decision so I can't say it was the best decision because of seeing Christian through all of you, but that would have been horrendous for everyone involved. However, she didn't deserve to grow up without a father or to discover how she was conceived, in deceit and lies and to be faced with the fact that her daddy loved his other children more than her and he chose them and his life with them over her."

Liv is crying silent tears now, their flow refusing to be stemmed by her hands that are attempting to wipe them away.

"I am sorry I didn't tell anyone. Sorriest of all that I wasn't more honest with Dec. I thought I could hide my shame, then I wanted to tell him but was scared he'd judge me badly, and once he told me about his own experience with Amber…I couldn't do it because I knew how hard he'd found it to be on the receiving end of that decision. I never wanted him to compare me to her, to judge us both to be peas from the same pod, and I wasn't sure he wouldn't. Turns out it was all in vain because that is exactly what he thinks."

"He loves you. He's a mess. Mase is worried about him."

My heart lurches, almost pleased that he's a mess too, but I quickly reason that he's a mess because I have reminded him of Amber and their child who he lost, not because of me directly.

"He'll get over it." I sound hard, but I don't mean to. I would do anything to turn the clock back and have things work out differently, but I can't, so I guess we'll all have to get over it as best we can one way or another.

****

I spend another hour or so with my sister, discussing baby names and all the possibilities of where I might end up once I get to the airport. She makes me promise to call her once my flight is booked and then when I land. I happily agree to her demands but refuse to check in at least once a day, although I agree to drop her messages regularly if nothing else.

It's time for me to leave and I really wish I didn't have to do this. I want to be here when the baby is born and continue to build my relationship with Liv, but I'm unsure how easy that would be right now because although he's been mentioned a few times, I haven't seen or spoken to Mase since that day in the kitchen and I get the feeling he is seriously pissed off with me.

"I love you and if you need anything." Liv is pulling me in for another hug. "Promise me."

"I promise."

She finally releases me and with my suitcase picked up, I hit the button on the lift, but it instantly opens to reveal Dec.

He does look like shit, but I can't even consider that right now. I need to leave. To get as far away from him as I can because my heart is breaking all over again at the sight of him.

We cross as he steps off the lift and I hurry in.

"Don't forget. Call me," Liv cries as the doors close between us.

Falling back into the corner of the lift, I hug myself and allow the tears to fall with a promise that they will stop by the time I am in a cab on my way to the airport. I don't even believe that will be the end of them once I reach my next destination because Declan Harding is without a doubt the love of my life and I will never feel for anyone what I feel for him. He is the one, and now, the one who got away.

Chapter Thirty

Declan

Liv is giving me daggers and is clearly upset, but right now, her sadness and annoyance are the last things on my mind.

"So, are you still up for the design work?" My words are clipped and my tone terse.

"Depends on whether you can stop being an arsehole."

She is sitting on the sofa and struggling to get comfortable by the looks of it. She looks fit to burst.

"I'm not being an arsehole." I kind of am with her but I am seriously pissed off with what she may have known about Anita and didn't see fit to tell me. "If you don't want the work, I can find another designer."

She laughs. "Yeah, in fact, I believe Christian would be happy to do your designs."

"Fuck off, Liv. I don't know why you're pushing my buttons and seem to be painting me in the role of villain in this, but I am the innocent party."

It's probably a good job that Mase isn't here, or he'd kick my arse for telling her to fuck off, but Liv can take it with the best of them.

"Fuck off yourself, and I am not pushing your buttons, your own stupidity is doing that for you, and you are innocent to a point, but so is Anita."

I let out a huff that turns into some kind of growl, startling Liv who closes her eyes and seems to be counting.

"You okay. I didn't mean to scare you."

She waves my words off. "You didn't. Look, maybe we should talk this through. You must have questions of me and my role in whatever it is you think has gone on."

She staggers to her feet and waddles towards the kitchen where she battles with the coffee machine before resorting to the kettle.

Once she has finished the drinks, I join her on the opposite side of the breakfast bar. We make polite chit chat for a few minutes and then she addresses the elephant in the room.

"Fire away, Dec."

"Did you know about the baby?"

"I walked in on a conversation…well, more a berating of Anita by Christian at your mother's house…at my baby shower."

That explains the weird moods and atmosphere after the shower at least.

Liv continues. "I heard him say she'd had an abortion. Anita avoided me and I didn't see Christian again until you found us in the kitchen. Anita hadn't got round to telling me everything when he burst in and acted like his usual dickhead self. He roughed me up and was vile to Anita, telling her if she didn't recommend using him on your new place, he'd tell you about her aborting the baby."

"Go on." I feel as though Mase earned the right to punch Christian, but I am really jealous that he did it and not me. My stomach churns at the thought of him daring to speak to Anita the way I know he did.

"Mase is angry with Anita, for not telling you and that has made it awkward for me and her to meet up, plus she was upset and trying to get her shit together. She's told the family everything and came to see me to explain it too."

"What's to explain?" I feel agitated again and want my sister-in-law not to justify what Anita did.

"She regrets not telling you everything."

I immaturely roll my eyes. Liv ignores that.

"When you told her about Amber, she didn't know how you'd react. She was scared that you'd lash out and behave, well, exactly as you did, so, maybe she was justified in keeping quiet."

"So, this is my fault? Unbelievable, both of you!"

"Not what I meant, and you know it. Look, unlike Amber she didn't have a good man who was going to take care of her child, she had a married man who lied to her and took advantage! Shit, he never even paid for the abortion he told her she had to have. He said he would but then backed down on it. This is not my story to tell, but she didn't put the baby up for adoption because she didn't want her or love her. Quite the opposite. She did it because she couldn't see an alternative. Her perception of abortion was that it equated to her killing her own child and that wasn't something she could do without good reason, but she wanted that baby to have the best life where she would be her parent's whole world and while I believe Anita could have given her that, it would have been hard and Christian would never have even acknowledged her existence, assuming their paths ever crossed again."

I let Liv's words sink in.

"She loves you Declan. Your comparison of her and Amber hurt her. Not as much as giving up her baby, nor losing you, but they did hurt her."

"I was so scared, Liv, risking getting hurt again, but I thought she was the one for me." I hear the break in my voice.

"Maybe she still is."

"How can she be? I want what you and Mase have, the marriage and family, but what if I never trust her to give me that?"

"Declan." Liv comes to my side and hugs me tightly. "I don't have the answers, but I know giving up the baby almost broke her. She was sad, hurting, angry and ashamed. She would never do that again, not least of all because you are not Christian any more than Anita is Amber."

I nod. I believe what she's saying. "Maybe we could talk. She could explain to me…I never gave her much of a chance before."

"Ah."

"Ah, what?"

"She's gone."

"What do you mean, gone? Gone where? When will she be back?"

"She was on her way to the airport, that's why she had the case."

"I thought she'd been staying with you."

"No. She came by to explain and to say goodbye. She was heading to the airport to grab a flight anywhere. One way with no destination or return date in mind."

"She didn't say goodbye to me." My petulant tone is quite pathetic.

"Declan, she thinks you hate her."

"Shit!" I am on my feet and pacing, roughly pushing my hand through my hair. "I need to speak to her. She can't go like this. I don't hate her, I love her."

Liv let's out a squeal as she grabs car keys and rushes for the lift. "Come on then. I'll drive, drop you at the airport and you can stop her leaving on the condition that you promise to listen to her and not just get mean."

"I promise." I have already joined Liv at the lift door that is opening.

"We'll call her on the way."

I'm not even sure how this has happened but just the thought of seeing Anita, of stopping her leaving and making things right makes me feel as though the weight of the world has been lifted from my shoulders.

Liv hits the button for the car park and the lift begins to move and then it stops dead. The lights go out briefly until the emergency lighting kicks in.

"What the fuck!" The lift has broken down. I have never known this to happen, and it has to be today when my sole mission is to go and stop my lady from fleeing to fuck knows where.

"Dec," Liv says, her voice almost a whisper.

I am still thinking of how long we're going to be stuck here when she repeats my name, but this time it's louder and filled with panic. Turning to face her, I can see she is clutching her belly.

"Dec," she says once more, "I think the baby's coming."

"No!" I tell her, almost forbidding her to confirm her thought.

Neither of us speak for a few seconds but we both hear and then see the pool appearing on the floor.

"Of fuck! My waters have broken. Get Mase!"

I hit the alarm button in the lift and it is answered immediately. I explain who I am, and that Mrs Harding is in the lift with me. I don't tell him she is in labour, but I do tell him to let Mase know. I don't need to tell him to send my brother to us, he will be beside himself at the idea of Liv stuck in a lift.

Liv looks shit scared as she clutches the handrail on the wall. "Shit, this hurts."

"Liv, I don't know too much about this, but I'm sure you'll have hours yet."

She nods and does look strangely reassured by my words. "I might have been in labour a few hours though…I thought the Braxton Hicks were just getting really strong." She doubles over as I assume another contraction hits.

Mase's voice comes through the panel on the wall, and he sounds concerned.

"Hey, Livy. Have you broken the lift?"

She laughs. "It seems that way, but slightly more concerning is the fact that I have broken my waters."

"Fuck!" Mase hisses and begins to bark orders to people to get us out of the lift, well, more Liv than me.

He then starts telling me to keep an eye on Liv. I resist the temptation to point out that as we are stuck in a six feet square box, I'd struggle not to keep an eye on her.

"Mase, just get us out of here. Midwife is not in my list of skills, and I need to get to the airport to find Anita."

He ignores the midwife comment. "Anita?"

"Yeah." I look at Liv and smile before looking back to the panel my brother's voice is coming from. "I love her."

"Okay," he says. "Why is she at the airport?"

"Because I was a dick and didn't listen to her."

"Okay," he repeats. "Oh, and Dec, the idea of you playing midwife chills me to the bone, plus, you do not need to see my wife's lady parts."

Liv and I both laugh but for our own reasons need to get the hell out of this bloody lift.

Anita

Arriving at the airport alone with no destination in mind is one of the scariest things I have ever done, and yet, it's one of the most exciting and liberating.

I look around at the various desks and kiosks before checking out departure boards; France, Italy, New York, The Maldives, Dubai, and then I see a flight to Greece leaving in a couple of hours' time. I laugh out loud as I consider that I am doing what my mother would call a *Shirley Valentine*. I remember watching it with her years before, one of her favourite films and it seems fitting.

Within minutes I have made my way to the airline's desk and handed my credit card over. I am going to Greece and for the first time in weeks feel a sense of positivity about my life. This is not the cure to everything, but it's a good start. I've made a decision about my future and one way or another I need to get on with a life that doesn't include guilt and shame, nor Dec. My heart lurches at the final thought. I love him and I miss him more than I thought was possible, but we are no longer together and one way or another, I need to deal with that reality and dealing with it in the sunshine on a beach for a while seems a better option than wallowing in it in an overcast England.

I wander through duty free and spy a couple of bargains I would normally pick up, but I resist. I have no clue how long I will be away and if I will remain in Greece. I have savings and my parents gave me a good chunk of cash to use. The thought of my parents and their cash saddens me, not that they haven't always been generous, but because I know they feel guilty about me giving up my baby. Guilty that they didn't know. That I didn't tell them and in that they were unable to help or support me. Their guilt is misplaced because if I had told them, they would have done everything in their power to enable me to keep her and with how things have turned out, that would have been a very awkward and painful situation for me and my daughter. I put down the perfume I have been looking at and feel a pang of

Family Affair

sadness at my bare ring finger. After that day in the kitchen, I returned my engagement ring via Scott who was seeing Liv. She in turn returned it to Dec. I know it was probably the coward's way to do it, but if that's the case, I am a coward.

****

Boarding the plane comes around quickly and every step I take towards my seat feels like a step closer to the weight that remains on my shoulders being lifted. I can't see another solo traveller, the plane seems to be filled with couples, families or groups of friends all heading into the sun for their annual holiday and although that should probably scare me, it doesn't, it does the opposite, I feel bold and empowered to have made this decision for me.

I prepare to switch my phone to airplane mode and see that the message I sent to Liv telling her I was going to Greece is sitting as sent. I don't read any more into that than the fact that when I left her Dec had just arrived and I assume she is still doing his design work despite her now being on maternity leave. My fingers hover over the keys, considering sending her further details, but I don't. Once I land and have found somewhere to stay, I will update her then, maybe even call her from wherever I end up. Until that second, I hadn't even considered the fact that I have nowhere to stay upon arrival. A little panic washes over me, but I push it down as I consider that there will be somewhere to stay, even if it's not the plushest of places and Greece is a big country to truly have no room at the inn. I giggle as I think that if all else fails, I'll buy a pool mattress and sleep on the beach, although that could get me arrested. I laugh as I imagine my parent's and Liv's face if someone has to come over and bail me out for sleeping on the beach.

With my phone now on airplane mode and my accommodation worries settled for a while, I get myself comfy and reach for the book in my bag. More people are boarding, and I just wish they'd hurry up so the plane can take off before I rethink everything and panic that this is a bad idea. No. I know staying at home was a worse idea. I give myself another pep talk and with my mind calm again, I open my book. Usually, I'd opt for a romance with a dashing hero and a heroine who feared love before giving in to the relentless chasing and pursuit of her by the hero and then together they'd find their happy ever after. No, that is not what I need right now. So, instead I have gone for a thriller with murder and mayhem and nothing to remind me of love, Declan, or my broken heart.

Turning the page, I see I am already on chapter three but still there is no sign of the plane moving and looking around there seem to be no more passengers boarding. I am sitting in a window seat and next to me are a couple of older ladies, sisters, going on their first girl's holiday. I smile across at them, loving their gumption in taking this adventure together. Maybe that's something Liv and I could do in the future, with her baby. I shake my head at the chances of that happening without Mase. Perhaps we could time it so that it coincides with some business trip of his and he could come to us later. I stop this train of thought before it leads me to Dec coming with him and us all having a wonderful time together. My wonderful times with Dec are over. I must accept that fully.

"Ladies and gentlemen, this is your pilot. Apologies for the delay, but we should be taking off very shortly..."

The cheer from the boarded passengers drowns out anything else he says, but just knowing my departure is imminent, I smile and go back to my book.

Chapter Thirty-One

Declan

"This cannot be happening."

Liv looks up at me and I immediately feel guilty. This is not how she planned on spending her afternoon either and she is the one in labour, not me.

"But it is." I try to lighten the mood. "We can do this together, right?"

"I think we're going to have to, Uncle Declan." Liv releases the strangest and loudest squeal I have ever heard, and I swear she is putting me off ever having sex again if this is a possible outcome.

"Baby," Mase's voice comes through the speaker of the lift.

"Mason, get me the fuck out of here!" she yells at him.

"I'm working on it, I promise. Livy, this will be okay."

I smile at their exchange, especially when Liv replies. "Babe, I need you here, holding my hand and telling me I can do this."

"I know and I need to be there too, and I will be, soon."

She does her squeal thing again. Yeah, this is not attractive. Maybe it's better that Mase isn't seeing this, or my niece would certainly be an only child.

"Dec." His attention is on me now. "I know I said I didn't want you playing midwife, but you may have to. Livy's contractions are speeding up and I can hear they're becoming more intense. There is an ambulance on the way, but in the meantime, I have a lady from the ambulance service on the line."

The next ten minutes pass by in a blur. Liv is propped up the corner and I have now seen her lady parts. Her contractions are almost constant, and I can see the baby's head doing something I now know is called crowning. The ambulance crew have arrived, as have engineers and the fire brigade. On one side we have the noise of people trying to get to us and on the other is the woman directing me and Liv on how to get my niece out. We also have a side order of anxious dad giving advice and muttering curse words.

I watch as Liv has another contraction, and the head begins to emerge.

"Fucking hell! I can see her. Her head is coming out! What do I do?" I am well out of my depth here but am also emotional to see this little person entering the world. Even the sight of Liv and her lady parts is no longer looking as traumatic. This moment is fucking amazing, and I feel privileged to be witnessing it, no, sharing it.

The woman is telling me to support her head but not to pull! She is talking about the shoulders, and I am panicking inside that I may break my niece as she enters the world.

Liv looks at me and smiles. She can see or sense my turmoil.

"Uncle Dec, we have got this. You wouldn't have been my first choice to do this with, but maybe you should have been. You've been amazing."

"Don't turn mushy on me now, Liv."

I am genuinely touched by her words and the sentiment of them, but I need not to get emotional because if I do, I will go to that place where I missed my own daughter being born and then I will inevitably end up imagining Anita doing this, going through this, only to give up the baby she loved and in other circumstances wanted. A baby she would have been an amazing mother to if the father had been different.

"Liv, I want a baby," I blurt out.

"That is not on the fucking table!" Mase hisses at me, making me laugh.

"Not with Liv, you dickhead." I look at Liv again, "No offense."

"None taken." She smiles briefly before another contraction

hits. She knows what I am saying.

Her scream is kind of blocked out by Mase shouting something about being on his way and the sound of metal scraping and then light hits us from outside of the lift. We have barely moved from the apartment. The men opening the lift are visible from just above the knees down.

The lift is suddenly filling up, paramedics appear a split second before Mase and before any of us know it, Liv is crying out again and I am literally catching a baby that resembles a bar of wet soap judging by how slippery she is in my grasp.

Her cry is the best sound ever. She is beautiful with dark hair and perfectly pink skin. I feel tears running down my face.

"She is fucking perfect. My little angel."

The paramedics intervene. I have no clue how long it takes but suddenly my brother is cutting my niece's cord while I hold her, both of us sobbing more than the baby and then she is being moved onto Liv who is also crying at the sight of her desperately wanted and loved little girl.

I get to my feet and look down at the sight of my brother holding his wife while she cradles their firstborn child and the phrase *a picture paints a thousand words* really makes sense. They are a perfect picture of happiness and love. I want that too. I had that and I threw it away because of my own ego and hurt.

"Liv, I want a baby." My repeated words make her grin up at me.

"Then go."

"What?" Mase is confused.

"I told you, Anita is leaving, and I can't let her. I love her and I need to listen to her, then most likely beg her to forgive and try again."

Mase frowns. He is still holding the grudge I am determined to let go.

"I. Love. Her. More. Than. Anything." Punctuating each word seems to get my message across.

"Where is she going?" Mase asks.

Liv and I both shrug.

"She said she'd let me know but she was going to the airport."

"Get the fuck out of here," Mase orders. "Call Dad, he'll find her."

I'm already climbing out of the partially accessible lift before dipping back in. "Congratulations by the way, and I'll be back for more cuddles with Auntie Anita." I feel the face splitting grin form as I hit my dad's number.

Anita

Chapter five has just ended and still I am sat on the runway. Cabin crew seem to be oblivious to what's happening or when we might take off. There has been one further announcement saying there will be a further short delay. No shit Sherlock.

The ladies next to me are planning their first drinks at the hotel bar and I admire their commitment to having a good time when they start mixing their own cocktails aloud.

I glance back down to my book when there's a commotion from the other end of the plane. I may lose my shit if we are about to be ordered off, although as I hear the family behind me discussing plane crashes and malfunctions, if that is what's causing the delay, maybe I'd rather disembark.

The sound of cabin crew's voices getting louder distract me slightly and then I hear something else and think I must be dreaming or having an out of body experience.

"Anita!"

I look around, checking for another Anita, but it can only be me this particular voice is calling.

"Cupcake! Where the hell are you?"

I stand up, unsure what I expect to see, but the sight of Declan Harding striding down the aisle of the plane towards me is far more than I imagined.

"Dec, what are you doing here?" I ask as he comes to a stop at my row.

"I've come to take you home."

I laugh. What the hell is going on here? We are not together and as recently as a few hours ago he despised me and looked at me with contempt. He's not looking at me with contempt now though.

"Dec..." I have no other words.

"Please. Forgive me for not letting you explain things. Give me a chance, one chance to listen, that's all I'm asking for."

I actually pinch the skin on the inside of my wrist, certain this is a dream. It must be because this cannot be real.

"If I need to get on my knees and beg, I will."

I watch in horror as he does just that and with his hands pressed together as if in prayer, he repeats his earlier words.

"Give me a chance."

I stare down at him, oblivious to all of the eyes I feel on me.

"Nothing will change the past," I warn him.

"It doesn't need to. I accept your past, as you accepted mine, but if you'll tell me everything, I promise to listen and not judge."

I am unsure if Dec expects me to reject him and the offer he's making. Hell, I have no idea if I am going to reject it based on the fact that this, us, is not going to be an easy or a quick fix.

Dec remains on his knees, adjusting his position until he is teetering on one leg and then, just when I think this can't get any more surreal, he produces my engagement ring.

"Liv gave me this. I don't want it. It's yours if you'll have it."

I hear giggles and people muttering oohs and ahs. He is not doing this, is he?

"Anita, Cupcake, marry me, please."

Okay, so yes, he is doing this.

"Declan, we can talk."

He grins up at me.

"But I am heading for Greece right now..."

"Then so am I," he declares.

"Not without a ticket you're not," one of the cabin crew says, coming alongside Dec.

"I have a ticket!" he snaps, holding up his boarding pass.

"Declan...why do you have a ticket?"

"Where you go, I go."

I have no words. He has no luggage as far as I know and is standing here in the clothes he is wearing, a very dishevelled outfit of jeans and a t-shirt, planning on coming to Greece with me! He has thrown all of my plans up in the air. I love Dec, of that there is no doubt, never was and as much as I want his pledge to not judge me to be true, what if it isn't?

"Cupcake, marry me?"

With no thought and very little co-ordination, I am climbing over the two ladies next to me and leaning down to kiss Dec.

"We need to talk first," I whisper as he gets to his feet and pulls me in, preparing to kiss me.

Looking down, I see blood on his top.

"What happened, are you hurt?" Panic grips me as I wonder what happened after I left him with Liv.

"What? No. Why?" He looks down to where my eyes have settled. "Ah, no. I should have told you…this is baby blood."

A couple of people nearby gasp at his phrasing.

He looks around. "Not like injured baby. I delivered a baby… my niece," he explains then turns to me. "Long story, but me and Liv got stuck in a lift and she went into labour. I delivered the baby just as Mase and the paramedics got to us…I should probably have told you that. Oh, I told the baby I was going back for cuddles and bringing Auntie Anita with me, so, are we doing that now or after Greece?"

This is unbelievable. For whatever reason, Dec wants us to try again. He has just slipped my engagement ring back on my finger which is something we need to talk about, but not with a whole plane as an audience. I now discover he delivered our niece in a lift and that one way or another we are going for cuddles. Even with the whirring of my mind and the chaotic thoughts of what this might mean long term, there is no way I am going anywhere besides off this plane.

"Now. Let's go." I reach for my hand luggage while Dec grabs my free hand and with a smile for the cabin crew we are passing, we're heading for the plane door that is thankfully still open.

By the time we are back in the airport, we are giggling like naughty schoolchildren until I stumble up a small flight of stairs. Dec pulls me back, preventing my fall and somehow, I end up pressed against a wall with his hands lacing through my hair.

"I'm sorry," he whispers as his face moves closer to mine.

I know that he is going to kiss me and although it's not our first kiss, it's a kiss I never thought I'd feel again. The softness of his lips as they gently find mine shocks me. His kiss is tender rather than frantic, cherishing me and this moment. I feel as though I am trembling, but not from arousal or anything that basic. This is love, real, honest, true love, coursing through me, telling me everything about how Dec feels as much as how I feel. In this kiss, I know that Dec is the one. The only one for me and I could live a thousand lives and never find this again and having had and lost it, but lucky enough to have a second chance, I will not waste it or throw it away.

Family Affair

Epilogue - One Year Later

Declan

Tonight is a big night and I am nervous, which is not something I am overly accustomed to.

After a few delays with planning permission and building work, not to mention Liv doing the design on the place, my new club in the old cinema is opening. It's not a full opening with customers, but a launch night for local businesses, friends, family, the press and a few local influencers.

My other business venture that I originally thought of as being a coffee shop come bistro, opened a few months ago. It is a coffee shop primarily, but from lunch time onwards we serve cocktails and wine. Due to its location on a High Street and being surrounded by nine til five shops, we opted not to open late nights, so it's now a nine til nine business. Anita is the manager and although she's not there full time, she keeps it stocked with her own cakes which are ridiculously popular, but she tends not to do the evenings.

I am going to maintain my role at Dazzler but as the new place, Jubilation, the name of another comic book heroine, opens, I will need to have managers too. In fact, Liv's brother, Scott has been working at Dazzler for about nine months now and has agreed to be the manager at the new place.

"What do you think?" Anita interrupts my thoughts.

I turn and drink in the image before me. She looks absolutely phenomenal standing in a white dress that after skimming over her chest and abs, nips in at her waist before flaring slightly into a skirt that finishes mid-thigh. I drop my gaze to her feet and lower legs that are encased in a series of silver straps, zigzagging from her stiletto shoes.

"I think I should have left an hour ago because we are at serious risk of being late for our own launch night."

Anita giggles then throws in a squeal for good measure as I pull her to me, crushing her against my chest.

"You look fucking phenomenal in white."

A tiny blush creeps across her cheeks. If she isn't the most adorable woman in the world.

"Thank you," she all but whispers.

"You are going to make a seriously hot bride."

Her flush deepens. "Eight weeks and counting, Stud."

Pulling her even closer, I prepare to kiss her. "Remind me again, why aren't you my wife yet?"

With precision timing, the sound of crying fills our home.

"Our yes, the birth of our son railroaded everything." I lean down and kiss the end of her nose before pulling away at the split second the intercom buzzes into life. "You deal with the intercom, and I'll deal with our boy, Charlie."

It's only a matter of a couple of minutes before I return to find my home filled with Liv, Mase, their baby, Phoebe, and my dad, the babysitter for the night.

Phoebe is already dressed in pyjamas and dozing off on Mase's shoulder. He really never has been so happy, and he's not the only one. We both have women we're crazy about and children we cherish.

Charlie who is only three months old, becomes a little restless as he is due a feed. Anita rushes to the kitchen to prepare a bottle before returning and handing it to my dad who is chatting to my son while Phoebe sits on Mase's lap gazing up at her father with clear adoration in her eyes.

With the baby now suckling on his bottle, my dad continues to chat to his grandchildren. "Are you going to be a good girl for Grandad and help me look after Charlie Boy?"

Phoebe gives him a gummy grin and chuckles before letting out a long, loud yawn.

"Do you hear that, Charlie? I think we might be on our own

tonight."

I smile, watching the amazing dad Mase and I were fortunate enough to grow up with, being an even more amazing grandfather.

"When this lot have all gone, why don't I tell you all about how I grounded your mummy long enough for Daddy to get his act together?"

Immediately, my eyes seek out Anita's who is arching a brow at my dad's words. "I still can't believe you did that. I don't even know how you did that!"

Phoebe begins to babble at her grandad, maybe sensing that his attention was solely on Charlie.

He looks down at her and with some juggling of my son and his bottle, he pulls her onto his lap. "And you, young lady, why don't I tell you all about how I had to literally watch your mummy's every move."

Liv rolls her eyes. "Or maybe don't because with how overprotective Mase is with me and Phoebe, you'll be implanting a tracking device in us both."

Dad laughs, but Mase doesn't. "Livy, I am not overprotective, just careful where my girls are concerned." He checks his watch. "Right, let's get moving then." Turning to Dad, he begins to give him instructions.

"Mason, I managed to care for you, your brother and your sister, so this won't be too difficult."

A little snort comes from Phoebe who has already fallen asleep in my dad's embrace.

"Any problems call, and we won't be late," Mase continues.

"Speak for yourself," chips in Liv making me and Anita who I have wrapped in my arms, laugh. "This is my first night out in over a year and I plan on making it count by working my way through your overpriced cocktail menu."

Anita appears to be about to throw in her support and I suspect, her companionship in this plan when I interrupt. "Good to hear, Liv, but you," I turn Anita to face me, "Are still breast feeding, so you will be on non-alcoholic options. Now, let's go."

Family Affair

Anita

Bouncing into the middle of the bed is not exactly romantic, but as I look up and find Dec standing at the side of the bed watching me, I decide this is possibly the most romantic thing ever.

Dec always looks amazing, to me anyway, but today, standing in a very well-cut three-piece suit, he looks out of this world handsome. I have no idea how this happened, me and Dec, not really. I should never have been lucky enough to find someone who would love me like he does and add to that the fact that I feel the same way about him, it just seems too perfect. It's not that we don't deserve loving like that, but the chances of finding someone who fits you so perfectly and feels the same is rare.

"So, Mrs Harding, at last."

My face is splitting in two with happiness and the grin I'm wearing supports that feeling. I am Mrs Harding as of about ten hours ago and the day has been perfect from the weather to the flowers, the venue to the food, but most importantly, the people; me, Dec, Charlie, our families, and closest friends.

This is the first night since Charlie's birth about six months ago that he hasn't been with us overnight. He is currently with my parents, for one night only as we spend our first night together as husband and wife. My grin only broadens when I think of my baby. He is perfect in every way. It was a huge shock to find myself pregnant rather than suffering from food poisoning a couple of weeks after Declan boarded my plane. I still can't believe he did that and moreover, I can't believe that my now father-in-law had the powers to ground my plane to allow Dec to. When I started vomiting, I assumed it was food poisoning or a bug, but it quickly became clear that it wasn't that and one pregnancy test later, confirmed that our first night together after disembarking that flight to Greece had resulted in Charlie. That night when I didn't even think about the fact that I'd stopped taking the pill weeks before when I was nursing my broken heart and the thought of contraception, never mind the discussion wasn't something either of us considered.

Dec was with me when I took the test and I think he was

nervous that I might not want the baby, but nothing was further from the truth. From the second I knew he existed there was nothing I wanted more than to carry my baby, deliver him, and this time keep him. Fortunately, Dec felt the same way and my nine months of pregnancy were some of the happiest of my life.

The only blot during that time was Christian. He incorrectly assumed I or maybe Mase and Dec was going to tell his wife, so he pre-empted it with a very distorted version of events which led to her confronting me at a family dinner where, after I tried to deflect her name calling and accusations, Liv came to my rescue, leaving her in no doubt of the truth. I felt guilty knowing whatever fallout there was, I had to accept some responsibility. The fallout was that she threw him out of their home and as far as we all know, he still has regular contact with the children, but his marriage seems to be over. I do feel bad about that when I think about it but as Dec, my family, and in-laws as well as Mase and Liv point out, I was innocent in the lies and deceit Christian perpetuated and now accept that, refusing to allow my past to impact any further on my future.

I see Dec's jacket fly across the room and then his hands move to his tie.

"Let me." I get up onto my knees and virtually crawl to him.

In the space of minutes, all clothes have been shed. My beautiful wedding dress lies in a heap on the floor somewhere. I remember trying the dress on for the first time and both Liv and my mum cried with me, knowing it was just perfect for me, simplistic with a boho-inspired twist. The V-neckline of my dress has linear dotted laces twisted and wrapped around it to make a banded detail, the same as the wide waistband. Even I had to admit it defined my shape but remained comfortable, unlike so many of the others I tried on. Having recently having had Charlie, I was thrilled to find a dress that had some stretch in it without it being a second skin. The flowing A-line skirt and elongated train complete the flattering shape that I felt both comfortable and beautiful in. My dad cried when he saw me in it and Dec was beyond complimentary.

"Fuck, you're beautiful." Dec gazes down at me, lying in the middle of the huge bed we have in the honeymoon suite we're in.

"You're pretty gorgeous yourself," I tell him, and he is. The most perfect specimen of a man I have ever seen.

"Sounds as though we're perfect for one another then."

I giggle until Dec moves closer, hovering over me, preparing to kiss me. As soon as his lips land on mine, nothing else exists. Our bodies work in perfect unison, fitting together seamlessly until we are one.

THE END

Have you read Mason and Olivia's story yet? Keep reading to find out how it all started for Mase and Liv.

About the Author

Elle M Thomas was born in the north of England and raised near Birmingham, UK where she still lives with her family. She works in local education and writes in her spare time with dreams of becoming a full-time writer.

Whilst still at school, and with a love of writing slightly risqué tales of love and romance one of her teachers told her that she could be the next Harrold Robins. Elle didn't act on those words for many years. In February 2017, with her first book completed and a dozen others unfinished, she finally took the plunge and self-published the steamy romance, Disaster-in-Waiting.

Elle describes her books as stories filled with chemistry, sensuality, love and sex that she always wanted to read and her characters as three dimensional and flawed.

Social media links for Elle M Thomas:

https://twitter.com/ellemthomas24

https://www.facebook.com/ellemthomasauthor/

https://www.instagram.com/authorellemthomas/

https://www.goodreads.com/author/show/16429813.Elle_M_Thomas

One Night Or Forever

Chapter One

Olivia

The sound of my alarm blaring comes all too soon and as I feel the throbbing of my head I groan loudly, however my groan is soon replaced with a shriek as an arm makes its way around my middle, and then it all comes flooding back to me.

Last night. Oh God! What was I thinking? Well I wasn't, at least not with my head, all of my powers of thought were coming from somewhere much lower down on my anatomy. This is my first one-night stand and as such I have no clue what the etiquette is here, if indeed there is any.

I realise my alarm is still droning on around us. Us? I really need to remember that as a newly single woman I am shit at drinking and it makes me behave strangely. It makes me do this with hot guys who show me attention and if memory serves me right my bed partner is hot, very hot, seriously hot, *volcanic* hot. I need to stop thinking about this and do something, something other than him.

"Turn it off," he moans from behind me, prompting me to actually slide my finger across my phone to shut the alarm off.

Whilst I usually go for a nine minute snooze I won't need that this morning because apart from anything else I will not be falling back to sleep with a man in my bed, even if I want to because there are other things I need to do this morning starting with getting my arse out of bed, but again I am at a loss as to how I am supposed to do that.

Shit! I suddenly acknowledge that if I get up before him then he is going to see me naked. I know he already has, but that was last night and I was under the heady influence of lust and vodka, but now I am not drunk, although I think lust may still be a factor.

For a brief moment I wonder if he will be fat, forty and balding when I roll over because last night he was late twenties, maybe early thirties with a full head of dark hair that I ran my fingers through countless times and his eyes, oh God, those eyes. In complete contrast to his dark hair his eyes were blue, dark, an almost twinkling navy. The memory of them makes me shiver with the sliver of lust I acknowledged earlier multiplying tenfold.

I am not exactly over-experienced with men, but I have seen enough to know that my bed partner is a fine specimen of a man with not an ounce of fat on him. I feel him pull me closer and although I want to soften against him I really need to get out of bed and go to work, even though I hate my job, kind of.

The arm around me is muscular which makes me smile as I look down at it and remember that his whole body is that way, ripped as my friend Sarah would say. In fact, I think she may have said just that last night when we saw him; *all hair gel, ripped muscles and tattoos* is what she'd said, and I am now familiar with each of his muscles and tattoos.

"Morning," he says, causing me to jump as his lips speak against my shoulder. "Any chance of coffee?"

"Course," I reply and instinctively prepare to leave my bed before I remember my naked state and his physical presence.

"Thanks," he replies before I feel his hand lift and the mattress shift beneath me, an indication that he is getting up first.

I blush, I can feel it, the burn of it on my cheeks as he comes into view; and seeing the naked glory of him I feel intimidated and jealous of his ease at being naked. I am staring at his naked rear view; his hair is mussed, very much a bed head, down to his broad and muscular shoulders that are flexing as he stretches, his narrower waist and then his hips and behind. Oh gosh, I had no idea any man could have such a beautiful arse.

I am unsure if he is putting on some kind of show for me but if he is then I really am very appreciative of it. Without warning, he turns, I blush further in the certain knowledge that he has caught me looking at him which his cocky smirk seems to confirm. I can't help myself now as I drink in his appearance from the front; his smooth chest and the tattoo that is a black, tribal design, all lines and curves covering one side of his chest. I know that at some point I traced the lines of it with my finger and then my tongue. Bloody hell, what happened to me last night? Next, it's the brown discs of his nipples that I suddenly recall sucking on, licking and nipping at. My colour rises a little more as I scan the hard, sculpted muscles of his abdomen and the trail of dark hair heading south from his naval past that muscular 'V' leading to, oh my, his erection!

I have no clue where to look or what to do so try to focus on something less sexual, if that's possible in these circumstances, but as I divert my gaze to his biceps I see another tattoo, this one is also tribal and covers the whole of his upper arm and incorporates a dragon or something similar and the sight of that reminds me of how I held onto those arms as he rested above me to drive into me, the way he held me in the same arms...

"Am I making my own coffee, or do you think you can take your eyes off me long enough to at least put a kettle on?" he asks, and I am even more embarrassed than previously. Not only because he has busted my ogling but because of the way he is speaking to me, abruptly.

The warmth of last night seems to be going fast, as if once he is out of my bed I am nothing. I know that I am nothing since we met last night and we don't know each other beyond the sex, the sex that was the best I think I have ever experienced. The way he touched me, talked to me, controlled the moments we shared. No doubt about it, he is the best I have had. I am beyond crimson now as I recall begging him to make me come.

Yes, I am nothing and am unworthy of anything resembling respect to have sunk to such depths is what I tell myself and yet the events of last night, if not this morning feel like they're significant. Not my Adonis of a quick shag himself but the decision to bring him back here and to forget, or at least ignore my self-doubt and loathing.

"I said," he begins as if he is about to repeat his coffee requirements and another layer of annoyance is added.

"Sorry, yes." I give him a weak smile as I wait for him to go to the bathroom or somewhere else, anywhere else, but he's still standing there, staring at me, waiting.

"Could you pass my erm, my robe?" I physically cringe.

"Why? It's not like you have anything I haven't seen already." He lifts my robe from the back of a chair.

I am sure that I breathe a sigh of relief that we both hear when he grips the satin fabric and prepares to throw it. Unfortunately for me he tosses my robe farther away, increasing my horror at the situation. Maybe he is going to increase my self-loathing rather than reducing it. When did he change from charming to dickhead? I immediately answer my own question, *when you brought him home and shagged him, like a slapper.*

"Did you want a shower?" My voice is so high-pitched that it sounds unfamiliar to me, but I am just trying to get him far enough away that I can put some clothing on and then I will make his coffee.

He shrugs and takes a long stride toward me. "You offering to join me?"

I am floundering, unsure how to deal with his suggestion, flat tone or the thrill that is humming through my body at the thought of it.

"We could finish the night off the way it started, or maybe I could have you on your knees again, begging to suck my dick. Do you remember how you begged for it?"

I can see and hear a hard edge to him, the torment clear to me, both qualities I don't like and yet my treacherous body is pulsating at the idea of what he's suggesting, my core turning to molten liquid as he stares across at me, waiting for me to do or say something.

His laugh startles me as does the action of him throwing my robe in my direction. I really, really need him gone, out of my bedroom, out of my flat and consigned to the large chapter of my life entitled, *The Many Mistakes I've Made.*

"Forget the shower, but the coffee would be appreciated. I have a long and dull day ahead." He smiles and a little warmth infiltrates his voice as he reaches for his own clothes that lie scattered around my room, well some of them do.

Looking down at the gathered clothing in his hands he heads towards the lounge and kitchen to find his missing items. I have enough time to put my robe on and fasten it before rushing through to the kitchen where I find him dressing.

The kettle seems to take an eternity to boil, but once I hand him a steaming mug we stare at each other for a while, him drinking his coffee and me hoping that I can avoid vomiting in front of him before I finally attempt to excuse myself.

"I need to get ready for work," I explain.

An understanding nod is his response as the coffee cup is placed on the kitchen counter before he moves closer, allowing me a final smell of his divine aroma.

"You have a nice place here. But as I said, a long and busy day awaits, so I'll be off. Last night was fun," he tells me then heads for the door leaving me wondering if this is the norm when you bring a stranger home with you.

"I didn't get your name," I blurt out and realise how slutty that makes me sound and feel, slutty and ashamed, both things I have rarely felt in the last seven years, but sadly both feelings I am more than familiar with courtesy of my damaged formative years.

"Nor I yours, so let's not spoil it. One night or forever, it was still fun, bye."

Then he is gone, and I have no way of knowing how I feel about the last twelve hours of my life beyond sad, I think. Unfortunately, I have no time to deliberate further as I must get ready for work and am already late. Rushing towards the bathroom I feel that my most delicate and intimate folds are sore and tingling, but in a good way and again I wonder what the hell got into me beyond my overnight guest.

Chapter Two

Olivia

The journey into work is a nightmare, more of a nightmare than usual; the train is packed, beyond packed, although I probably need to accept some responsibility for being on the late train, the one that gets me to work on time, just, but I usually avoid taking it because it means I can't experience any further delays without being late and as I previously noted, it's crowded.

I am standing, along with many other commuters and I have managed to find myself wedged between an occupied seat and a slightly overweight man who is standing close, too close, closer than I believe he needs to be. I can feel his belly pressed against my back, his breath on my neck and worse still a fledgling erection that I am sure he is rubbing against my behind. I want to get off the train, be sick or cry, maybe all three, so I turn slightly to try and compose myself, to centre and refocus on something not involving the violation I currently feel. As I turn my head, I get a whiff of my dry humper's breath causing my stomach to churn, so much so that the acidic taste in the back of my throat indicates that vomit isn't far behind.

"Would you like a seat? I'm getting off at the next station," the man sitting in front of me says as he prepares to stand.

"Thanks." I sigh with a grateful smile and am unsure if I allow him to fully get to his feet before I am sliding into his space where I feel more settled, safer.

I avoid looking at the man who was getting off on our close proximity, focusing instead on the other commuters around me. Some are reading or working on computers, others are talking on phones and a couple of women are putting on make-up. Me? I'm just wishing the minutes away until the train is pulling into my station.

I disembark quickly and with my feet safely enclosed in trainers I begin a swift walk come jog until I reach the foyer of the office building where I work. Kicking my trainers off in a corner I dig through my rucksack for my heels that today are teal and perfectly match the button through blouse I'm wearing whilst my black pencil skirt that finishes just above my knees provides the ideal contrast.

There's an odd sensation washing over me, as if I am being watched, scrutinised, but as I look around the only person I see glancing in my direction is the security guy on duty, my favourite, Sid. He's about fifty and very sweet, like a favourite uncle.

"Morning, young lady, you're cutting it fine," he tells me with a smile and a wink.

"I know, I know," I reply, already dashing towards the lift doors that have just closed. "Finer still now," I add with a smile for Sid.

The next lift arrives and is empty. As I get in, I take the opportunity to give my appearance the once over. My near black hair has been very cooperative this morning and is up in a perfect messy bun. I don't wear much make-up for work, well at all really, but due to the bags under my eyes I have used a foundation rather than my usual tinted moisturiser and highlighted my cheeks with a pink blusher that goes someway to mask just how pale I am, ridiculously so. In fact, I sometimes think I'm almost transparent, especially in the summer when I can burn from looking out of the window without sunscreen. My eyes look jaded and so they should with my lack of sleep, excess alcohol and equally excessive shagging. I have highlighted my lids with a golden coloured powder then added a touch of brown eyeliner and some dark brown mascara, the overall effect lifting the shadows and drawing attention to my actual eyes that are technically hazel, however they are more green than anything else and my look is completed with clear lip gloss.

I roll my canvas jacket up and push it into my rucksack with my trainers and wonder what I must look like to other people in my business dress and trainers and then my business dress and shoes with a great bloody rucksack on my back. I regret that it wasn't on my back this morning preventing the creepy guy on the train from being able to get quite so close.

I take a deep breath as I step off the lift and head through the double glass doors of Peterson Michaels which is where I work. They're a company of interior designers and whilst that is what I'm trained for I took the job here on reception because I needed the cash, but also because Mr Peterson assured me there would be opportunities for me to work in interior design. However, eighteen months later I am a permanent fixture on reception and design jobs total zero, although I have done a few jobs on the side, mainly for friends of friends, but it's not the same as doing it as a real job.

I throw my bag under the reception desk and then head to the coffee machine. At least the coffee is complimentary, and this will be my first cup as my companion this morning made me so uncomfortable that I could barely breathe never mind drink coffee.

Returning to my desk I'm beginning to chicken out of the decision I made in the shower this morning where I go charging into Mr Peterson to demand that he keeps his word and allows me to build some design experience when the phone rings.

"Hello, Peterson Michaels, how may I help you?" I take my seat.

Sean, a real interior designer saunters in and waves at me with a big smile on his face. Sean is pretty gorgeous, tall, blonde and bronzed but a little too perfect for me, not quite rugged enough. Not that any of that stopped me dating him briefly, very briefly, about half a dozen dates over a couple of weeks when Brad and I were having some space, but when I didn't shag him in that time he realised I wasn't the girl for him and that was fine. We're just friendly colleagues really.

The woman ranting in my ear is pissing me off in my semi hungover state as she tells me that the design work done on the sunroom in her five-million-pound mansion is a disgrace. Apparently, when her design remit was described by her as *give me sunshine* she hadn't meant literally. Unfortunately, she hadn't told Cathy, the designer who used lots of yellows and oranges.

I am struggling to stifle a giggle until she says, "You see dear, I expected a sedate room that made me warm and relaxed, as the sun does, not to feel as though I have entered the ninth circle of hell."

The caller, Mrs Tyrell is a regular customer and loaded, seriously loaded. Like richer than God but her favourite designer, Ronaldo has left after falling in love with an Italian that he's followed back to Milan.

"I love *Dante's Inferno*," I tell her for no reason I know. This could go horribly wrong because she, Mrs Tyrell, is a bit awkward at times and can be more than a little testy when the mood takes her, but I do love *Dante's Inferno* and I like the fact she knows it. "Although from what you're saying you probably only have the yellow face of Satan in that room, maybe the red one too," I say, finally giving in to laughter, laughter she actually joins in with.

"I demand to speak to Christian, Mr Peterson. I expect a full refund and a reworking of my room," she tells me as I roll my eyes in Sean's direction.

"Let me just check if Mr Peterson is available for you, Mrs Tyrell." I bring up his online diary on my screen. While I wait for it to load, I make conversation. "How's Mr Tyrell?" I do it as a time filler but also because the subject of him calms her. She clearly loves him, adores him from the way she speaks about him.

"Oh, aren't you a sweet girl," she coos down the line meaning both of my objectives in using his name have been achieved.

I allow her to continue talking as the diary appears on my screen showing nothing at all for my boss until almost noon, meaning he should be free, but as Mrs Tyrell is in full flow, I allow her to continue.

I recall that she is an attractive woman in her mid-fifties with highlighted hair and blue eyes. I remember seeing her, the first and only time when Ronaldo was leaving and was shocked at how in condition she was, still is. Obviously, she's a gym bunny, or more likely has a personal trainer on the payroll.

Mrs Tyrell is always nice to me when we speak, except when she is getting stressed or pissy, like today, but in fairness she never directs her anger at me personally. I think Ronaldo told me that her husband is not her first husband but is her favourite one. The richest one I assume. I reckon in her younger years she was a goer, a real goer and absolutely stunning.

Briefly, I wonder if she was the sort of woman to partake in one night stands, she kind of looks the sort, although if that is the case I must look like her because I am now the sort of woman who partakes in them too. But last night was different and I have never done anything like that before and in my own defence am unlikely to again.

We, my friend Sarah and I went out, her idea to cheer me up since I have recently split up with Brad properly and although I insist I have not been moping Sarah disagrees. She is smugly in love and engaged to Jed who she is marrying in a couple of months' time. They are just perfect for each other, so perfect that Sarah wants everyone in the world to feel the same.

Brad and I ran its course several months ago but neither of us admitted it until more recently and although we were together for almost two years, we were the on/off couple. Sarah romanticised it into a Burton and Taylor, *can't live with 'em, can't live without 'em* scenario and refuses to accept that I'm not heartbroken on some level. We never were that couple and I think we were simply relieved to just be off with no pressure to get it back on again.

Last night we went to a club which is where I met *Mr hair gel, ripped muscles and tattoos* as my friend named him. Once she was happy that he wasn't a mad axe man she bailed, called Jed and left me to it. I don't mind that she left and when she did, I was as sober as a judge, almost, so I was safe. I haven't yet plucked up the courage to call or text her with the details of what happened next, although I am sure I recall my overnight guest texting Sarah from my phone when we got back to mine, he didn't want her to worry. I really need to check what he sent to her, possibly just check my phone because he could have text anyone, well anything'd anyone from my number.

"But apart from that he's okay," Mrs Tyrell informs me, reminding me that I am supposed to be working and checking where Mr Peterson is and as if by magic, he appears from his office.

He's a strange man really, nice enough I suppose, but strange. He is only a couple of inches taller than me at about five and a half feet and whilst not fat he is what you'd describe as stocky. His hair is a mass of soft, messy, mousy curls. He is only thirty but seems older with his tales of mortgage rates, catchment areas and keeping a family that consists of a wife, three children, two cats, a dog, a hamster and six goldfish.

"Mrs Tyrell," I begin, about to tell her that I am putting her on hold when Mr Peterson, who insists on being called Mr Peterson at all times during office hours is shaking his head and doing some strange hand signal to say he won't be free until later and then he disappears into his office with his fresh coffee. "I have Mr Peterson's diary here and he is quite busy today," I lie. "I can get a message to him and have him call you as soon as he's free and in the meantime, I will email an outline of your dissatisfaction to him," I offer.

"Thank you, dear."

Before I know it, I've hung up and wonder why my boss was unwilling to speak to someone who puts a lot of business our way, her own and that of her friends which equals big bucks.

After fielding another couple of calls and with Mr Peterson in a good mood, a very good mood I rediscover my earlier conviction to confront him about my own future. Grabbing my condensed portfolio that I put together some time ago for prospective clients and employers I head towards his office, stopping at the desk of a junior admin worker to ask her to cover reception. The door to my boss' office is ajar and I can see him through the gap, sitting at his desk sipping his coffee between taps on his keyboard.

"Mr Peterson." I gently knock the door and enter, my appearance startling him.

"Sorry," he says, causing me some confusion with his apology. "Mrs Tyrell," he expands. "I will call her back after lunch," he assures me in a confusing near whisper.

I feel a little irritated at his assumption that Mrs Tyrell is the only reason for me entering his office.

"She was really upset about her sunroom," I explain, getting side-tracked from my real reason for coming in. "She's talking refund and free reworking."

"Okay, okay," he says, almost dismissing me, but not quite so I seize my moment before I lose my nerve.

"Look Mr Peterson, I need more than you're giving me here," I tell him and am thankful that nobody else is here to hear how those words sound when spoken aloud to my boss because what I want is entirely professional.

"Excuse me?" He looks directly at me giving me his undivided attention.

"Professionally, I need more. I am not a receptionist, well I am because that is what I do here, but that is not really what I am, you know that. You know I have a degree in art and design and the reason I applied for my job here was because of the business it is. I told you that when you interviewed me over eighteen months ago. I was honest about the fact that I wanted to gain design experience and you encouraged that idea, but nothing has been forthcoming." With all the words out, I finally take a breath.

"I see." I am not convinced that he is taking me seriously. "We should talk about this later, maybe Wednesday. I am free on Wednesday afternoon," he replies, and I am irritated further because as far as I can see he is available right now.

I huff and glance around the room willing myself not to tell my boss to stick his job up his arse. My focus is drawn to the open door that leads onto the balcony that Mr Peterson insists on calling a terrace, but regardless of the noun we use to describe that area, I love it. I love the idea of one day having my own office with a balcony. I smile at that thought and then my smile drops through the floor as a body comes into view, in the open doorway of the balcony and I immediately recognise him as my one-night stand.

Shit, could this day get any more surreal?

"Christian." He steps into the room he is now crossing. "I am happy for you to deal with your staffing issues." He remains focused on my boss. "In fact, I would be interested to hear your receptionist's ideas."

I am staring between my boss' face and the back of my, my

what? My shag piece from last night? Whatever he is, I am still staring at his back that is turned towards me as he faces my boss.

"No, no, this can wait," Mr Peterson assures my whatever.

"Christian, it would appear that it has been waiting for eighteen months so maybe it can't wait any longer."

"Oh, okay then." My boss sighs and for the first time the possible consequences to my actions begin to register in my mind and I start to panic that I may get the sack.

"Good, let's familiarise ourselves. It would be remiss of me to sit in on your meeting and not know your name," he says turning to face me.

I know I'm staring wildly, mainly because it seems odd that he needs to exchange names to sit in on a meeting with me but not to fuck me. Fortunately, Mr Peterson has his mind together enough to introduce us.

"Mason Harding." He gestures to the man whose deep blue eyes are boring into me.

"Olivia Carrington."

"Pleased to meet you," Mason says.

"You too." I accept his outstretched hand, immediately regretting it as the burn of his touch registers and my nostrils are assaulted with the scent of him, the same scent from last night and this morning; woody, clean and citrusy at the same time. I pull away quickly as I feel my pulse rate increasing and my libido going into overdrive.

He smiles, convincing me that he knows the effect his touch has on me.

"You don't mind if I sit in do you? I don't want to be intrusive or overfamiliar." His words make me stare even more thinking that he couldn't be more familiar if he tried after last night.

"No," I reply in a hushed tone, unsure who or what this man is.

He smiles, a triumphant smile as I take the seat he's gesturing to, putting me next to him and opposite Mr Peterson.

Unsure how best to sit I cross my legs and instantly regret it because not only does that position push my skirt up giving Mason a flash of my legs, moreover because the soreness I feel between my legs after my night with the aforementioned Mason is increased in this position.

Almost immediately I unfold my legs and place both feet flat on the floor to see him smirking. I would actually like to punch him for that smirk alone because I know he knows why I changed my position. That he is responsible for my soreness. That he fucked me senseless last night.

"Is that your portfolio?" Mason asks, pointing to the folder I'm holding, interrupting my thoughts.

I nod and hand it to him. "It's an edited version of my full one."

As he skims through my things Mr Peterson turns his attention to me. "Olivia, I know you may feel a little frustrated by your role here but you are an asset to the company, on reception." He gives me a sense of optimism until he added the last two words of that sentence.

"You have some good ideas," Mason throws in. "A good eye."

I am still waiting for Mr Peterson to say something positive about my opportunities in the company, but he appears to have nothing else to say so I speak.

"Mr Peterson, that doesn't reassure me or offer me any kind of incentive to remain here long term. Reception work is all well and good and the fact that I can placate Mrs Tyrell when she is seething about the state of her sunroom isn't enough for me. It's not what I want to do, so maybe I should look elsewhere for opportunities that don't seem to exist here."

Mason is looking across at me with a frown before turning to Peterson, "You have a dissatisfied customer?"

"What? No, yes, kind of, but Olivia has passed those concerns on and I will deal with them later. Mrs Tyrell likes Olivia, she calms her when she's fraught," he tells Mason and I have no clue where this fits in with anything but I can't miss the scowl tossed my way by my boss or the one Mason throws at Mr Peterson.

"Miss Carrington, I am here to engage Christian's services for some of my offices and I like your stuff." Mason hands my portfolio back. "I have listened to your desire to gain professional experience and admire it so what if I agree to let you work on my building, with a more experienced designer of course?"

"Why would you do that?" I find myself asking and hope to God that his response doesn't reveal our night together.

"Why do you think?" His eyebrows quirk making me panic that I am the one who is about to reveal our history to my boss now.

"I, erm," I stammer.

"I said, I admire your desire," he says, making me blush. "Professional desire, but if you're not interested…"

"No, no I am, thank you, if Mr Peterson is agreeable."

I want to slap my own face for handing control for the future of my design career back into Mr Peterson's hands and if he says no, well, I will have nobody to blame but myself.

"Fine." My boss sighs, shocking me slightly because this all seems a little too simple. I have been trying to get a break here for the best part of two years with no success and now, one word from Mason and a door is opening for me. "I was thinking of putting this design Sean's way and I know you and he get on."

I notice Mason frowning at me when my boss refers to me and Sean getting on, but that can't mean anything, can it? No, because he never even gave me his name.

"Miss Carrington, I'd appreciate a further discussion with you at my offices. Three o'clock this afternoon is good for me." His tone somehow offers no room to debate or discuss. "For us to establish exactly what you can and can't do without consulting the lead designer or me. You're good with Miss Carrington cutting work early to come to me, Christian?" he asks. It is more of a statement than a question.

"Of course. So, if you're finished Olivia, maybe you could send Sean in," Peterson says, and I know I am definitely being dismissed now.

I get to my feet and walk towards the door when Mason calls to me, "I'll let you have the address on my way out, Miss Carrington."

An hour and a half later Mason is leaving Mr Peterson's office and heading towards me.

Family Affair

"Do you drive?"

"No."

"Okay, I'll pick you up at two, downstairs," he says and is already on his way out.

"No, just give me the address and I'll make my own way to you for three," I insist.

He turns and studies me for a few seconds and then smiles. God, I remember that smile from last night and it still has the same effect, it's melting me.

"If you insist, just this once." He returns to my desk with an overconfident swagger. "Here," he says, offering me a business card. "Address and my direct line, in case you get lost, but don't be late, I hate tardiness, especially when I have offered you a way to be on time. Three o'clock, Miss Carrington."

I turn away as he leaves and find Cathy and Sean grinning at me.

"What?"

"He is seriously hot," Cathy replies.

"And he fancies you," Sean adds.

"Erm, can we get on with work," says Peterson from his doorway with a frown before he returns to his office, slamming the door shut behind him.

Printed in Great Britain
by Amazon